Couldn't Ask for *More*

KIANNA ALEXANDER

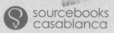
sourcebooks
casablanca

Published by Sourcebooks Casablanca, an imprint of Sourcebooks, Inc.
P.O. Box 4410, Naperville, Illinois 60567-4410
(630) 961-3900
Fax: (630) 961-2168
sourcebooks.com

Printed and bound in Canada.
MBP 10 9 8 7 6 5 4 3 2 1

Chapter 1

STRETCHED OUT ON THE FLOOR OF HER LIVING ROOM, Alexis Devers flipped through the pages of her sketch pad. Sunlight flooded through the bay windows of her downtown Raleigh condo, illuminating the images she'd created. The soft, white carpet beneath her cradled her body, threatening to put her to sleep. It was only the sheer thrill of artistic expression that had kept her awake for the three hours she'd been lying there in the same spot.

She smiled. The sketches filling the book's crisp, white pages represented the final iteration of what would be her first independent fashion line. She already had the perfect name for it: Krystal Kouture One. She planned to keep it simple, numbering her lines and using her company name, to keep her brand top of mind with fashion consumers as well as movers and shakers in the industry.

Alexis hadn't left her house for four days, she was so wrapped up in getting the pieces in the line just right. She'd barely slept, unable to stop visualizing her designs. She'd entered her kitchen maybe twice, and that was to get coffee or water. Everything she'd eaten had been delivered to her door, courtesy of the many nearby restaurants.

Seeing the completed sketches made all her hard work worthwhile. Pride surged through her, because she knew she'd created something sorely missing in the fashion world. Her clothes would blur the line between sexiness and practicality, giving women the option to cover up their bodies without losing any of their natural allure. This line would be perfect to launch for fall, as chilly air encouraged people to layer clothing and shield their bare skin from the elements.

She blew out a breath, anticipating the time crunch she and everybody at Krystal Kouture would soon enter. In order to get the One line ready for launch at the upcoming Carolina Music and Fashion Festival, they'd have to make samples, test and photograph them on the fit model, do preliminary press... Thankfully, she knew her small but brilliant staff would be fully capable of pulling it off. It just meant they were all about to put in some serious overtime.

The festival, cosponsored by the North Carolina Arts Council and the Greater Raleigh Convention and Visitors Bureau, had been created five years ago to showcase the talent of musicians, singers, fashion designers, and models all over the Tar Heel State. The festival brought in a diverse, sizable crowd each year, and Alexis was thrilled that her fashion line would make its debut there. Not only would her clothes be on display for the very women she hoped would wear them, but there would also be retail buyers present. The festival fashion show could be her opportunity to break into the retail market.

Everything was in place for making the One line a reality—*almost* everything. She'd have to call her best friend and business partner, Sydney Greer, and let her know that the sketches were finalized. But first, one important question remained to be answered.

What's my tagline? She tapped the end of her graphite

pencil against her chin, turning ideas over in her mind. She needed something catchy but not cheesy or cliché. Something that would express the purpose behind her designs in just a few succinct words. She sat up, scooting her back against her white couch, listening to the whir of her ceiling fan.

The ringing of her smartphone snapped her out of her thoughts. Twisting around, she grabbed it from the couch cushion. Seeing Maxwell's name on the screen, she answered it. "Hey, Bro."

"Honestly, Alexis. I've been calling you for the past two days. And so has Mom. What in the hell is going on with you?"

"I was working." She balanced the phone between her ear and her shoulder as she climbed up from the floor. Her back muscles immediately contracted, cursing her for spending so much time on the carpet. She settled onto the couch

"Good grief. So you mean you were on another one of your 'art benders'? Where you're so busy being creative that you can't even bother to take calls from your family?" His tone held a mixture of mockery and annoyance.

She shook her head. Her brother had a penchant for dramatics. "Maxie, I'm fine. This is how I work."

"The way you work is weird."

"I'm an artist. I'm allowed my eccentricities."

"Eccentrics do things like wear paisley with polka dots or talk to their potted plants. You're just an oddball."

"Shut up, Maxie." She teased him right back, calling him the nickname he hated. He thought "Maxie" was too feminine a nickname for him. He was four years older and had been teasing her for as long as she could remember. "Besides, you're kind of an artist. Don't you ever get wrapped up in a project to the exclusion of everything else?"

He feigned offense. "'Kind of an artist.' Lex, please. I am *the* artist. I'm responsible for some of the most breathtaking buildings in this country."

The Devers children were an artsy bunch, all right. All were North Carolina Central University alumni, having attended the college where their parents had met and fallen in love. Alexis was a fashion designer, Maxwell owned an architectural firm, and… She stopped herself, not wanting to think about something that would ruin her celebratory mood. "Arrogant much? Now you see why I didn't answer the phone when you called yesterday."

"Not arrogant. Confident. There's a big difference, but that's beside the point."

"Then what is the point?"

"Just answer my calls, and we won't have a problem. Oh, and you should probably answer Mom's calls, too, because if you don't, she'll assume you've been kid-napped, murdered, and decapitated."

On that, she could agree. Their mother, Delphinia, pro-fessed nonstop worry about her children, all of whom were well into adulthood. At thirty, Alexis was the baby, and Delphinia worried about her the most. "Mom does tend to go from zero to worst-case scenario in ten seconds."

"Yes, she does, so stop raising her blood pressure."

Alexis ran a hand through her short-cropped curls. "Fair enough. Why were you trying so hard to reach me, anyway? Is something wrong?" She paused as a ter-rible thought entered her mind. "Did something happen with Kelsey?"

"No, Kelsey's fine. I mean, considering the situation." He coughed. "Everything is fine. I was just trying to invite you to something."

"Invite me to what?" She stretched out her legs in front of her and leaned forward, releasing tension in the angry muscles of her lower back.

"There's a step show tomorrow at Central. It's a Theta Delta Theta thing, but you know your girls from Alpha Delta Rho will be there, too, since that's our sister sorority."

Her mood brightened at the thought of returning to her alma mater. "Oh my gosh. I forgot about that. Teresa texted me about that, like, two weeks ago. It's tomorrow, for real?"

"You do realize that time is still passing while you're locked in your little creative bubble, don't you, Lex?"

She rolled her eyes. "Yes, I do."

"Just thought I'd ask. So are you going or not?"

"Yeah. I'm finished with my project. What time does it start, and where?"

"Two o'clock, at the gym building."

It had been ages since she'd seen her sorority sisters, and it was high time she rectified that. Based on Teresa's text, at least a few of her girls would be turning out to watch the brothers of TDT rep their organization at the step show. "I've got a lunch meeting, so I might be late. But I'm definitely coming."

"Good. It's time for you to get out of the house and rejoin the living."

"When I see you, I'm gonna give you a smack right upside your head, Max."

He laughed. "Whatever. I'm, like, twice your size."

"Then I'm just the right height to punch you in the stomach," she retorted playfully.

"I'll see you at the step show. I *dare* you to leave your sketch pad at home this time, Lex." Without waiting for her response, he hung up.

She set her phone aside, shaking her head. *Max and his stupid dares...*

A squeal of delight passed her lips as the perfect tagline came to mind. "Dare to Be Demure!" she shouted into her empty condo. As much as she detested Maxwell's tendency to "dare" her to do things, she was glad he had today. The tagline was succinct, evocative, and not at all cheesy.

Jumping up from the couch, she jogged down the hallway to her master bedroom. After several days trapped in the house, a shower would be the first order of business. Then she'd have the pleasure of calling Sydney and telling her they were ready to roll.

———

Bryan strolled into the gym at Central, his eyes scanning the space. The bleachers on either side of the polished basketball court were already partially filled with spectators. It was just before two o'clock, and people continued to stream in around him. He moved farther in, searching the bleachers for Xavier and Maxwell.

He spotted them in the center section on the western side of the gym, toward the top. Jogging over to the bleachers, he slowed to climb the steep stairs. When he reached his boys, he gave them both a brief handshake. "Did I miss anything?"

"Nah," Maxwell said, keeping his eyes on the

preparations happening down on the gym floor. He wore a Theta Delta Theta tee and a pair of khakis. "The kids are still lining up to do their routine." He leaned back, letting his elbows rest on the rung behind him.

"They did practice a few steps, but it hasn't really kicked off yet." Xavier loosened his tie. Now that he served on the city council, the man was rarely seen in public in street clothes.

"Where's Tyrone and Orion?" Bryan asked.

"Tyrone's working late on a deposition or some thing," came Xavier's absentminded reply as he kept his eyes on the floor.

"Orion's on tour with Young-n-Wild. You know those kids need a chaperone everywhere they go." Maxwell stifled a yawn. "He'll be back in a couple of weeks, I think."

Bryan eased into an empty spot on the end of the row next to Xavier. Xavier glanced at his watch. "Looks like they're going to start late. Apparently, our little brothers aren't as organized as we were back in the day."

Maxwell elbowed him. "Xavier, come out of that tie and sport coat. It's obviously making you uptight."

Shrugging out of the sport coat, Xavier removed the tie and tucked it into an inner pocket. He draped the coat over the bleachers and clapped his hands together. "That's better. But they're still running late."

"Come on, X. Don't you remember that step show we did during junior year?" Bryan tapped his shoulder. "That one didn't start on time, either."

"Oh yeah. The one where Maxwell got caught in the broom closet with one of the girls from Alpha Delta Rho." Xavier swiveled around to look in his direction.

"I don't know what y'all are talking about." Maxwell's eyes twinkled.

As the marching band filed into the gym, Bryan and his boys turned their attention back to the floor. The drum major stepped forward, and the drumline began to play a complex, catchy rhythm. Soon, the entire Eagles Marching Sound Machine was playing in all its glory. The rousing music cued the entrance of the young brothers of Theta Delta Theta, proudly wearing the fraternity colors, complete with faces painted half silver, half green.

As was customary, the senior member of the younger set took the mic and called out for all elite alumni of TDT to "represent." All around the gym, whole sections of the bleachers rose to their feet, cheering and pumping their fists. Bryan, Maxwell, and Xavier joined in, standing and raising their hands and voices in celebration of their fraternity's proud legacy.

After they returned to their seats and the show kicked off in earnest, Bryan watched the complex formations the little brothers made as they stepped to the music. Putting in extra effort, strictly for visual appeal, was part of the TDT tradition. "Look at those young brothers. They are killing it."

"I gotta admit, I'm impressed. That ain't easy." Maxwell nodded in the direction of the gym floor.

"Whew!" That came from Xavier as one of the young brothers executed a perfect backflip. "He nailed it."

"Hey, X. How's married life treating you, man?" Bryan leaned back against the rung behind him.

A goofy grin spread across Xavier's face. "It's beautiful, man. Waking up to Imani every day is way better than I could have imagined. We always make sure to eat breakfast together before we go in to work, and—"

Maxwell's dramatic gagging effectively interrupted Xavier's sentence. "Please, dude. You're killing me."

Xavier punched him in the shoulder. "What are you, twelve? If you knew like I know, you'd be looking for a good woman yourself."

"Whatever," Maxwell sat up a bit and appeared to be looking around. "Where is she? She's gonna miss the whole damn show."

"She who?" Bryan asked.

"My sister Alexis. She said she was coming today." Maxwell stood, peering down toward the entrance. "Never mind. I see her."

Bryan followed his gaze. A group of Alpha Delta Rho women was entering at that moment, decked out in the sorority colors of purple and blue—or "lavender and lapis" as ADR ladies referred to them.

The young brothers on the floor ended their routine, and everyone applauded, including the sisters holding court by the door. As the applause began to die down, Maxwell cupped his hands around his mouth. "Lex!"

As Maxwell's shout rang out, one woman in the group turned her head, frowning as she searched the crowd.

Bryan's eyes were glued to her as she started walking toward the bleachers. *That's Maxwell's baby sister?*

Gone was the cute little teen who'd visited Maxwell on campus. The woman currently coming their way oozed femininity from her every pore. She was tall—at least five eight—and she walked with confidence. Her lithe, curvaceous frame was draped in a fitted lavender top bearing her sorority letters and a knee-length denim skirt that revealed the tempting bronze length of her legs. Short brown ringlets of hair framed a heart-shaped face that could only be described as elegant, and her hazel eyes were fixed on Maxwell.

"Damn." The word fell out of Bryan's mouth before he could stop it.

Maxwell cut him a look. "Damn what?"

As Alexis came abreast of them, Bryan blurted, "I can't believe you're Maxwell's baby sister."

One of her perfectly arched brows hitched, her rose-tinted lips thinning. "Who are you?"

Chapter 2

ALEXIS WAITED, WATCHING THE STRANGE MAN'S expression. Clearly, he had expected her to know him. She assumed he was a friend of Maxwell's, since he wore a Theta tee. But beyond that, she had no idea who he was.

He was handsome, even with that look on his face. The jeans and tee he wore weren't tight but fit him well enough to give a clear idea of the strong, muscular frame beneath his clothing. His face was angular, his hair neatly trimmed. His lips looked full and supple, and he had a gorgeous pair of cocoa-brown eyes that were assessing her at the present moment.

"You don't remember me."

She shook her head, feeling her brow knit with confusion. "Should I?"

"I'm Bryan." He stuck out his large hand. "Bryan James."

She shook with him. "I'm Alexis. Nice to meet you."

"The pleasure is mine." His tone of voice sounded like a manifestation of the pleasure he spoke of. He kept his hand wrapped around hers for about two beats longer than necessary.

She drew her hand away, feeling the beginnings of a smile tilting her lips. Apparently, her brother's friend liked what he saw. She found him pretty easy on the eyes, too, but knew better than to say that out loud.

Maxwell, on the other hand, didn't look very happy. "Bryan, I know you better quit looking at my baby sister like that." Maxwell appeared less than pleased.

"I can't help it." Bryan kept his eyes on her as he made the remark. "It's just that I see no similarities between the little high school girl who used to show up and eat lunch with us in the college cafeteria and this gorgeous woman."

Heat rushed to her cheeks. *He's not short on charm.* She gave a nervous chuckle. "Thanks?" Needing to take the attention off herself, she gestured to her girlfriends. "These are my friends Teresa and Claire."

More pleasantries were exchanged between the men and women.

"Okay." Maxwell entered Bryan's space. "You cut your eyes at Lex like that one more time, and I'm gonna have to rearrange your face."

She rolled her eyes. "Maxie, sit down." Pressing her open palm to his chest, she pushed past him and took a seat next to her girls on the rung behind them. On the way, she noticed the other man sitting with them, who'd been quiet the entire time. "Oh, hey, Xavier. How are you?"

Xavier smiled her way, waved in her direction. "What's up, Squirt?"

She punched him gently in the shoulder. "I'm too old for you to still be calling me that. Hey, Maxwell told me you got married. Congratulations."

"Thanks."

Everyone was seated now, and Bryan stole a glance in her direction, then looked back toward the floor.

He was good-looking, no denying that. But she was sure Maxwell would have a stroke if she dated any of his friends. She knew Xavier, because he and Maxwell had been in the same graduating class. Back in the day, Xavier had always been nice to her, at least aside from calling her Squirt. She'd even had a little crush on him, but that seemed like a million years ago.

She looked down toward the gym floor, where the show had entered an intermission of sorts. The band played the school's fight song as the next group to perform took their positions on the floor. Did we miss the Thetas!"

"Probably. You were half an hour late." Teresa ribbed her with an elbow.

"The young brothers were pretty good, too, based on what I've heard." Claire adjusted her ponytail, then draped one leg over the other, assuming her usual demure posture.

"Well, as long as we haven't missed our little sisters." A smile spread over Alexis's face as she saw the girls lining up on the floor. "Looks like they're up next."

Teresa nudged her. Leaning close, she whispered, "So, what's up with you and Bryan?"

At first, Alexis didn't acknowledge her. She loved her girl, but Teresa's idea of a whisper was still pretty damn loud. Alexis knew that answering Teresa's question might encourage more of her failed attempts at discretion.

Teresa nudged her again, fixing her with an expectant gaze. "Well?"

Alexis sighed, sensing Teresa wasn't going to let this go. She answered, in an actual whisper, "Nothing. I don't even know him."

"He sure looks like he wants to change that."

"Shh!" Claire chastised in a hushed tone. "They can probably hear you two hens clucking."

A prickle of awareness running up her back, Alexis hazarded a glance in Bryan's direction.

His dark-brown eyes were waiting. A smile tipped the corners of his mouth. "Your friend's right. I can hear you." Still smiling, he turned back around.

Her cheeks hot like the sun on a summer day, Alexis leaned back against the cool cinder-block wall behind her. "Geez, Teresa."

"Sorry, girl." Teresa slunk back, wearing an expression of amused embarrassment.

Rolling her eyes, Alexis put her focus on the floor for the remainder of the show. She purposefully avoided eye contact with both Teresa and Bryan.

After the step show ended, Alexis grabbed her handbag. She wanted to join the crowd leaving the gym and make it back to the car, even though she knew she'd likely be stuck in traffic for a while on the way out. At this point, she was eager to get out of what had become an awkward situation and get back to her sketches.

That dream was crushed when she stood too fast. Her upper body tipped forward, and the rest of her was about to follow when Bryan's hand shot out to balance her.

"You okay?" He kept his hand clamped on her forearm, as if waiting for her to steady herself.

Straightening, she nodded. "I'm fine. Thanks for the save."

"Don't mention it. I sat on a nail myself. Damn bleachers are a death trap."

Amused by his cheesy joke, she smiled. "I plan to write a sternly worded letter to the alumni association. I want my donations to go to work on these bleachers right away."

He laughed, a deep, pleasant rumble erupting from his throat. "I'm with you."

She felt her smile brighten. The humor between them had done wonders at allaying the embarrassment she normally would have felt. Laughing with him almost made her forget how close she'd come to face-planting on the bleachers.

Teresa cleared her throat. "I'm out, Lex."

She eased back, letting her girlfriends go by.

"Meet us by the car," Claire called as she and Teresa descended the steps.

With her girls gone, Alexis turned her attention back to her handsome rescuer. "So I gather you went to school here with Maxwell." She'd spent some time on the campus while she was still in high school and met plenty of the guys her brother hung out with. She guessed Bryan had been among them, but she hadn't paid much attention to any of them, other than Xavier, who'd been closer with Maxwell than anyone else.

He nodded. "I did, but I was a year behind him."

That meant he was a little closer to her age. *Why am I even thinking that?* "You were long gone by the time I came here to study, then."

"Your brother said you're a fashion designer."

"I am. Graduated top of my class."

"That's funny. Apparel and textiles was my minor. I'm in textile manufacturing."

"I see." That was something of an odd coincidence, one that begged to be further explored. With the crowd teeming around them and all the accompanying noise, this wasn't the time or the place to get into a deep discussion of the apparel industry. Pity, though, because she sensed Bryan could hold his own in such a conversation.

Before either of them could say anything else, Maxwell appeared. "I go to the men's room, I come back, and what do I find? My boy trying to push up on my baby sister." He folded his arms across his chest, frowning.

Alexis sighed, rolling her eyes. "Bye, Maxie." Turning to Bryan, she added, "It was nice talking to you. Thanks again."

"No problem." He gave her another megawatt smile, even as her brother punched him in the arm.

She walked away, taking care to watch her steps as she moved down the bleachers. She could feel Bryan's eyes on her back, and she didn't want to end up taking a fall while he was watching her.

Once she reached the bottom, she looked up toward him again.

She could see her brother's back as he lectured Bryan, but Bryan's sole focus remained on her. Throwing him a sexy wink, she turned and joined the crowd exiting the gym.

Outside in the parking lot, she found Teresa and Claire waiting in Claire's luxury sedan.

The minute Alexis climbed into the backseat, both women swiveled toward her.

Fastening her seat belt, Alexis settled in. "What?"

Teresa sucked her lip. "Girl, if you don't quit playing and tell us what happened with Bryan…"

"Nothing. We just talked for a few minutes."

"I bet Maxwell lost his shit, didn't he?" Claire navigated the car out of the parking spot and into the long line of vehicles trying to get out of the lot.

"Yeah. But he's not the boss of me." Alexis loved her brother, but she was so over his meddling in her life.

"I'm telling you. That man wants you." Teresa turned back around in her seat.

"I know." Now she just had to figure out what, if anything, to do about that.

Bryan lifted his mug of *café con leche* to his lips, taking a tentative sip. The brew was still hot but not enough to burn him and went down smoothly. He wished the same could be said for the conversation he was currently enduring.

His father, Oscar, sat across from him, grousing. Entering the latter half of his sixties, Oscar James was about as set in his ways as a man could be. His head was bald; he'd shaved it several years ago to avoid, in his own words, "chasing a receding hairline." His upper lip was just as bare, but his chin was home to a neatly trimmed beard. He had assessing brown eyes, lips that were turned down most of the time, and a pair of wire-rimmed glasses that rested on the bridge of his nose. He was dressed casually in a light-blue button-down shirt and a pair of chinos, but his manner was anything but relaxed. Every button on the shirt was fastened, right up to the base of his throat.

Just looking at that top button made Bryan feel confined, and he scratched his own neck in response.

Father and son were sequestered in a booth at Comer Bien, a local Spanish restaurant. They had brunch here two Sundays a month, and one would think it was a time of male bonding between a man and his only child.

Bryan knew different. Oscar James wasn't that kind of person. He wasn't cruel, but he'd never been particularly affectionate, either. As a child, Bryan had longed for a friendlier, more laid-back relationship with his father. By the time he reached adolescence, though, he'd realized things weren't going to change between them. Bryan had learned to accept his father for what he was and tried not to take the old man's moodiness personally.

Oscar took a drink from his own ceramic mug of *café solo*. "Son, I don't think you understand just how important it is for you to secure accounts."

Swallowing a mouthful of his vegetarian omelet, Bryan shook his head. "Dad, I do understand. I promise I do."

"Then why haven't you brought in a major contract over the last few months? If Royal Textiles is to thrive, we need a number of lucrative contracts. Have you been making the rounds?"

"Yes, I have. I've spent most of this past month either in meetings, on planes, or in airports." And he had. The nonstop travel, in search of their next big account, had begun to take its toll on him. Physical and mental exhaustion dogged his steps. Why couldn't his father see his efforts?

Oscar nodded, but his expression didn't brighten. "You have been traveling a lot. I think I'm going to keep you close to the office for a while. If you're not bringing in accounts, I can't really justify all these travel costs to the board and the shareholders."

"That's fine, Dad." He was grateful for the break from the grind of airport security lines, long flights, and sleeping in hotels. He didn't elaborate on any of that,

COULDN'T ASK FOR MORE 19

knowing his father wouldn't be particularly interested in hearing his complaints.

"It's so much more expensive to do things the way we do, to keep all of our production here in the United States." Oscar sipped from his coffee again. "But I wouldn't change a thing. Your grandfather loved this company. He started it from almost nothing, built it up with his own sweat. He would never have wanted to see operations go overseas, taking jobs away from the folks in his hometown."

Bryan's answering nod was solemn. His paternal grandfather, Martin James, had been a hard-working, pragmatic man. Bryan knew his father was right; Martin had pushed back against every suggestion of moving operations until his retirement some twenty years ago and had continued to resist the notion until his death eleven years later.

Sitting back in his chair, the old man scratched at his chin, raking his fingers through a gray beard streaked with white. "I wonder what Wesley is doing these days. Haven't heard from him in a while."

Bryan put down his mug, as hearing his cousin's name soured his stomach and ruined the flavor of his coffee. Wesley, the only son of his father's brother, Otis, was the golden child of the James family. "Honestly, I don't care what he's doing, and I don't see what that has to do with what we're talking about."

"Otis tells me Wesley's got his MBA now. Maybe he can come in to the company and turn things around."

Bryan wanted to groan aloud but didn't. Instead, he placed a hand to his temple. "Dad, Wesley doesn't know a thing about the textiles business. He and Uncle Otis are in automotive." Otis owned a luxury car dealership, and Wesley managed it while his sisters worked in the office. "It's a totally different industry."

"I know that. But Wesley knows the art of the deal. He knows how to make potential buyers open up their wallets." He shrugged. "That may be just what we need. Someone from outside the field, with a fresh perspective."

Bryan remained silent. He saw no similarities between the clothing textiles industry and the automotive sales industry and didn't think Wesley would add anything positive to the company. This wasn't just an issue of skill; it was one of temperament. As of now, Royal Textiles was a hectic but pleasant workplace. Bringing in someone like Wesley, who possessed the same megalomaniacal personality as an overfed house cat, would ruin that balance.

"You know, Otis told me Wesley sold twenty of their flagship model last month. Think about that. He sold twenty cars, at forty thousand dollars a pop, in a month. You have to admit it's impressive."

As his father went on and on about Wesley and the fascinating world of swindling people out of their hard-earned money for a bunch of add-ons they didn't need, Bryan's mind began to wander. His father's voice faded into the background as he recalled the previous day's encounter with the leggy beauty who was Alexis Devers. In his mind's eye, he could see the long, dark lashes framing those beautiful hazel eyes, the pink-painted lips spreading into a smile. She was a woman made to be admired like a fine work of art, and he would love to spend more time doing just that.

She'd been somewhat standoffish, and he supposed he understood that, since they'd been under Maxwell's watchful eyes the entire time. Still, he was attracted to her, and he sensed she felt the same way. Now he just needed to figure out a way to see her again, without Maxwell looking over his shoulder.

"Bryan. Did you hear what I said?"

He hadn't. "I'm sorry, what did you say?"

Oscar shook his head. "I said, what are you willing to do to show me you want to stay in your position at the company?"

Bryan pushed his plate and mug away. All through his childhood, he'd lived in the shadow of Wesley's accomplishments. Otis was always bragging to Oscar about what his son had done. Oscar, due to a sense of competition between him and his older brother, had projected his desire to be the best onto his own son. "Listen. I'm going to bring in an account soon. I have some very promising leads. But don't bring Wesley in. He's just going to distract me from what I'm trying to do."

Oscar looked skeptical. "How soon can you bring in a new account?"

"Three weeks, tops." Bryan knew it was a lie the moment he said it, but he didn't care. He'd do whatever was necessary to avoid dealing with his asshole of a cousin. Wesley was book smart but a little dense when it came to the social graces. Having internalized his father's constant praise of everything he ever did, Wesley had grown into the biggest jerk Bryan ever had the misfortune of knowing.

"That's reasonable. I'll give you the three weeks, and we'll see what happens."

Bryan leaned in, tenting his fingers. "And what's going to happen if I don't bring in a contract by then, Dad?"

He shrugged. "I don't know. I suppose we'll have to reevaluate."

His brow furrowed. "Dad. Why not just be straight with me?"

The old man sighed. "I'm going to see if Wesley will help us out. We can't afford to keep losing money, and he may be our only way to keep the books in the black."

Bryan's frown deepened. "Thanks for the vote of confidence."

"Now, Son, you know this isn't personal."

"I know, I know." Shaking his head, he repeated the same words he'd been hearing from his father for years. "Business is business."

Oscar drained the last of his coffee and set the empty mug on the white tablecloth. "You still have the three weeks. I want you to get out there and do everything you can to lock down an account. Show me you still have the fire in you."

He said nothing, sensing his father had more to say.

"Work your contacts, Bryan. Have you reached out to everyone you know, either personally or by extension, who could help you get this done?"

He thought again of Alexis, easily the most intriguing designer he'd ever met. "I have a few more people I need to speak to."

"Then do that, Son. Your three weeks starts tomorrow." Oscar's lips tilted up slightly, his expression getting as close as it ever did to an encouraging smile. "Make me proud, Bryan."

Mirroring his father's fraction of a smile, Bryan nodded. "Don't worry. I will."

Chapter 3

ALEXIS JOGGED ACROSS THE CARPET COVERED FLOOR of her office in an attempt to answer her ringing smartphone. The device was on the edge of her desk, vibrating like crazy as it played Rufus and Chaka Khan hit "Tell Me Something Good" to alert her to an incoming call.

Just as she reached for the phone, the vibration pushed it off the desk. It hit the carpet with a thud, and she squatted down to scoop it up. With the phone finally in hand, she swiped the screen to answer it. "Hello?"

"May I speak with Ms. Alexis Devers?"

"Speaking." She tried to sound calm, despite being breathless from the mad dash through the building to answer the call.

"Good morning, Ms. Devers. I'm Stephanie Monroe, account rep for Clarkson Apparel Producers. Have you received the kit of information we sent to you a couple of weeks ago?"

"Yes, I have. Thank you."

Ms. Monroe continued. "We've heard good things about your Krystal Kouture One line, and we would love the opportunity to manufacture your clothing."

This was the sixth such call she'd received in the hour since she'd come in to work. Fighting down the

giddy excitement spreading through her, she kept her
tone professional. "Why, Ms. Monroe, I'm so flattered
to hear that. We're in the process of choosing our textile
partner right now."

"Lovely. Please do reach out and let me know what
Clarkson can do to turn the tide in our favor. Have a
good day."

"You do the same, Ms. Monroe." Disconnecting the
call, Alexis set the phone down, a little farther away
from the edge of the desk this time. Once her hands
were free, she pumped her fists in the air, doing a little
celebratory shimmy.

Sydney Greer, her friend and business partner,
entered the office then. She was of average height, about
four inches shorter than Alexis. She had olive skin,
brown eyes, and long, dark hair with blond streaks. As
usual, she'd parted her hair in the center and left it hanging down past her bare shoulders. Dressed in a cream-
colored shell blouse and brown, wide-legged slacks,
Sydney's arms were loaded with papers and folders.
"Lex, what the hell are you doing?"

"Celebrating. The One line is going to be the hit of
the fall fashion season." She gave her friend a bright
smile, continuing to wiggle her hips.

"Celebration is in order. But I know you can dance
better than that." Sydney moved farther into the room,
placing the stack on the desk.

"True. But in a pencil skirt and heels, this is the best I
can do." Rather than subject Sydney to more of her bad
dancing, Alexis eased into the leather executive chair
behind her desk. "What's all this?"

"Sample contracts and information so that we can get

a manufacturer for the line." Sydney flopped down into the seat across from her. "We need to get someone on board right away."

"I know. The phone's been ringing off the hook all morning." Pride surged through her as she thought of the interest textile mills had shown in her debut line. "It's rare to get this kind of attention before the debut fashion show."

Sydney gave her a sly smile. "I told you that if we shot Vivian in the clothes, pulled together an info kit, and sent it out, we would get at least a few bites."

"You were right, as usual."

She waved a hand in the air, feigning modesty. "Oh, how you do go on. But enough about my genius. We really do need to decide on a manufacturer, because without that, we've got nothing."

Alexis ran a hand through her hair. "Are our sample pieces still in-house?"

Sydney shook her head. "Girl, no. I sent out all five of them."

Her brow knitting with confusion, Alexis asked, "To whom?"

"Celebrities, duh." Sydney chuckled. "I took a look at some of the fashion magazines and blogs, as well as a few of the gossip shows. I've followed this stuff for years, so I have an idea of who would be most likely to wear what, and I acted accordingly."

Alexis couldn't hold back her smile. That was precisely why she loved Sydney. While Alexis fell down the rabbit hole of artistic inspiration, she could always count on her partner to be thinking about the business side of things. "So who did you send the Rochelle dress to?"

"Angela Bassett, of course. That dress practically screams her name."

When Alexis had sketched the design of that dress, she'd had Ms. Bassett in mind. But she wouldn't even have thought to send her the dress. She was a huge star, and who knew how many packages she got on a daily basis from random designers hoping to win her favor. "You're serious? You sent my dress to *the* Angela Bassett?"

With a shrug, Sydney nodded. "Yes, I did."

Shaking her head in amazement, Alexis leaned back in her chair. "And how did you pull that off?"

"Easy. I just contacted her favorite designer, got her measurements, had Pam alter it, and sent it off by courier. Then I lathered, rinsed, and repeated."

At this point, Alexis struggled to keep her mouth from hanging open, especially in the face of Sydney's matter-of-fact tone. "So who got the other four samples?"

"Kerry Washington, Glenn Close, Jazmine Sullivan, and Tamron Hall."

Alexis felt her eyes widen. "Wow. You've really covered all the bases, then."

"Yep. Television, film, and music." Sydney tossed one leg over the other, looking rather satisfied with herself. "You just keep doodling, and I'll keep moving the merchandise, girl."

Normally, she would have lectured Sydney about the complexities of fashion design and how it was much more than just doodling, but she refrained. She'd known Sydney since they were roommates during sophomore year at Central. Even back then, business and finance major Sydney had added a bit of balance and practicality to Alexis's free-spirited, creatively fueled life. How could she be annoyed with Sydney when she'd been working so hard to make the One line a success? So she said the only logical thing. "Thank you, Sydney. I don't know what I'd do without you."

"I don't either. So be glad I love ya." She blew her a kiss.

Alexis's intended response was interrupted as the office phone started ringing. "Is there anything in particular that I should be telling the retailers?"

"Have you talked to any of them? I thought I'd taken all the calls."

"Somehow, an account rep from Clarkson's got my cell phone number. I talked to her right before you came in here."

Sydney's brow lifted. "Well, damn. What did you tell her?"

"Nothing, really. Just that we're in the process of choosing manufacturing partners. I kept it pretty light and noncommittal since we haven't made a decision yet."

"Good." Sydney got up, headed for the hallway. "I'll take the call in my office. And if anyone else calls you, just send them my way. We both know I'm the business manager for a reason." With a wink, she disappeared around the corner.

A few seconds later, the ringing of the phone ceased. The wall between their offices was thick enough that Alexis couldn't hear a conversation, but she knew Sydney had answered it.

Krystal Kouture's office occupied a small building in downtown Raleigh, located only a few blocks from her condo. Since the design house didn't share the space, there was plenty of room for the five employees. Alexis and Sydney each had a private office, while Dawn, their receptionist and office manager, worked in the reception area. A third, larger space served as a workshop for Pam, the seamstress, and Vicki, the fit model. Pam brought in part-time seamstresses to assist her as necessary, but the five of them made up the entire permanent staff of the company.

Alexis's eyes drifted to her bookcase, eyeing the small angel statuette symbolizing Krystal Kouture's beginnings. She had been a senior designer for Torrid for eleven years. The brand, known for its edgy, modern take on plussized women's wear, had proven integral in helping her develop her design skills. From day one, she'd squirreled away money from each paycheck in her "DHF," Design House Fund. She'd managed to amass a tidy five figures on her own, through frugality and a simple lifestyle.

When she'd approached Sydney, who owned her own successful financial advising firm, three years ago about opening Krystal Kouture, Sydney had agreed to come on as business manager with the understanding that Greer Financial would remain open. With her savings and a boost from an angel investor Alexis met at an arts council event, she'd opened the design house two years ago. Alexis had continued to design for Torrid until she left her position in early spring, and Sydney still ran her firm. Neither of them drew a full salary from the design house, having agreed to wait until their first line took off. Only the other three staffers drew paychecks, with the receptionist working part-time and the others coming in on an "as needed" basis.

Alexis leaned back in her chair, imagining Angela Bassett emerging from a limousine in the Rochelle dress.

If the actress decided to wear the dress, it would be a life-changing event, not just for Alexis, but for everyone who worked at Krystal Kouture. Actually, if any one of the people Sydney had sent a sample to wore it in public, things were bound to get very busy, very fast.

Sydney poked her head around the doorframe. "Listen, that was another mill. We need to get a manufacturer, stat. That makes eight mills that have called us…today. Is there anyone else you want to consider before we choose?"

Alexis tapped the tip of her index finger against her cheek. "I think Maxwell's friend said he was in textiles…"

"Well, girl, get him on the damn phone!" Sydney gave several rapid snaps of her fingers to indicate the urgency of her words. "We gotta get this done."

After Sydney left, Alexis recalled her brief conversation with Bryan at the step show. Could his company really handle a contract this size? The only way she knew to find out was to reach out to him. Sure, there was the issue of the attraction she'd felt crackling between them like dry brush dropped into a campfire. But she needed a manufacturer, and fast. There wasn't time to go through a drawn-out process.

I'll call him. She didn't even know what to say to the man. Thinking she could get some information from her brother, she decided to talk to him first. Maxwell would know if Bryan's company was a possible fit.

After all, she had no time to waste.

———

Bryan walked the main first-floor corridor of Royal Textiles with four young men trailing behind him. The boys were from Revels Youth Outreach Center, the brainchild of his friend Xavier. Xavier's recent win of a seat on Raleigh's city council had only intensified his passion for working with youth, and he'd enlisted his friends to help mentor the kids who visited the YOC. Xavier had spent his first nine months on the council championing after-school programs, parks and recreation, and other causes that would positively impact the lives of the city's youth. Bryan was happy to do his part by introducing these young men to the world of fashion textiles.

The four ranged in age from twelve to seventeen and were all wearing bright-orange tees that proclaimed them as "Revels Youth." They remained quiet while moving through the building and managed to maintain something similar to a straight line. Bryan didn't consider himself a taskmaster, and he found their behavior satisfactory, so he didn't press them to straighten up.

Turning around, Bryan walked backward so he could face the youngsters as he spoke to them. "Today, I'm going to take you all to a few important areas in the building. We'll view the factory floor, where clothing is manufactured, as well as some of the machinery. We'll also view the corporate offices on the upper floors, and the sales department, where the deals are made."

They nodded and murmured in the affirmative, each face displaying varying degrees of disinterest. Bryan turned around again, continuing to lead them. He didn't blame them for seeming bored; even he could admit they hadn't done anything particularly exciting. He remembered what he was like as a teenaged boy, so he understood why they looked so unmoved. This wasn't an action film full of explosions and car chases, nor was it meant to be. Today was all about giving them a peek into the industry, the workplace, and adult life.

Bryan took the group to the factory floor first. The five of them rode the elevator down to the basement level in relative silence, other than the clicking sound of one of the boys typing on his phone. Bryan shook his head, lamenting the obsession this generation possessed for their electronic devices. He'd managed to survive high school without a cell phone, but he doubted kids of today would be willing to do the same.

As they walked off the elevator and entered the factory floor, Bryan stopped them near the entrance. "This is where all the clothing Royal Textiles manufactures is made. Machinists keep the equipment in good working order, and skilled technicians operate it to produce our goods." He gestured around with his hand, pointing out the employees currently at work on the floor.

He checked to see if he had the boys' interest. Three sets of eyes were looking his way, while the other remained focused on his phone. Bryan continued, "Our factory floor is divided into two sections. This smaller section is where denim goods are made. The larger section, on the other side of those dividers"—he pointed to indicate the steel shutters—"is for the manufacture of other clothing."

Kelvin, the youngest of the boys, raised his hand.

"What's your question?" Bryan gave the youngster his full attention.

"What are they making right now?"

He smiled. "Today, we're running an order of men's jeans."

That seemed to get their attention. Even Liam, the one involved in a love affair with his phone, glanced up from the glowing screen.

Sixteen-year-old Peter asked, "What brand?"

"Funny you should ask. Actually, the rapper J. Cole just launched a line. These are his jeans."

"Wow." Peter looked impressed. "And how many pairs can y'all make in a day?"

"Well, Peter—"

The young man stopped him. "My friends call me P-Dawg."

Bryan chuckled. His opinion of the nickname aside, he was happy to have made some kind of connection with him. "Okay, P-Dawg. By the end of the day, we'll turn out about two thousand pairs."

Peter appeared impressed but didn't say anything else.

"Does anybody else have any questions?" Bryan looked around at the faces of his mentees.

Liam, tucking his phone into his back pocket, asked, "Can we get closer to the machines? You know, to see how they work and all?"

"Sure. But you'll have to keep a safe distance. I don't want any of you hurt." Bryan led the group to a spot near the bank of sewing machinists, who were busy stitching the pieces of denim together. "Making these jeans involves a lot of time. Most of the process is completed by hand."

After they'd remained for a few moments, Bryan left the sewing machinists to their work and took the boys upstairs for a brief tour of the corporate offices on the second floor. Returning to the first floor, he then headed for the sales department. The main room, set up to look something like a department store, had sample pieces on display.

"This is our sales area. Here, members of our sales force speak with fashion designers and their representatives to secure production contracts." He pointed to a polished oak table. "Actually, I sat across from J. Cole, right over there, about seven weeks ago when we closed the deal with him."

All four of the boy's heads swiveled to look at the table.

He didn't mention the fact that he hadn't closed another deal since that day; they didn't need to know that. Instead, he tried to push away thoughts of his father's constant nagging and of the looming threat of his jerk cousin showing up to relieve him of his job.

Peter broke away from the group, his focus on a suit hanging on one of the display racks. "Do you ever sell the clothes that are hanging up here?"

"Those are sample pieces, and yes, we do sell them. When a designer changes direction for their line or the contract falls through, we sell the samples."

"This is a nice suit. I like the cut." Peter reached out to touch the lapel. "Slim fit, right?"

Bryan felt his brow rising. "Yes, it is a slim fit. Are you into suits?"

He shrugged. "Not really, but I know them. My pops is a tailor."

That caught him by surprise. Peter didn't look at all like the son of a tailor, but then again, Bryan knew better than to judge someone based solely on appearance. "Are you interested in textiles?"

He shrugged. "I don't really know what I wanna do. I'm just trying to graduate, you know?"

He nodded. "I feel you. But based on what you've seen today, do you think you would consider working in this field?"

Peter looked thoughtful for a moment, then grinned. "Yeah. I think I would."

"Sounds good." Bryan shook the young man's hand, and in that moment, he felt he'd reached him. From his chat with Xavier, Bryan knew Peter had recently been in trouble because of some bad decisions. Maybe all he needed to get on the right path was a little encouragement.

For the rest of the tour, Bryan noticed how Peter's behavior changed. He was more engaged, asked more questions, and made insightful comments. The young man's interest seemed to have been awakened, and for Bryan, that felt good. He realized that mentoring gave him an entirely different sense of accomplishment from the one he got by doing his job each day. Courting designers, fielding phone calls, and securing contracts was great and kept him employed. But he knew that his day-to-day work made very little impact on the future, because the fashion industry was an ever-changing beast. Reaching out to these young people, though, felt like touching the future. If he could make a difference in their lives, the impact of that could last long after his time on earth had expired.

He thought of his grandfather, Martin, who'd taken some of the other neighborhood boys along on their fishing trips. And of Oscar, who had led scout troops and coached peewee football teams when Bryan was a child. Both men had taken on those positions without being cajoled by their wives and had seemed to genuinely enjoy the time they spent with kids. As he thought back on those days and of the ways the men who'd raised him had reached out to other young men who lacked supportive role models, he supposed mentoring was in his blood. If only that notion had been passed on to Otis and Wes, Bryan imagined he might not find his uncle and cousin quite so insufferable.

As the tour wrapped up, Bryan was doubly determined to keep Wes from infiltrating the Royal organization. Family or not, Wes simply wasn't a good fit for the company. And as he saw the light in Peter's eyes, Bryan knew he would never stand by and see the mentoring program shelved. Not now, not after bearing witness to the impact the program could have. In a matter of an hour, Peter had gone from barely aware to fascinated. The young man, who'd come in with the simple desire to graduate, might now be considering just how broad his horizons could be.

By the time Bryan escorted the boys to the youth center's van and watched them pile in, he understood why Xavier spoke so passionately about mentoring.

It was one thing to make a living, but it felt far better to make a difference.

Chapter 4

BRYAN JOGGED UP THE STAIRS IN THE FRONT OF THE Arts Council building Tuesday morning with his leather portfolio tucked beneath his arm. The North Carolina Arts Council, located on Jones Street in the heart of downtown Raleigh, pursued a mission of supporting artists and advocating for the arts throughout the state of North Carolina. Knowing he was within a few minutes of being late for his appointment, Bryan entered the double glass doors and quickly made his way through the lobby of the building, intent on his destination.

When he entered the office of Mrs. Meyer, the program coordinator, he could see her seated behind her desk through the glass panel in her door. She was currently speaking with another woman sitting across from her, so he took a seat in the reception area adjacent to the office to wait. Opening the black leather portfolio he'd brought with him, he shuffled through the five pages of paperwork he was to turn in today. He doubled-checked the forms, making sure he'd filled in each slot. Instead of passing the forms and their delivery off to his assistant, he'd taken on the tasks himself.

The forms were to allow his participation as an industry guest in the upcoming Carolina Music and Fashion Festival. This would be the inaugural event, and success could mean it would become annual. The Arts Council and the Greater Raleigh Convention and Visitors Bureau were cosponsors and planned to showcase the state's talented musical artists and fashion designers. Several musicians from North Carolina were already enjoying national success in music; country singer Scotty McCreery and rapper J. Cole were the first two names that sprang to Bryan's mind. He couldn't name a famous designer that had come out of the Tar Heel State, but he hoped the festival would play a role in changing that.

As one of the few textile manufacturers that had kept its operations U.S.-based and one of only two left in the state of North Carolina, Royal was a rare company. Event organizers had reached out to Royal several weeks ago to gauge interest in the festival, and the members of the board had been excited. Bryan had volunteered to attend the festival as company representative, because he enjoyed seeing what was new on the arts scene. He wasn't the kind of executive who was content to sit behind a desk all day. He loved to get out into the community and see the latest trends firsthand.

The door to Mrs. Meyer's office opened, the sound drawing Bryan's attention out of his own thoughts and back to reality. He closed his portfolio and placed it on the empty seat next to him. As he swiveled his head, he could see a woman stepping out of the small room. The woman took a few steps backward, still engaged in conversation with Mrs. Meyer. She was clad in a blue skirt, crisp white blouse, and blue pumps. He let his gaze drift up to the back of her graceful neck, revealed by the short, dark curls of her glossy hair.

His brow crinkled. Is that…

Before he could complete the thought, the woman

turned around. As she fully entered the reception area, Bryan could feel the smile tilting his lips. It *was* her.

"Good morning, Alexis. Lovely to see you again." He stood up, leaving the portfolio as he walked toward her, hand extended.

Her dark eyes swung his way, and she smiled as well. "Bryan. Good morning. What are you doing here?"

The question reminded him of his abandoned portfolio, and he picked it up and tucked it beneath his arm again. "I'm dropping off paperwork for the festival. What about you?"

"The Carolina Music and Fashion Festival?" Her eyes sparkled with interest. "That's why I'm here. My fashion line is going to make its debut at the festival, so I'm here making sure all my loose ends are tied up."

Mrs. Meyer, wearing her usual sunny smile, interjected. "I didn't know you two were acquainted. I'll let you catch up, then. Bryan, just come on into the office when you're ready." Mrs. Meyer reentered her office and pushed her door closed behind her.

Alone in the reception area with the beautiful Alexis Devers, Bryan shifted his focus back to her. "Looks like we're here for the same reason. I'll be attending the festival as an industry guest, representing my family's textile company."

She swept a hand through her glossy curls. "Oh, I see. I remember you saying at the step show that you were in the textile business."

Watching her touch her hair that way made him wonder if her locks were really as soft and touchable as they appeared. Pushing that thought away, he nodded in response to her statement. "Yes. Royal Textiles was started by my grandfather, and my father is the current chief executive."

"So your offices are here in Raleigh, then?" She adjusted the shoulder strap of her handbag.

"Yes, we're headquartered here. Our building is located on a hundred or so acres in between the Crabtree and Brier Creek areas." The area along U.S. 70 had been experiencing a population boom as more retail and residential properties moved there.

She nodded, appearing impressed. "That's a nice area. And where are your products manufactured?"

"Right here in Raleigh, in our headquarters."

Her brow cocked. "Really? Most mills have moved production offshore."

He chuckled. "Not Royal. My grandfather always insisted on hometown workers making a quality product. The state has given us some tax advantages, but I think we would have kept production here even without them."

"I'm impressed." She met his gaze. "Maybe I will have to talk to you about my fashion line."

"I'm always looking for the next big thing in fashion, so I'd be happy to hear from you." He held her gaze, knowing that he could easily pass several hours considering her gorgeous eyes. "Meanwhile, congratulations on getting accepted into the festival. I know they only had room for three designers statewide."

She smiled, a subtle blush filling her cheeks. "Thank you. Sydney and I worked hard to win the opportunity to participate. I'm really honored that I'll be able to launch my line at the festival."

He returned her smile, noting how humble she was.

Her statement had lacked any bluster or puffery; she seemed genuinely excited and grateful for the chance to showcase her work. Humility was an appealing quality, especially in someone so attractive and talented.

She cleared her throat. "Look at me, standing here holding you up."

"You haven't heard any complaints from me, have you?" He was enjoying her company, and he wanted to prolong this encounter as much as possible.

She giggled, a tinkling sound that reminded him of a wind chime on a breezy day. "I'm sure you're just being polite. Anyway, you need to meet with Mrs. Meyer, and I have to get back to my work, so I'll let you go. It was nice seeing you again, Bryan."

"Likewise. Have a good day, Alexis."

"You, too." As the words left her glossy lips, she turned and walked down the corridor toward the elevator.

He watched her exit, mesmerized by the way she moved. Despite the height of her heels, she seemed to glide effortlessly down the hall. The mixture of confidence and grace she exuded made it hard to tear his eyes away from her. She pressed the elevator button, and when she stepped into the car, he was still watching her. Unable to look away, he continued to watch until he saw the elevator doors slide shut.

Mrs. Meyer opened her office door and poked her head out. "Ready, Bryan?"

Turning away from the now-closed doors of the elevator, Bryan gathered his focus and offered her a smile. "Sure."

Wednesday morning, Alexis stood by the island in the kitchen of her parents' home, filling her plate. Every other Wednesday, she and Maxwell joined their mother and father for a huge breakfast and some family bonding. Today, she still felt giddy from all the offers that had flooded her office from mills that wanted to manufacture her new fashion line. Once she got a manufacturer on board, she'd be golden.

After she'd loaded her plate with scrambled eggs, crisp strips of bacon, a couple of her mother's homemade biscuits, and a few fresh strawberries, she made her way from the counter to the breakfast nook. The round table, sitting in a sunny spot between the kitchen and the formal dining room, was situated in front of a window seat. Alexis and Maxwell customarily sat on the cushion of the window seat, while their parents sat in chairs facing them.

Humphrey Devers, ever the classic family patriarch, held open the pages of the *Wall Street Journal* in front of him. He'd been retired from his career as a bank executive for more than four years, but he still liked to "keep up with the stocks," as he often said. "Maxwell, are there any more biscuits, or have you devoured them all?"

Maxwell, who still stood at the counter with his plate, quickly dropped the last biscuit back on the serving platter. "You're in luck, Dad. There's one more left."

Alexis giggled. When it came down to her mother's biscuits, it was every man for himself.

Delphinia leaned down to remove something from the oven. "Don't worry about it, honey. I'm just taking another pan out of the oven."

Hearing that, a smiling Maxwell swooped in and claimed two of the steaming biscuits.

Alexis inhaled deeply as the heavenly aroma of her mother's hot biscuits filled the kitchen. She already had two on her plate, but just smelling them made her want to get up and grab a few more. Instead, she tucked a slice of bacon into her mouth.

Folding up the newspaper, Humphrey took a sip from his coffee mug. "Your mother tells me there's quite a lot of interest from the mills for your fashion line."

She smiled. "There is, Daddy. Sydney and I were overwhelmed with calls on Monday. The hard part will be deciding which one we want to use."

"I'm sure you two will figure it out." He smiled his daughter's way. "I'm proud of you, Alexis."

"Thanks, Daddy."

Maxwell slid onto the window seat next to her, setting down his plate on the table. Before digging into his mountain of scrambled eggs, he asked, "Lex, do you all have a manufacturer yet?"

She shook her head. "No. And with all the buzz we're getting, we need to get one. Like, yesterday."

Chewing and nodding, Maxwell waited until he swallowed to speak again. "You know Bryan's family business is textiles, right?"

"I ran into him at the Arts Council, and we talked briefly. Are they in clothing specifically?" She knew that the textiles industry was broad and varied. Being in the field could mean manufacturing anything made of fabric, from rugs to awnings.

He nodded, attacking his biscuit.

She thought back, recalling what Bryan had said about his family's company. She'd wanted to hear more from him at the Arts Council, but hadn't wanted to monopolize his day. She'd also been worrying about the upcoming show. But beyond that, she'd been distracted by Bryan—his looks, his smile, and his easygoing charm. Everything about him had appealed to her, and even though she'd come prepared to shoot down any man who spoke to her, he'd disarmed her right away. She sipped from the steaming cup of white tea by her plate, a smile tilting her lips as she remembered how he'd prevented her from tumbling down the bleachers. Maxwell hadn't been pleased with them speaking to each other, but she didn't care. Her big brother occupied a special place in her heart, and she knew he only wanted to protect her. Still, sometimes his oversight of her personal life grated on her nerves. She couldn't wait until he got involved with someone so she could become the nosy little sister and give him a taste of his own medicine.

Delphinia joined them then. As usual, she was the last person to sit down with a plate. "You know, his mother, Francine, and I were sorority sisters, may she rest in peace. She pledged Alpha Delta Rho the same year I did."

"And what year was that?" Maxwell teased.

Delphinia's brow furrowed. "Boy, if you don't quit. A lady never reveals her age, and if you keep that up, I'll cut off your supply of biscuits."

Looking appropriately chastised, Maxwell turned back toward his sister. "Seriously, Royal Textiles makes apparel of all kinds. They just locked down the contract for that rapper's new denim line a couple of months ago. I'm sure they could handle your line."

Alexis sat back in her chair, thinking on her brother's

words as she polished off the last of her bacon. Handsome as Bryan was, she knew she wouldn't mind working with him. That was a face she could look at all day. "Maybe I'll reach out to him."

"You should," Maxwell insisted. "As long as you plan to keep things strictly business."

Her brow hitched. "What do you mean by that?"

"I saw the way he was looking at you at the step show. And the way you were smiling at him." He stopped eating and gave her a stern look.

She rolled her eyes. "You're imagining things, Maxie. And besides, I'm grown."

"Whatever. Just keep it on the business level, and everything will be fine." He went back to his eggs.

Delphinia laughed. "You two are a mess."

"She may be an adult legally, but she's still my baby sister." Maxwell made the declaration while raising his glass of orange juice over his head.

Alexis fought down the urge to punch him in the shoulder, knowing he might spill juice all over their mother's tablecloth. She loved her brother, but she worried that he'd never see her as an adult, no matter how old they both got. She was thirty years old, and yet he still felt he had a right to "screen" every man she became involved with. Once, she'd thought it was cute, but Maxwell's meddling had become a nuisance. Having him as a big brother was like having two fathers.

"Maxwell, you can't keep your sisters under your thumb forever," Delphinia remarked. The moment the sentence left her lips, her smile faded. A sadness crossed over her face, dimming her expression the way a passing rain cloud temporarily blocked out the sunlight. Pushing back from the table and her nearly untouched plate, Delphinia stood. "Excuse me." She turned and hurried out of the room.

Humphrey watched his wife's departure with concern. Turning back to his children, he asked in a hushed tone, "Have either of you heard from Kelsey?"

"I haven't." Alexis turned to her brother. "Has she reached out to you, Max?"

Maxwell shook his head. "No. Not recently."

Humphrey sighed. "She's all right. In order for me to keep my sanity, I have to believe she's all right."

A silence fell over the table as conversation ceased.

Alexis eyed her mother's empty chair, and it reminded her of her sister's absence. It had been months since Kelsey had attended one of their family breakfasts. And as things stood now, no one knew when — or if — she'd ever return.

Not wanting to dwell on the sadness that rose within her, she put her focus back on her breakfast. She loved her sister, and though Kelsey was in a complex situation right now, Alexis still had hope that one day, she'd return to the family that loved her.

———

"Son, are you busy?"

Seated behind his desk, Bryan raised his head and looked toward his father. The old man had poked his head around the doorframe of Bryan's private office on the third floor of the Royal Textiles building. "Just going over some paperwork. Do you need something?"

He shook his head. "No. But your c—"

Before Oscar could finish his sentence, Wesley James strode into the office.

Bryan's face immediately folded into a frown. He looked to his father, who'd suddenly vanished. He supposed the old man didn't want to be around for Bryan and Wesley's interaction. It was well known among everyone in the company that the two cousins didn't get along.

He shook his head again and folded his arms over his chest. *Thanks for the warning, Pop*.

"So how the hell are you, Cuz?" Wesley, a notorious loudmouth, nearly shouted the question.

"Good morning, Wesley. I see you still don't have enough manners to knock."

He shrugged. "The door was open, dude." Wesley, though a good five inches shorter than Bryan, walked with the air of a man seven feet tall. He wore an expensive Italian suit, matching wing tips, and an overconfident smile. His tie, a hideous paisley number, had probably set him back a good three hundred dollars. As he moved toward the desk, he tugged on his lapels in a self-important way that made Bryan want to kick him in the shins.

"Why are you here, Wesley? Shouldn't you be convincing some old man to spend his entire 401(k) on a car he doesn't really need?" If he'd had a second cup of coffee, Bryan might have minced words with his cousin. But since he'd yet to make the return trip to the break room, he simply said what was on his mind.

Wesley placed his hand over his chest, feigning injury. Sitting down in the chair across from Bryan, he remarked, "That's really harsh, B."

"I can't help noticing you didn't say it was a lie."

COULDN'T ASK FOR MORE 47

Another shrug. "Whatever. I make ass-loads of money, so…"

Bryan rolled his eyes. "Again, why are you here?"

"I'm on vacation. Besides, Uncle Oscar called me."

Bryan groaned. So his father's attempt at warning him of Wesley's presence had been fueled by guilt, not concern. "I'm sure Pop knows I have important work to do, so I don't know why he asked you to come here and interrupt me."

"He didn't ask me to come here. I decided that on my own." Wesley made himself comfortable in the chair, tenting his fingers in front of him. "I thought I'd see if I could offer you some advice on how to close a few more deals. Uncle Oscar says you haven't been getting the job done lately."

Bryan chose to let that remark slide and to play along with his cousin's sudden urge to "help." "Okay, Wes. Why don't you tell me what you think I should do?" Settling in to his executive chair, he waited to be dazzled.

Clapping his hands together, Wesley launched into a speech. "I know you're all about the straight and narrow. And that's good and all. But why don't you try gassing your clients up a little bit? You know, embellish. Make them an offer they legit can't refuse."

Bryan listened to him rattle on, knowing Wesley liked nothing better than the sound of his own voice. He was indeed dazzled by his cousin's strong tendency toward dishonesty. "So, just so we're clear, what you're saying is I should overpromise? Lie to potential clients about what Royal Textiles can offer them, just to get them to sign on the dotted line?"

Wesley frowned and shook his head. "No, no, no.

Not lie. Lie is too strong a word. I said embellish. Just tell them what they want to hear. Close the sale at all costs, man."

"That's not how I do business, Wes." Bryan repositioned himself so that he was tenting his fingers, mimicking Wesley's positioning. Due to the height difference, he had to look down slightly to make eye contact, and it felt good to do so. "I get my accounts by laying out what we have to offer, not by making grand promises I can't keep."

"Listen, B. No offense, but it's been working for me all these years," Wesley insisted, sitting up straighter in the chair. To Bryan, it almost seemed like he was attempting to appear taller.

Bryan thought back to the conversation he'd had with his father over brunch. This was exactly what he'd meant when he said Wesley knew nothing about the textiles business. The questionable practices Wesley employed to sell cars simply could not be applied here. "You can't compare the two things. We don't sell a product here; we provide a service. You can rip someone off and never have to see them again. But things don't work like that in the textiles industry."

Wesley's jaw tightened. "You calling me a rip-off artist?"

"I don't have to." Bryan stood from his seat, now towering over his cousin. "We both know that's exactly what you are."

"I don't like your tone, B."

"And I don't like you being in my office. Yet here you are." Bryan leaned in, letting his cousin know the deal. If Wesley thought he was going to back down, he had another thought coming.

Wesley slid the chair back and stood. "Excuse me. I was just trying to help you out. But since you wanna get an attitude, I'll just stand back and watch you fail." He rubbed his hands together. "Just don't get mad with me when I swoop in to rescue the company and take your job in the process."

"This isn't just about turning a profit, Wes. It's about doing things the right way." Even as he spoke, Bryan didn't have any indication of whether his meaning had reached his cousin. "That's why I don't lie to potential clients. Why I work hard to make sure my team has everything they need. Why I mentor."

Wes scoffed. "You mean you think you deserve a cookie for bringing those little brats into your place of work? Personally, I think it's a waste of time. Kids these days are hardheaded. They're gonna do whatever stupid stuff they want regardless."

Bryan shook his head, taken aback by his cousin's callous statement. Then again, he'd never known Wes to be overly concerned with anything that didn't have a direct effect on him. "I'd rather take the chance that I might reach one of them."

"You're a hopeless case, Bryan. You're so busy being Mr. Upstanding Citizen that you're letting Uncle Oscar's company go down the tubes."

Bryan clenched and unclenched his fists. "Since we're family, I'm not gonna pop off and punch you in the throat, even though you deserve it. But I am gonna tell you to get the hell out of my office. Some of us have actual work to do." He made sure to hold eye contact with Wesley.

As expected, Wesley backed down. Throwing up his

hands in a show of surrender, he turned away. "Fine. We'll see what happens next."

"Yeah, Wes. We will see." Sitting back down, Bryan watched his cousin stride out of his office. Alone again, he took a few moments to compose himself. While he didn't hate his cousin, he wasn't particularly fond of him, either. Wesley's personality made him difficult to be around for more than a few minutes, and Bryan could safely say he'd had his fill of him for at least the next month or so.

Even when they were kids, Wesley had been the same way. Having picked up on the competition between their fathers, Wesley had tried at every turn to show himself superior to Bryan. Bryan couldn't be bothered and had refused to participate in his cousin's pointless contests, which only served to annoy Wesley.

With his eyes back on the paperwork he'd been looking over, Bryan recaptured his focus. His team had sent him a set of new marketing materials that needed his approval. Flipping through the pages of the spiral-bound booklet, he marked the places where he thought improvements could be made. He also made sure to point out things he liked, because he believed in encouraging his team. He knew he couldn't expect them to do their best work if he consistently pointed out their shortcomings but didn't praise them when they got it right.

His encounter with his cousin only made him more determined to turn things around. He would pull in all the accounts he could, but in his own way: with honesty and integrity. He sensed that if he didn't and Wes came in to take his position at the company, his first act would be to shelve the mentoring program.

This wasn't just about Bryan anymore. He didn't

want to see those kids kicked to the curb, just because Wes didn't see the value in mentoring. Now that he thought about it, maybe it was the lack of a supportive and positive male role model in Wes's life that had made him the way he was. While Oscar hadn't been affectionate in an overt way, he'd shown Bryan love by spending time with him and by taking Bryan's friends under his wing. Uncle Otis, on the other hand, had seemed offended by the very presence of children and avoided them whenever possible. Aunt Rita seemed to have shared the sentiment, because Bryan couldn't remember her ever doing anything one could consider "maternal." She'd seemed more interested in manicures and shopping than in baking cookies; that hadn't changed even though she was now nearly seventy.

Wes had attended boarding school from kindergarten through twelfth grade, spending only summers and holiday breaks at home. And even during those occasions, Otis and Rita usually left him with Oscar and Francine, Bryan's mother. Wes had spent those times terrorizing Bryan, and for the first time, Bryan realized why. The conclusion made him feel sympathy for his cousin, but not so much that he'd let Wes walk all over him.

Shutting down the mentoring program could mean unleashing a whole new crop of men like Wes on society—men who'd felt unwanted as children and would spend the rest of their lives overcompensating. Bryan certainly didn't want any part of that.

Pulling out his phone, Bryan began skimming his contacts.

Somebody out there needed the expert services of Royal Textiles, and he was going to find them.

Chapter 5

ALEXIS STOOD IN HER OFFICE THURSDAY MORNING, staring at the idea board in front of her. The board, a large sheet of white cardboard, was propped on an easel in the center of the room. Sydney had hauled it in and set it up minutes earlier.

Sydney, sitting by Alexis's desk with one shapely leg thrown over the other, waited in silence. She favored little black dresses, and today's long-sleeved number was a mini, the hem just grazing her lower thighs. She'd paired it with low-heeled, knee-high black boots.

Alexis, dressed in a pair of slim black pants, a sleeveless white button-down tunic, and black ballet flats, had chosen a more casual look for the day. She expected to spend the entire day in her office, brainstorming and ironing out concepts. Today's mission would be determining the best way to get the Krystal Kouture One line launched successfully.

Alexis let her eyes sweep over everything Sydney had set before her. The board held fabric swatches, color samples, and handwritten notes, all surrounding the Krystal Kouture logo. Seeing her line brought to life this way brought a smile to her face. Turning to look at her business partner, she asked, "Where do you want to start, Syd?"

Sydney shifted in her seat. "I thought we'd talk about where we think the line would sell well on the retail side. That will help us target our efforts. I've spoken to a few of them, and there's something I need to tell you—"

Alexis stopped her. "Remember, we need a manufacturer before we can commit to any retailers. Somebody has to make the clothes, and all we have right now is the photographs of the samples on our fit model."

"Yes, I know. We've had brochures and calls coming in from quite a few retailers." Olivia paused. "We're to a young company, and you're a new designer, so the retailers aren't exactly clamoring to work with you."

Alexis pursed her lips. "Did you tell them how much interest we've generated?"

"Of course I did. But it doesn't amount to much until we settle on a manufacturer."

Shaking her head, Alexis turned her attention back to the board. "We might have a better shot if we were doing haute couture. But that's just not my thing, never has been." As much as she enjoyed flipping through magazines to see what was new in high fashion, Alexis had always known she wanted to design clothes that were more approachable. Working with Torrid had allowed her to do just that. While haute couture's glamour generated plenty of buzz and media interest, many of the designers seemed hopelessly stuck in the past. They labored away, designing clothes mainly in sizes zero through four. And while those pieces looked great on the waifish models strutting the runways, the average American woman, who wore a size fourteen, just wasn't going to buy them.

Her goal for the One line was to blur the distinction between ready-to-wear and mass-market fashions. Her clothes were attractive, high quality, and structurally complex, yet simple and practical enough for wear by everyday women. Beyond that, they were sized to fit fuller figures and cut in a way that didn't constrict or bind. In her opinion, being gorgeous and well-dressed shouldn't mean being unable to move freely. Not every line could be high fashion. Regular people had to have something to wear, too. It wasn't as if a teacher or a librarian could afford Issey Miyake.

"I think I have somebody in mind for the manufacturer."

Sydney's brow rose. "Are we talking about your brother's friend?"

She nodded.

"Great. So when is he coming in?"

"I haven't called him yet," Alexis answered sheepishly.

Sydney frowned. "Girl, get your life together and call that man!"

"I will." Alexis touched one of the fabric samples on the board, avoiding eye contact with her partner. "I just haven't had a minute yet."

"Right. Anyway, stop putting it off." Sydney side-eyed her, sounding skeptical.

Alexis remained quiet for a moment, considering her options. She'd been avoiding making the call, but she had no intention of revealing that to Sydney. There was something about Bryan that made Alexis nervous. Not only was he fine, but he just had the air of a man who could make even the most scrupulous woman suddenly decide to mix business with pleasure. She thought back on their encounter at the Arts Council and how seeing him in a suit had nearly rendered her speechless. Putting off making contact with him about this important business matter was little more than a defense mechanism.

"Listen. I really have to talk to you about the situation with the launch." Sydney's voice cut into her thoughts.

Alexis walked around the easel and returned to her seat behind the desk. "What situation? You're not talking about changing our strategy, are you?"

She shook her head. "No. We're still aiming for three retailers: one boutique, one volume, and one high-end department store. That strategy is too brilliant to change."

"Good. Because I want this line to be available in every major city in America. If it does well, we'll have the pull we need to take it global." The very idea of seeing her clothes worn by women in Paris, New York, Cape Town, and Tokyo filled Alexis with immense excitement. Swinging her gaze back to Sydney, she noticed how nervous her partner looked. "Syd, what's the matter?"

"Well…" Sydney looked away, glancing over her shoulder at the idea board.

Alexis could feel the vibes rolling off Sydney's body; she could sense her hesitation. "Okay. What is it that you're not telling me?"

Sydney's brown eyes were wide as she spoke. "It's going to sound a lot worse than it actually is, so don't freak out."

Now I know she's about to say something off the wall. "Just tell me."

"Promise me you aren't going to freak out."

Brow furrowed, Alexis leaned back in her seat. "The longer you stall me, the more worried I get. So just spit it out."

Sucking in a breath through her clenched teeth,

Sydney launched a speech. "Okay. So I was talking to Maria Valasquez. And you know how you came up with that brilliant slogan, 'Dare to Be Demure'?"

"Yes. My slogan is brilliant, and thanks for pointing it out." Alexis wondered what Maria, a reporter for the local network news, had to do with this. "But why were you talking to Maria anyway?"

"Duh. We need as much positive press as we can get. Maria has been following your career ever since we opened the design house. So why wouldn't I reach out to her?"

Alexis nodded. "That's true. I certainly won't turn down any good publicity. Go on with the story."

Sydney took a deep breath. "Well, I told Maria the slogan and the idea behind it. She seemed a little skeptical that a line focused on covering up instead of revealing a woman's…assets…would do all that well in the current market."

Alexis sighed, bracing for what would come next. Knowing Sydney, she'd probably let her passion for the line get the better of her and said something crazy. "That's a little presumptuous of her, but I'm sure you set her straight. What did you tell her, Syd?"

Her face shifting into a sheepish half smile, Sydney admitted her deed. "I told her that you had a super sexy, wealthy fiancé and that you'd won him over when he saw you in a sample piece."

"Let me guess. The whole love at first sight, this is destiny, kismet story?"

"Yes."

"Good grief, Sydney. This is nuts, even for you."

"I know, I know. But you should have seen the

reaction it got. I mean, not every woman who wears something from the line is going to bag a rich, handsome man. But Maria loved that angle. She ate it up, and she's probably going to float that line in the story she's doing about our show at the festival."

Alexis felt her brow crease. "And when's that going to air?"

"In a few minutes. That's why I'm telling you about it now." Sydney grabbed the remote from the edge of the desk and flipped on the wall-mounted television. Once she put it on the right station, the two of them settled into tense silence to wait for the segment.

Maria's face appeared on screen, and Alexis watched nervously, hoping that Sydney's fabricated tale would be left out of the story. For the first few minutes, Alexis thought she'd be okay. But then, as Maria ended the segment, Alexis cringed.

"It seems like Alexis Devers has it all. A design house, a new line that's sure to make waves in the fashion industry, and, as my source tells me, a handsome and well-to-do fiancé. Talk about a local girl made good. I'm Maria Valasquez for Channel Six News."

Alexis rested her forehead in her palm. "So these people all think I have a rich fiancé?" It sounded even more ridiculous coming out of her own mouth. She didn't so much as have a serious boyfriend, and Sydney had just assigned her a husband-to-be. She had a unique lifestyle that revolved around her artistic process and wasn't exactly conducive to dating.

Sydney clasped her hands in her lap. "I'm sorry. But I knew that was what she wanted to hear, you know, to put us over the top."

"Over the top is right." Alexis shook her head. "And what happens when people ask to meet this fiancé of mine? Because you know they will."

"I haven't figured that part out yet. I figured we'll just say he's out of town on business the first few times they ask."

"And if they persist?"

Sydney shrugged. "I honestly don't know."

Leaning back until her executive chair went into recline, Alexis groaned aloud. "Sydney, if I didn't love you, I would fire you. You know that, don't you?"

"Don't worry, Lex. We'll find somebody who fits the bill." Sydney stood, clapped her hands. "Right now, it's not even an issue, because so far, no one has asked to meet him. So that buys us some time at least."

Alexis rolled her eyes.

Sydney spoke again, looking genuinely repentant. "Again, I'm really sorry. But this just goes to prove that I'll do anything to see Krystal Kouture thrive. This design house is our baby."

That much was true. Alexis and Sydney had started the house two years ago with a grand vision in mind. They'd both worked hard, side by side, to build up a stable footing so that they could launch their first line.

"When you're world-famous, you'll look back on this and laugh." Sydney's expression conveyed far more assurance than her tone did.

"I hope so." For right now, Alexis had to figure out a solution to the situation Sydney had gotten them into. Truth be told, a part of her admired Sydney's gumption. She'd been dishonest but not in a way that would hurt or defraud anyone. "By the way, Syd. I applaud your passion, but let's keep it aboveboard going forward, okay?"

"You got it." Sydney winked as she made her way toward the door. "I'm headed down to my office to draft a sample contract for the retailers. I'll swing back by with it before lunch."

As Sydney left, Alexis straightened in her seat. Booting the computer, she opened her browser's search bar and typed in "Royal Textiles NC."

Waiting for the results to load, a crazy thought occurred to her.

Nah. She pushed the thought aside and concentrated on finding out everything she could about Bryan's family business. Before she called him, she wanted to make sure she would be an informed consumer.

———

Bryan swung open the door of Krystal Kouture Design House. The building, a contemporary structure of steel and glass, stood four stories. Located in a recently updated section of downtown Raleigh, it was prime real estate.

Stepping inside the office, which encompassed the entire first floor of the building, he paused for a moment. The interior, well-lit and inviting, was painted in pale pastels. The framed art pieces, mostly modern minimalist works, conspired with the paint job to create a calm, peaceful environment.

A tall reception desk centered the main lobby, but at the moment, no one was there. Bryan made himself comfortable in one of the plush upholstered chairs lining the walls. He'd already shown up here unannounced, hoping Alexis would see him. He wasn't about to make it worse by barging into her office. Rudeness was more Wes's style.

Opening the brown leather briefcase he'd brought with him, he shuffled through the stack of papers inside. His secretary, Joan, had loaded the case with the typical items he took with him when he spoke with potential clients. Glossy, full-color brochures touted the cutting-edge technology, quality materials, and highly trained employees utilized by Royal Textiles. There were spec sheets, news releases of the recent contracts he'd acquired for the company, and a list of current designers who used Royal as their manufacturer.

He shut the briefcase, settled into the chair. He'd use everything Joan had sent in his presentation while adding his own personal touch. As with every pitch, he'd tailor everything he said to Alexis, her line, and her unique needs. *That is, assuming she'll see me.*

He thought back to Tuesday, when he'd run into her downtown. She'd mentioned her intention to discuss her line with him, yet he hadn't heard from her. It had only been two days, but since she'd pointed out her time constraints, he wanted to get the ball rolling. He'd called the office earlier and left a voicemail. Rather than wait to hear back from her, he'd decided to cut his losses and visit her in person. Hopefully, he'd picked an afternoon when she'd actually have time to speak with him.

A short, slender brunette walked into the lobby then, from the east corridor. Dressed in a black skirt and white top, she took her post behind the desk and looked his way. "Hello. Can I help you, sir?"

He rose from his seat, taking the briefcase with him as he approached. "Hi. I'm Bryan James from Royal Textiles. Is Ms. Devers available to take a meeting with me?"

"Welcome, Mr. James. I'm Dawn." She lifted the receiver of the phone on her desk. "I'll check with her. Just a moment, please."

He took a step back and waited while Dawn used the phone. When she put it down, she looked his way with a smile. "You're in luck. Ms. Devers will see you in few minutes. Wait here, and she'll come and get you as soon as she's ready."

"Thank you." He stepped back again, giving her space to go about her work.

A few minutes later, Alexis appeared in the west corridor.

His eyes swung to her immediately. Something about her presence dominated everything in the room, capturing his attention right away. She wore a pair of slim black pants that clung to every line of her long legs. A white top flowed easily over the curves of her upper body. Her hair was held back from her face by a jeweled black headband, leaving her face unobscured. Her skin glowed, but he couldn't detect any makeup.

As his brain worked to process how gorgeous she was, he shifted his weight from his right foot to his left. "Hello, Ms. Devers."

Her hazel eyes fell on him, and she gifted him with a smile. "Hi, Bryan. Nice to see you again."

"Same here. Thanks for taking time out to see me."

"You lucked out today. But next time, make an appointment."

He chuckled, detecting the teasing in her tone. "I promise to do that, Ms. Devers."

She shook her head. "Just call me Alexis. No need to be so formal." Curving her index finger, she beckoned him to follow her. "Let's continue this in my office."

Taking a moment to compose himself, he followed her down the hall. He always gave himself something of a silent pep talk before a presentation, but that tradition was quickly quashed as his eyes landed on her shapely backside moving a few feet in front of him. There wasn't much else he could do but take in her magnificent "rear view."

He inhaled deeply, breathing in her scent. She smelled of citrus and flowers, clean and enticing. The confines of the hallway seemed to magnify the fragrance. The scent was familiar and comforting, like the refreshing scent that hung in the air after a spring rain. He smiled at the thought. He hadn't spent much time with her yet. But being in her presence seemed to refresh him as well.

They entered her office, where the pastel theme continued. Instead of modern art, though, framed sketches were displayed on the walls of the space.

She gestured to the chair in front of her desk. "Have a seat."

He did as she walked around to the other side of the desk to claim her own seat. Still admiring the sketches, he asked, "Did you do all of those?"

She nodded. "I did. Sydney, my partner, has some sketches up in her office as well."

"They're very impressive. You're a talented designer." Bryan's eyes swept over the sketches once more before returning to her face. "You look skeptical."

"You did come here to make a pitch, so..." She paused, gave a little shrug of her delicate shoulders. "Let's just say I'm a little jaded."

"Trust me. I wouldn't have complimented you if I didn't mean it." He held her gaze a few beats, hoping his expression would communicate his seriousness. If they were in a different setting, he'd be complimenting more than just her skills as a designer.

A ghost of a smile lit her beautiful face. "Thank you."

He slung the briefcase onto his lap, opening it. "I know you've got other things to do, so do you mind if I go ahead with my presentation?"

She shook her head. "I don't mind. Go right ahead."

He cleared his throat, loosened the Windsor knot in his tie. "Let me start by telling you that Royal Textiles is the largest, most efficient clothing textile manufacturer in the southeastern United States. What sets us apart from our competitors is our dedication to excellence."

She nodded. "How so?"

"We don't make rugs and curtains and tents. Our sole focus is on apparel manufacturing, and we put our absolute best into it. We have only the most state-of-the-art equipment and the most highly trained technicians working on our factory floor." He handed over the materials he'd brought, two brochures and a full color booklet, for her to peruse. "You should also know that we've been honored for quality by both the American Council of Textile Production and the International Apparel Society."

"I'm impressed." She looked through the material, addressing him as her eyes scanned the glossy paper. Her expression was difficult to read. "Okay. So tell me about the most recent apparel line your company has acquired a production contract for."

He straightened in his seat, holding eye contact with her. "We recently started manufacturing J. Cole's denim line. The first pairs of jeans rolled off the line in the past two weeks."

Her lips curved, and she appeared impressed. "Sounds good. There isn't any denim in the Krystal Kouture One line."

"I know. I've seen the designs."

One perfectly shaped brow lifted. "And how is that? My partner only sent out promotional items to the retailers."

"I have connections in retail. A friend of a friend let me take a look at your materials." He leaned back, tenting his fingers. They'd reached the juncture of his pitch where he needed to appear casual but still show that he was serious about closing the deal. "Like I said, I think you have a lot of talent. As a textiles guy, I'm also mindful of how regional weather patterns can affect buyer expectations, especially in women's wear. You have a good variety of pieces, and they're sized right as well. I can see the appeal of your line for women all over the country."

Closing the booklet, she set it aside. Lacing her graceful fingers, she placed her hands on the top of her desk. "I see you've done your homework. And I'm impressed with everything you've shown me." She gestured to the stack of paper he'd given her.

A smile crossed his lips, and he clapped his hands together. Reaching into the open briefcase, he started to extract a preliminary agreement. "Wonderful. To get started, all I'll need is for you to fill this out."

She blinked a few times. "I'm sorry, I think you

misunderstood me. I'm impressed, and everything looks good. But I have to take this up with my partner. I'm not going to make a decision, especially not one as major as this, without speaking to Sydney first."

He tucked the agreement back inside, snapped the briefcase shut. "I understand completely." Inside, he could feel the disappointment welling up inside him He'd expected to win Alexis over with his brilliant presentation and return to the office with a signed agreement. Now, he'd have to go back empty-handed. While that wasn't the outcome he'd hoped for, he did respect Alexis's regard for her business partner. They were obviously a tightly knit unit, and he could see that reflected in Alexis's manner and her words.

"We'll get back to you with our decision by Monday at the latest." She let her gaze travel over his upper body, then back to his eyes. "Is that acceptable?"

"That's fine." This time, his brow hitched. *Was she just checking me out?* He shifted in such a way that the muscles in his forearm flexed, and noticed the brief look of approval that flashed over her face. It flattered him and tempted him to let her know just how attractive he found her. But on the off chance that might make her uncomfortable, he kept it to himself.

She stood then, extended her hand to him across the desk. "Thank you for stopping by, Bryan."

"Thank you for seeing me." He stood up with the handle of his briefcase in one hand. He closed his free hand over her smaller one and shook it, feeling the tingle of heat that radiated from his palm. The warmth spread through him, bringing back the feeling of comfort he noticed whenever he was in her presence. He released her, pushing aside his urge to linger. As much as he wanted to bask in her glow, they both had work to do, and he didn't want to monopolize her entire afternoon after dropping in on her the way he had.

Turning away from her, he started walking toward her office door.

"Bryan?"

Standing in the doorframe, he turned his head toward the sound of his name. "Yes?"

"Nice suit." She winked. "You wear it well."

He couldn't stop the grin that stretched his lips. *So she felt it, too.* Keeping his tone even, he responded to her compliment. "Thank you. Have a nice day, Alexis."

"You do the same."

Knowing that if he stayed any longer he would start "pitching woo," as his father often said, he strode out.

Chapter 6

LYING ACROSS HER SOFA, ALEXIS STIFLED A YAWN. It was a foggy, overcast Saturday with thick, gray clouds rolling past her window. Even though it was close to noon, she still wore the white cami and red boxer shorts she'd slept in the previous night. With the weather being so gloomy and her being so tightly wound from a whirlwind week at the design house, she'd decided to rest today. Her entire agenda for the day consisted of three things: lounging, puttering, and snacking.

Grabbing the remote, she flipped on her television. She surfed the channels for a few moments before stopping on the classic comedy film *Harlem Nights*. A smile came over her face as she watched the movie, even though she'd seen it six or seven times.

Just as Della Reese's character began complaining about being shot in the pinky toe, Alexis felt the couch cushions vibrate. Picking up her phone, she looked at the screen to see whose call was causing the device to buzz so insistently.

Her eyes widened as she saw the name on the display. Swiping to answer the call, she said, "Kelsey? Is everything okay?"

"Hey, baby sis. Yes, I'm okay. Scott isn't here, so I thought I'd give you a call." Kelsey's tone held a false brightness, one her family members had become accustomed to.

Alexis cringed at the mention of Kelsey's boyfriend. "How long will he be gone?"

"I don't know. He went to the store, so maybe a half hour." She sighed into the receiver. "I miss y'all. How are Mom and Dad? And Max?"

"We're all fine, Kelsey. Just missing you." Alexis struggled to keep the emotion out of her voice, knowing things were already hard enough for her sister without her getting weepy.

"You know, I woke up in the middle of the night. I just had the strangest feeling. And I rolled over, and Scott was wide awake. Just staring right at me."

Alexis swallowed but didn't say anything, because she sensed there was more.

"I asked him if he needed something. You know what he said? 'Just go back to sleep, so I can watch you some more.' I don't know how long he was lying there like that, just staring at me. It was so eerie." She paused, sighed. "It took me a long time to go back to sleep."

A chill ran down Alexis's back as she listened to Kelsey's story. "Kelsey, you have to get out of there. Please."

A soft, sarcastic chuckle met that plea. "I can't leave. And you know why. Every cent I make goes into our joint account, and I only have access to the money he gives me."

"We'll help you. Whatever you need. Mom and Dad and Maxwell and I, we're all willing to help you."

"I have to do this for myself, Lex. In my own way."

"But Kelsey, I…"

"What about Naji? I can't leave him here with Scott. He won't be safe, and you and I both know that."

Alexis sighed.

A moment later, a small voice called out Kelsey's name.

"Speak of the devil. Come here, Naji."

Alexis could picture Naji, Scott's five-year-old son, climbing up in Kelsey's lap. Even though Kelsey wasn't Naji's mother, it was obvious that she'd grown to love him in the two years she'd been with Scott. Your heart is in the right place, Kelsey. But you have to think of your own safety."

"I know what I'm facing here, Lex. But I can handle it. Right now, Naji needs me."

Alexis heard a door slam in the background, then the call disconnected. Sighing again, she tossed the phone aside. Scott must have come back, and he'd trained Kelsey well. She knew better than to be caught talking on the phone when he wasn't present.

Tears welled in her eyes, threatening to spill on to her cheeks. Wiping them away with the back of her hand, Alexis took several deep breaths to try and calm down. The fear she had for her sister's safety had risen again, stronger this time. Not knowing what else to do, she grabbed her phone to call Maxwell.

Once he was caught up on the details of the conversation between his two younger sisters, Maxwell had questions of his own. "What happened? Did she say anything before she hung up?"

"No. I just heard a door slam."

"Shit."

"I know." She shook her head as she wondered for the millionth time why Scott was such a jerk. Kelsey was about as sweet as a person could be, as evidenced by her dogged determination to protect a little boy who wasn't even related to her from potential danger. "I don't know if there's anything we can say to her that will get her to leave without Naji."

"She can't help caring about the kid. That's just the way she is." Maxwell sighed. "I'm not sure what to do here. I mean, I don't want any harm to come to Naji, either. She's asked us not to interfere, right?"

"Yes. She claims she can handle it, though I'm not sure I believe that."

"We don't have a choice here. She's an adult, and if she says not to get involved, then we have to stay out of it."

Alexis could only sigh in response. *Max is right.* She would simply have to do her best to tuck away the worry rolling around like a ball in the pit of her stomach.

"If you hear from her again, let me know. And I'll do the same." Maxwell's voice brought her back to the present.

"Okay. Later, Max."

"Later." He disconnected the call.

Setting her phone back on the couch cushion, she got up from her comfy seat. Heading into the kitchen, she made herself a cup of herbal tea. The blend she preferred usually went a long way toward calming her nerves, and after Kelsey's call, she needed it.

Monday morning, Bryan found himself back in Alexis's office, sitting across from her again. She'd summoned him there to give him her decision on the possibility of Royal Textiles manufacturing her new clothing line.

Today, she wore a black button-down blouse and a white pencil skirt. Black-and-white striped pumps on her feet capped her long bronze legs. Silver hoops hung in her ears, and her hair was pinned back from her face with two bedazzled bobby pins. He loved the way the hairstyle left the elegant lines of her face and the hollow of her throat unobstructed from his view.

Aware that they were not alone, he swung his gaze away from Alexis to settle on the face of her partner, Sydney Greer. She sat in an armchair against the wall of the office, adjacent to Alexis, her ankles crossed. Sydney's black jumpsuit looked as if it had been chosen to coordinate with Alexis's outfit.

Alexis's cherry-red lips parted as she spoke again. "Sydney and I read through all the material you left with us last week, and we discussed the feasibility of having your company make our clothing line."

"I appreciate your careful consideration of my offer." He couldn't read anything from her expression or her body language. *She's got a mean poker face.* He braced himself for rejection, in case that was where the conversation was headed.

She shifted in her seat, lifting one leg and crossing it over the other.

He sensed the gesture was force of habit, but he noticed it nonetheless. She was the picture of elegance, and he felt fortunate to be in her presence.

"We've decided to go ahead and sign on with Royal. Sydney and I agree that it will be a good fit."

A smile tilted his lips. Her approval meant a lot to him, and not just because it meant he would meet his goal of securing a contract from her.

Sydney nodded. "Yes. Having a local company handle our manufacturing will allow us to be involved in the process, from beginning to end."

Alexis spoke again. "It's important to us that all our pieces be made in America and with the highest of environmental standards. I also demand a safe and comfortable workplace for the people who'll be making my clothes. I know that textile manufacturing overseas can be pretty dicey, and I want to make sure that the production of my line is good for the environment and for your employees. Can you guarantee me that?"

"Yes, I can." Yet again, she'd impressed him. Her concerns seemed to reach everyone and everything involved in the process, and that stood out. He'd met many a designer whose only concern was how much money they'd make off the final product.

"Good." She sat back in her seat. "I'll come by to inspect your facilities, of course. But I think we're all set."

"Thank you, ladies. I promise Royal will produce your line to the high standards your designs demand." He stood and reached across to shake Sydney's hand, and the contact remained very brief, cordial, and professional. When he clasped Alexis's hand, he felt a charge the moment his skin touched hers. He released her hand, stepped back, and returned to his seat.

Sydney stood. "Alexis, I'm going to look over the last few samples Pam has sewn." She looked his way. "Welcome aboard, Mr. James."

"Thanks again." He gave her a nod as she passed him and left the office.

"I'll take a look at the paperwork now." Alexis leaned forward in her seat, lacing her fingers together.

"Here you go." He opened his briefcase to retrieve the papers, then handed them over the desktop to her.

She took them, immediately set them down. "Before I sign these, there is one more thing I want to request from you."

Meeting her gaze, he asked, "What can I do for you?"

"Funny you should pose that question. I'll warn you, what I'm about to ask is very unorthodox."

His brow twitched. "I see the immense value in this account, Ms. Devers, and I plan to do whatever you require in order to gain your business." He used that line often when a new account was on the line, but he didn't remember ever meaning it as sincerely as he did at the present moment.

She smiled, gave a small chuckle. "I'm about to test that. Call me Alexis."

"Okay, Alexis." He settled in, giving her his full attention. "Let's hear it."

"When my partner was out drumming up retailer interest in our fashion line, she told one reporter that I was engaged to be married. For some reason, that made the line more saleable. Sydney's little falsehood is now part of the public discourse, because the reporter mentioned it on television."

He could feel his brow scrunch with confusion. "That's an odd way to go about it, but whatever works. Though I'm not sure what this has to do with me."

Another soft chuckle. "I'll just ask you straight out, then. Would you be willing to pose as my fiancé? At least until the line gets off the ground and becomes well-established?"

He blinked several times. *Did she just say what I think she said?* "I'm sorry, what?"

"I told you it was unorthodox. I need a wealthy, handsome fiancé on my arm, and my cursory research tells me you fit the bill. So will you do it?"

"You researched me?"

She shrugged, her expression remaining casual. "All it took was a little bit of digging online to find out a few things about you. I also looked into Royal's company history, and based on that and your illustrious educational and professional background, I'd wager you are financially set."

He blinked a few times, unable to disagree with her assessment. "Okay, then."

"And as far as the other thing, I'm not blind." She fixed him with an appreciative stare. "You're very easy on the eyes."

His pulse quickened, his throat becoming dry as his body reacted to her words and her tone of voice. "You were right. This is the first time I've had a request like this."

She said nothing but kept her eyes on him.

He met her gaze, arrested by the dark pools of her eyes, framed by a thick fringe of black lashes. "And what exactly would I have to do as your faux fiancé?"

"It depends on whether the line catches on. You have to be seen in public with me. We'd need to appear affectionate toward each other, of course."

"I can handle that. Is there more?"

"If things go well, there will probably be television interviews and press. So you may have to appear affectionate in front of cameras. I won't ask much else of you."

He cupped his chin, thought about what she was asking him to do. He couldn't deny that it appealed to him. "Is this strictly a business offer? Or is there more to it?"

"What do you mean?"

"I mean, I'm sure you could ask someone else, but you asked me. So what does that mean? How should I take that?" He searched her face, attempting to gauge her motivation.

She pursed her lips momentarily before answering. "I'm attracted to you; I can admit that. The way I see it, that will only make this easier. Our engagement will look like the real deal."

She just admitted that she's attracted to me. He'd thought as much, but to hear her say it was the best kind of confirmation. He quieted as he let the satisfaction of her admission sink in for a few moments.

"I apologize if you think I'm out of line or if I made you uncomfortable. If you'd like to think about it, I understand, and I can wait a few—"

"I'll do it."

Now she appeared surprised. "Really? Just like that?"

"I'm attracted to you as well. But I think you know that."

She broke eye contact for the first time in several minutes, and a hint of redness crept into her cheeks. "I know."

"And since I'm marriage agnostic, I don't have any qualms about the whole fake engagement thing."

One arched brow lifted. "Marriage agnostic?"

"I don't have any strong feelings about the institution, one way or the other."

"Hmm." She seemed to turn that over in her mind for a moment. "So you're sure you want to do this?"

"Why not? The two of us can have fun, at least until this little arrangement has served its purpose."

She said nothing, watching him intently.

"You need a manufacturer as well as a fiancé. I need this contract. I'd say this is a pretty good way for us both to get what we want." He nodded as he thought about it further, because he planned to make full use of his time as Alexis's intended, fake or otherwise. "Whose brilliant idea was this, by the way?"

The blush in her cheeks deepened. "Mine. I haven't even told Sydney about it. You may think it's brilliant, but she'd probably think I was nuts."

"She got you into this mess. Now you're getting yourself out." He grinned. "So now that we're agreed, are you ready for the paperwork?"

She nodded. "I'll take care of it right now."

He watched as her graceful fingers wrapped around a silver-plated pen, extracting it from a small mesh cup full of writing implements. She buzzed Sydney back into the office, and together, they spent time reading through the contract. Bryan answered their questions and explained the finer points of the agreement. He tried to be attentive to both of them, but as always, his eyes were drawn back to Alexis. Again, he was refreshed by her savvy. Her business acumen was as good as that of any man he knew. Yet Alexis was so undeniably feminine, it took his breath away.

When everything was signed and initialed properly, Sydney slipped out and returned to her own office. Alexis slid the stack of papers toward him. "Anything else?"

He shook his head. "No. We're good. Although…"

"Yes?"

"If we're going to carry on a decent fake engagement, I really think we should sit down and iron out our story. You know, get our facts straight. Maybe over dinner."

She appeared amused. "Are you asking me out on a date?"

He gave her his best and brightest smile. "I guess you could say that."

"Why don't we start with coffee?"

"I'll take it."

"Here." She held her hand out. "Give me your phone, and I'll put my number in."

He took the phone from his pocket, unlocked it, and slid it across to her. Watching her tap her number into the phone's memory, he noticed the way her lips flexed as she completed the task. Did she always do that when she was thinking about something? Soon, he would know, because he'd be learning all her quirks if he had his way.

"There." She slid the phone back to him. "You can call me and we'll pick a time and place."

"Sounds good." He tucked the phone away again, then stood, briefcase in hand. "I don't want to take up your whole day."

"I don't want to monopolize your whole day either. Have a good afternoon, Bryan."

"You, too, Alexis." And as he turned and left the office, he thought about the interesting and wholly welcome turn the day had taken.

Chapter 7

AFTER BRYAN LEFT, ALEXIS SAT AT HER DESK FOR A FEW silent moments, reliving their interaction. *Did he really just agree to be my pretend fiancé? Just like that?* She'd expected to have to do some cajoling, but he'd been much more receptive than she would have guessed he'd be. She didn't know how to take that, but she supposed it didn't matter. After all, they'd come to an agreement that would be mutually beneficial. Now she just needed to apprise other people of the situation, and since Sydney was her partner, she figured that would be the place to start. Using the intercom system, she summoned Sydney to her office.

When Sydney appeared in the doorway, Alexis beckoned her inside. "Come on in, Syd."

Easing into the chair on the other side of the desk, Sydney fixed her with a questioning stare. "So, what were y'all talking about in here? Bryan stayed for a good little while after I left."

"How do you know that?"

She scoffed. "Girl, please. We all know every move of any rooster that visits this hen house. Besides, he passed by my office door when he left about fifteen minutes ago."

Alexis giggled, shaking her head. "You're a mess. Anyway, my conversation with Bryan is why I called you in here. Bryan has agreed to be my fake fiancé." She left out the whole discussion of their mutual physical attraction to each other; as far as she was concerned, Sydney didn't need to know that.

Sydney's eyes widened with shock. "What? You didn't tell me you were going to—"

Alexis pursed her lips. "You mean, like you didn't tell me you were going to invent a man for me?"

Sydney sighed, letting her gaze drop as if she were ashamed. "Yeah, okay. You got me there."

"As I was saying, I asked Bryan if he would fill the role, and we came to an agreement. I'm telling you first, because you're going to have to help us maintain the ruse."

Sydney nodded. "Okay. And just how long do you think this is going to continue?"

Alexis shrugged. "I don't know. But he agreed to keep up appearances until I feel the line has a stable footing."

Sydney's eyes narrowed, and she appeared to study her friend's face. "And what happens after that?"

Alexis remembered then that they hadn't discussed the end game of their little deception. "We never talked about that. But I guess we'll come up with some statement about how we love each other deeply but have decided to go our separate ways. You know, the whole damage control, we'll-always-be-friends narrative."

"Sounds like you two have it all figured out."

"You didn't really give me much choice, Syd. I had to do something."

Sydney leaned back in her chair, crossed her legs. "Y'all obviously hashed out a lot of the details, but I think there are two important factors you haven't considered."

Leaning in, Alexis asked, "And what are they?"

"First of all, you need a history as a couple. How you met, how he proposed, and everything in between. I know y'all haven't worked that out. He wasn't in here long enough."

She smiled, struck by how often she and Sydney thought alike. "I'm way ahead of you. We're going to set up a date and come up with our origin story then."

Sydney nodded to express her approval. "Okay, okay. That sounds good. Make sure to write it down, and get me a copy."

Alexis chuckled. "Sure. Now what's the other thing we need to address?"

"Maxwell." Sydney fixed her with a knowing look.

"Shit." She'd been so busy working out the details with Bryan that she hadn't even considered her older brother.

"You've got that right." Sydney shook her head. "When Maxwell finds out, he's going to lose his entire mind. He's going to freak the hell out, and we both know it."

Alexis groaned. She could clearly recall the dirty looks Maxwell had given her just for talking to Bryan. He would definitely not approve of them dating; he'd made that clear. Once he discovered their so-called engagement, Maxwell's head was liable to explode. "You're right, Syd. What am I going to do about Maxwell? And my mom and dad?"

Sydney shrugged. "Girl, I wish I could tell you. But I don't know if there's anything you can do to smooth this over."

"I don't suppose you can go back to Maria and admit you were lying?"

"Now, after it's been on TV?" Sydney shook her head. "No, boo. We're way past the point of no return. We're just going to have to make the best of it."

Alexis nodded, resigned. If Sydney went back on her story, they'd likely only generate more press, but not the positive kind they were seeking. With their fledgling fashion collection at stake, they couldn't afford to bear that potential loss.

"I know I said it before, but I'm really sorry about all of this. I never expected it to blow up in my face this way." Sydney looked genuinely remorseful.

"I know. But it's like you said. We'll just have to make the best of it."

"I'm just thinking out loud here, but maybe this will go over better with your families if they never know it's fake."

Alexis felt her brow hitch. "How do we pull that off?"

"Tell them you've been spending time together since you ran into each other at the step show. That it was love at first sight, and you just couldn't help yourself." Sydney tapped her chin with her index finger. "I think they might buy it."

Alexis thought back on that afternoon at Central. She'd definitely felt something when she first laid eyes on Bryan's tall, muscular frame. But what she'd felt would come under the heading of lust, plain and simple. She'd watched him, even ogled him at times. Hell, she couldn't help herself. He was super easy on the eyes, and it had been a long time since she'd encountered such a handsome man. But love? "Maybe." Her skepticism seeped into her tone.

"Well, unless you're itching to tell them you're

faking this whole thing, I don't think you have much choice. When it comes to family, y'all better make it look real."

Alexis let her head fall back on the headrest of her chair until her gaze raked over the ceiling above her. This was a fine kettle of fish. She'd have to convince her family and the entire world that she and Bryan were a love match, brought together by fate and hit by the thunderbolt of true love the very moment they met. She let her mouth fall open into an O shape, exhaling in a whoosh.

Sydney chuckled. "I'll leave you to think about how you're going to play this game. I'll come back at lunchtime." She rose from the chair and slipped out.

Still staring up, Alexis sighed. This little ruse was bound to be a wild ride, for everyone involved.

She'd recovered from the conversation and settled onto the love seat in her office to read the latest issue of *Real Simple* when her phone rang. Setting aside the open magazine, she answered the call. "Hello?"

"Alexis? It's Maria Valasquez."

She tucked away the urge to sigh. It was true that Sydney had started this whole thing, but it was Maria's television segment that had sent it into overdrive. "Yes, it's me. Hi, Maria. How are you?"

"Great, great. I just wanted to reach out and ask you for a quick favor."

Wondering what this favor could be, since Maria already had the latest scoop on the goings-on at Krystal Kouture, Alexis took the bait. "What can I do for you?"

"Are you familiar with the *Morning Buzz*?"

Alexis's brow crinkled. "You mean the morning news show?"

"Yes, that's it." Maria, who generally spoke very fast, took a rare pause. It sounded as if she were shuffling through a stack of papers. "My college buddy Veronica is a producer on the show. I had lunch with her when she was in town earlier this week, and she's looking to fill a slot on the show. Because of Fall Runway Week in New York, they want something with a fashion angle."

"Okay. So tell me more." Alexis tucked the phone between her shoulder and her ear and balanced it there.

"Naturally, I suggested you. With your line about to launch, I knew you'd appreciate the publicity."

She blinked. "Wow, Maria. Thank you for thinking of me. When is the taping?"

"On the fourteenth."

She clapped her hands together. "That works, actually. I'm going up to Manhattan that week to have lunch with Tracy Reese." She'd scheduled the lunch months ago, because her mentor was notoriously busy. Now, she smiled, thinking how nicely things had lined up.

"Great. I'll let Veronica know you can do it. There's one more thing, though."

"What's that?"

"Do you think you could bring your fiancé along? I know Veronica said the host loves to include angles like this in her stories. You know, to help the viewers make a real connection with you."

She understood that. A bit taken aback by the request, she said, "He's pretty busy, but I'll ask him. I'm in either way, though."

"Great. Just send me a text and let me know." Maria paused, her tone changing. "By the way, Sydney never told me what his name was. Can you fill me in?"

Drawing a deep breath, Alexis said, "His name is Bryan James." He'd agreed to her bold offer, so she might as well put him to work.

"Cool. Got it. I'll wait to hear from you again, then. Bye, now."

After she disconnected the call, Alexis let her head drop back against the cushions. She wondered how Bryan would react to the news of this interview, especially since they hadn't yet worked out their origin story.

Deciding she'd find out soon enough, she directed her attention back to her magazine.

Behind the wheel of his late-model luxury sedan, Bryan navigated the streets of Raleigh. Evening approached, and as he passed by the illuminated signs in the windows of the businesses downtown, he shook his head. He could recall a time when there were corner stores, eateries, and more, owned by people who reflected the diversity of the neighborhood. Now, as real estate developers continued to descend on the City of Oaks, building their fancy condos, the very people who'd made the neighborhood so vibrant were being pushed out. Downtown was all high-end retailers and fancy restaurants, a product of the gentrification sweeping through cities all over the nation. He understood economics, and he generally welcomed new jobs and an infusion of wealth into his hometown. But parts of him lamented the lost city he'd grown up in, the one that nurtured him and made him the man he'd become.

South of downtown, he made a right turn toward his destination. He'd found Peter's sketchbook on the

corner of his desk and wanted to return it to the young
man. Mentoring sessions at Royal happened only twice
a month, and he felt pretty certain that Peter wouldn't
want to go that long without his book. Fortunately, a
sticker inside the back cover had Peter's address written
on it. So after he'd left work for the day, he'd grabbed
dinner and was now headed toward Peter's house on
Raleigh's south side.

The farther he drove into the heart of the neighborhood, the more he noticed the decline and decay around
him. The houses were small, the yards cramped. Some
of the homes were vacant or in various states of disre-
pair. He wondered if fixing up some of the homes that
were occupied but had seen better days could be added
to the list of community service projects for the kids
at the YOC. It would certainly be a worthwhile project
and would give them a sense of accomplishment while
relieving the burden of some of the residents, especially
the elderly and infirm.

He made a right turn, continuing to take in the
environment. People stood on corners, conversing,
smoking cigarettes, or simply hanging out. He nodded
and waved to those he passed, and most responded in
kind. A few simply stared at him, and he knew they
were probably wondering what he and his expensive
car were doing on this side of town. He had no ill will
for these people, nor did he feel threatened by them.
After all, most of them looked just like him, minus the
three-piece suit, a haircut, and a shave. As long as he
lived, he'd never understand the utter disdain some
people showed for those they deemed beneath them.
He hoped that through his involvement with mentoring,

he could help create a generation who put aside those divisive views.

When he arrived at the address inside Peter's book, he pulled his car close to the curb. Cutting the engine, he got out with the book tucked under his arm and walked to the porch. The little house had green siding and white shutters and a few pink azaleas blooming in the yard.

He rapped on the door, waited.

A few moments later, Peter swung the door open. Shock registered on his face. "What's up, Mr. J? What you doing here?"

Bryan chuckled. "You don't usually just fling open the door when somebody knocks, do you?"

Peter shook his head as he propped open the wooden screen door with his foot, standing in the gap. "Nah. But I could see you through the peephole."

Holding out the sketchbook, Bryan passed it to him. "You left this in my office. I thought you'd want it back."

Peter smiled as he took the book. "Yeah, thanks. I was looking for it."

"No problem. I knew it would be a while before you kids came back over to the office." He looked past Peter, over his shoulder into the darkness of the house, but couldn't see anything.

As if sensing his scrutiny, Peter volunteered, "Oh, my pops isn't here. He's pulling a late shift. Says a lady brought him three suits to alter, a half hour before closing time."

Bryan nodded. "I'm sure you're capable of taking care of yourself. But if you need anything before your dad gets back, just give me a call. You still have my card, right?"

"Yeah, I still have it." Peter backed up, letting the screen door close. "I need to finish my homework. But thanks for dropping off my sketchbook, Mr. J."

"No problem. See you later." Bryan turned and started walking toward his car. Behind him, he heard Peter close and lock the heavy wooden door.

A few minutes later, he was back in his car and on the Beltline, headed home. He thought back to what he'd seen at Peter's place. He was a bright kid, even though he lived in one of the city's poorer neighborhoods. Seeing the environment Peter lived in compelled Bryan to want to help him, but first, he had to figure out a way to do it that wouldn't cause embarrassment.

Putting that aside for now, Bryan engaged his hands-free calling. Soon, the car's interior was filled with Oscar's voice as he answered the call. "Hello, Son."

"Hi, Dad. Sorry I cut out early today, but I had a ton of errands to run." He had been there for part of the morning but hadn't returned to Royal after that fateful meeting with Alexis Devers.

"I understand. So what's going on with you?"

"I didn't get a chance to tell you earlier, but I secured a new contract for us that I think is going to be very lucrative." He felt pretty satisfied knowing he'd pulled a contract in only a week, two weeks shy of the timeline he'd promised his father.

"Wonderful!" Oscar's voice conveyed his enthusiasm. "With what design house?"

"You've heard about the debut line that Krystal Kouture is doing, right?" He flipped his turn signal on as he waited in the left turn lane.

"Yes, yes. I've read about it in the trade bulletins.

Retailers will be clamoring for it the moment it comes off the line."

"Then you'll be glad to know that we'll be their sole manufacturer." Bryan let the satisfaction of his accomplishment roll through his body as he executed a left turn into his neighborhood.

"Excellent. Great work, Son."

"So, there's really no reason for Wesley to stay, is there? Now that I've locked down an account, he can go home, right?"

"Well, actually, he's going to stay for a few weeks. He's using the guest cottage at our house."

Bryan frowned. Navigating his car into his driveway, he rolled his eyes. "Don't they need him back at the dealership?"

"Apparently not. But look on the bright side. If anything should go wrong with this new contract, he'll be here to help us out."

Bryan pulled his car into the empty slot of his three-car garage. As he cut the engine, he switched the call back to his handset. "You and I obviously have very different opinions on the meaning of 'the bright side.'" He saw nothing positive about having to deal with his jerk cousin during the first few weeks of a new contract.

"Look, I know you and Wesley have your differences, but remember, he's family."

"Unfortunately," Bryan groused while using his key to let himself into the house. There were many traditions of the black families in the South that he loved and espoused. There was the obligatory electric slide, performed without fail at every gathering. Or the rules that only one person in the family could make the potato salad, and that you didn't visit without bringing a dish. But this whole idea of dealing with people you didn't like simply because they were "family" wasn't something he could get with. "Whatever you say, Dad."

"Anyway, it's great news. What time are you coming in to the office tomorrow?"

"I'll be there around nine. But I may have to leave around four." He planned to ask Alexis out for coffee then, to discuss their new arrangement, but he saw no need to disclose that to his father. His preference would have been to take her out to dinner, but since everything was so new, he could understand why Alexis had suggested something more informal. There would be plenty of time to wine and dine her over the coming weeks.

"Okay. I'll see you in the morning. Good night, Son."

"'Night, Dad." He disconnected the call as he entered his living room. Setting the phone on the charging dock on the side table, he shrugged out of his sport coat. He had his mind set on a hot shower and then crashing into his bed.

Because with any luck, tomorrow would be just as eventful as today had been.

Chapter 8

TUESDAY EVENING, ALEXIS SHOWED UP AT THE
Raging Bean about fifteen minutes prior to the appointed
time. She'd walked there, since the coffee shop was less
than two blocks from her building. It was a temperate
early fall evening, and other than the thick cloud of
ragweed pollen swirling around her like a fog, it was a
beautiful day. The shop had an area set up on the sidewalk in front of the building, where wrought-iron tables
and chairs beckoned patrons to sit outside. But like just
about everything else outside, the furniture already bore
a generous coating of pine pollen, which fell steadily
from the trees above like snow. She covered her nose
to stifle a sneeze and, in the interest of her breathing,
entered the shop and sought out a seat inside.

The moment she stepped inside, the rich aroma of
roasting coffee beans filled her nostrils, replacing the
scent of the copious evidence of plant reproduction
she'd dealt with outside. She inhaled, a smile stretching
her lips. The shop wasn't too crowded, but she could
see there were a good ten or so people inside, seated at
tables, on benches, or in the fluffy armchairs. She eased
her way to the counter, reading the chalkboard that displayed the day's special concoctions.

Bryan strode in.

The moment he entered the space, she felt his presence. It was as if her senses awakened whenever he was

near. She looked toward the door, letting her gaze sweep over him. He wore a pair of navy slacks and a light-blue button-down shirt. He'd forgone a tie, and the top two buttons of his shirt were undone. His black dress shoes gleamed in the overhead light. A pair of dark sunglasses obscured his eyes but could not hide the smile that brightened his handsome face when he saw her.

He removed the sunglasses, tucking them into the hip pocket on his slacks. Their gazes met as he crossed the space.

Her heart pounded in her ears. What was it about him and his killer smile that made her feel like an overzealous fangirl in the front row of a concert? Even now, she could feel the rise in her body temperature, and she could tell it had nothing to do with the climatic conditions of the coffee shop.

No. This man was hot, plain and simple.

Standing abreast of her, he spoke. "Have you been waiting long?"

"No. I was a little early, but I haven't been here that long." She blinked, hoping to break the spell he seemed to be casting over her. "Do you want to order something?"

"I'm gonna grab a mocha. You look nice, by the way." He let his gaze travel over her body.

She glanced down at her simple outfit of a long gray tunic, black leggings, and metallic silver ballet flats. "Thanks." She hadn't changed clothes after leaving work. As a designer and as a consumer, she held firm to the belief that comfort should coexist with looking put-together.

The young woman working behind the counter asked, "What can I get you, ma'am?"

Alexis turned toward the menu again but found it hard to decide. Nothing there looked quite as delicious as the tall drink of man standing behind her. In the end, she went with her usual. "Can I have a medium French roast with cream and a caramel drizzle, please?"

"No problem, ma'am. Anything else?"

"No." She occasionally ordered a muffin or some other pastry to accompany her dark roast, but the butterflies in her stomach left little room—or desire—for food. She reached into her black shoulder bag for her wallet, but she heard Bryan speak as she rifled around inside her purse.

"I'll be paying for the lady's drink. And I'd like a medium mocha, please."

She snapped her head up in time to see him hand the barista his credit card.

As if he sensed her wide-eyed stare, he turned her way. "What is it?"

"I was intending to pay for my drink."

"Nonsense. It's the least I can do for my beautiful fiancée." He winked.

Her mouth watered, and she swallowed. Was it from the heady scent of coffee and baked goods arousing her taste buds? Or from the way he looked at her, which aroused her in an entirely different way?

"Did you already pick somewhere to sit?"

His question drew her back to reality. She shook her head. "Like I said, I haven't been here that long."

He gestured to a table for two, situated in the far back corner of the coffee shop, to the left of the counter. "That looks nice and private."

She couldn't help noticing the way he seemed to emphasize the word *private*. She swallowed again.

"Sounds good." Based on what they were about to discuss, it made sense for them to seek a table away from the other patrons.

Once the barista handed them their steaming ceramic mugs, he started toward the table he'd chosen. She fell into step behind him, and her traitorous eyes dipped to his hips. He had a glorious backside that nicely filled his slacks. It looked tight enough to bounce the proverbial quarter off. Chastising herself for the direction of her thoughts, she jerked her gaze upward as they reached the table.

And found him watching her, an amused grin on his face.

Her hands began to tremble beneath his scrutiny.

He set his mug down, then grabbed hers and put it down as well. "You okay?"

She nodded, slipping into her seat. "Yes, I'm fine."

He sat in the chair across from her. "I know where you were looking."

Her eyes widened, and she slid her cup to the side so she could rest her forehead on the cool surface of the tabletop. She certainly hadn't intended to be so obvious in her ogling. She remembered that she'd caught him doing the same thing when he'd first visited her office. His inability to hide his behavior had amused her, yet here she was, doing the very same thing.

He chuckled. "Don't be embarrassed. The fact that we're attracted to each other will only add to the realism of this little game we're playing."

"I guess that's true." She slowly raised her upper body and sat back up, determined to soldier on. "So where do we start?"

He took a sip from his mug. "We need to learn as much as we can about each other for this to work."

"What about the details of our relationship? Our first meeting, how you proposed…"

"We'll work that out. But let's start with the truth and use it to build the basis for…everything else."

She nodded, seeing the logic in his suggestion. If they were going to go ahead with this crazy undertaking, they might as well do it right. Reaching to her purse, she extracted a small notebook and a pen. "Okay. You start. When's your birthday?"

"November 1."

A Scorpio. So that's why he exudes such powerful sensuality. With that mystery solved, she moved on to her other queries. For the next fifteen minutes, he answered the slew of questions she asked, and she made notes. "Tell me about your family background. What was it like growing up in your household?"

He scratched his chin. "Let's see. I'm an only child, so no siblings. My cousin Wesley was around a lot when I was growing up, but I can't say we're close."

She heard the tone of his voice change, as if to communicate his dislike for Wesley. "May I ask why?"

He shrugged. "Wesley's just a difficult person. Enough about him, though. Royal Textiles was my paternal grandfather's business. My father always worked in the executive offices. My mother, Francine, supervised the embroidery department."

Her brow crinkled. "Will I get to meet your parents when I come to tour your facilities?"

"Sure, you'll meet my father. But my mother passed away about twelve years ago."

She cringed. "I'm sorry to hear that."

"Thank you. She was a master at embroidery and could do it by hand. As machines became advanced, she switched to machine embroidery, but strictly for speed. No one could match her skills."

"Impressive."

"You bet she was. I needed a costume for a play when I was in middle school, and she made me the most epic embroidered vest you could imagine. After I wore it in the play, she was always getting calls from the school, wanting her to design things." He chuckled. "One day, she said, 'Tell your teachers I can't take any more custom orders.' They had her phone ringing off the hook." His expression changed, a hint of sadness entering his eyes. "I miss her."

She gave him a soft smile. "I hope my prodding hasn't caused you any pain, Bryan."

He shook his head, seeming to recover from the momentary emotion she'd seen flicker across his face. "It's fine. I loved my mother very much, and talking about her is good for me. Sharing my memories of her is a way of keeping her close, do you know what I mean?"

She nodded, because she understood. "Memories are precious, especially when it comes to someone you love." She put her pen down, fixed her gaze on him. "Thank you for sharing her with me."

His eyes held hers. "Thank you for listening."

After a few silent moments, she started asking questions again. "Any serious relationships?"

He shook his head. "Nah. I've dated but never got serious with anyone." He sipped from his mocha.

"Why is that?" She was probing again, but she didn't

expect it would make him uncomfortable this time. He spoke of his romantic past so nonchalantly, it bordered on aloof.

He looked thoughtful for a moment before he answered. "Honestly? None of those women moved me enough to make a commitment."

Apparently, they moved you enough to take them out. Where's the line?

She could question him further about the topic, but she decided not to give voice to her thoughts. They were at the beginning of their little experiment, and she didn't want to antagonize him. Besides, since this was just a pretend relationship, why should she care about the details of his dating history? Beyond any potential interference from his ex-flames, it had no bearing on what they were doing.

"Is there anyone you were involved with who took things more seriously than you did? You know, someone who might make trouble for us once the news of our engagement really gets out?" She watched him, wanting to gauge any changes in his expression or body language.

He shrugged. "I don't think so. I can't think of anyone who thought of being involved with me as anything particularly serious."

She hadn't picked up on any change in his demeanor to indicate dishonesty. All she noted was his continued casual manner. Mindful of that, she said, "Okay. We'll move on, then." By the time she'd asked everything she thought she'd need to know, they'd both finished their coffee.

He brushed the back of his hand over his forehead,

making a show of exhaustion. "Wow. I've never been grilled like that, not even at a job interview."

She smiled. "Don't worry. Now it's your turn to ask me questions."

So he did. To her surprise, he didn't write anything down or even enter it into his phone. He simply asked her question after question, ranging from her favorite color to her family dynamics, until she stopped him.

"What is it?"

"Don't you need to take notes? How are you going to remember all this?" She watched him expectantly.

He shrugged, his expression nonchalant. "I'm not worried."

"Why not?"

He fixed her with a stare that seemed to penetrate her clothes and touch her like a lover's caress. "I never have trouble recalling things that are important to me."

Her brow rose. She hadn't come to this meeting expecting him to flirt with her, at least not as openly as he seemed determined to do.

As if sensing her thoughts, he spoke. "I've been completely honest with you about the fact that I'm attracted to you. And because of that, I plan to milk every drop of enjoyment out of this arrangement that you allow." He reached over, grasped her hand.

Before she had a chance to react, he gently tugged her hand to his lips, placing a kiss on the back of it. The contact was brief but sent tendrils of warmth dancing up her forearm to radiate through the rest of her body.

By the time he released her hand, she knew they would have no trouble convincing people that they were a couple.

But how hard will it be to convince myself that this isn't real?

Wednesday morning, Alexis reclined in the leather chair behind her desk at Krystal Kouture. While she scanned her computer screen to read a buyer's response to her inquiry for the new line, she sipped from a mug of Morning Volcano herbal tea. She swallowed a mouthful of the tangy brew, the hints of citrus and ginger tickling her throat as they went down.

Her full focus went to deciphering the terms the retailer generally offered to new designers to see if they were reasonable. This line was her baby, and she wouldn't see it mispackaged by a retailer who didn't understand her vision. She was so engrossed in the offer that she tuned out the rest of the world.

So when Sydney came barreling into the office, shouting, it startled Alexis.

Her hand shook, and tea sloshed out of her mug. She shoved her wireless keyboard out of the path of the falling liquid just in time to prevent it from being fried. Setting down her mug a safe distance from the computer, she slid back from her desk. Leveling Sydney with an annoyed expression, she asked, "Girl, what the hell?"

Sydney, flailing like an air traffic controller signaling a wayward jet, squealed. "Omigoshyouhavetoseewhat…"

"What?"

"Turn on the TV!"

Shaking her head, she got the remote and pointed it at the wall-mounted flat screen in one corner of her office. Once it was on, she looked to Sydney again.

COULDN'T ASK FOR MORE

"Put it on the *Today* show. Quick!"

Still wondering what all the fuss was about, Alexis changed the channel. When she saw the picture on the screen, her mouth fell open.

There was Angela Bassett, being interviewed by Tamron Hall. Per the strip across the bottom of the screen, she was starring in a new biopic about educator, author, and women's rights activist Anna Julia Cooper.

Standing, Alexis laid her palms on her desk, careful to avoid the puddle of spilled tea. "Oh my God, Syd. Angela Bassett is wearing our sample dress."

"I know! That's what I wanted you to see!" Sydney's eyes flashed with excitement.

Alexis felt the smile stretching her lips. "Looks like you were right. That dress was made for her. She looks fabulous." She couldn't help admire the way the black dress, with its one-shoulder design, white peplum skirt, and knee-grazing hem, looked on the talented actress. As a testament to her impeccable fashion sense, Ms. Bassett had paired the dress with the perfect pair of black-and-white pumps.

"Those shoes, though." Sydney's transfixed gaze and tone of voice conveyed her admiration.

"I know. They look amazing with our dress."

For a moment, the two of them watched the interview in awed silence. Angela and Tamron talked about the film, which costarred Idris Elba, Tika Sumpter, and many other talented actors. It sounded like it would be a spectacular movie, and Alexis made a note to see it when it came out.

Tamron eyed Angela's outfit. "I know this is totally unrelated to the film, but you always look so amazing. I love your dress!"

The ever-gracious Ms. Bassett offered a smile. "Thank you, Tamron."

"Who's the designer? I have to know."

"Oh, it's from a newer fashion label called Krystal Kouture. The designer sent me this dress, and the minute I received it from my assistant, I couldn't wait to wear it."

Alexis clamped her hand over her mouth to cover her scream of delight. For the next few minutes, she and Sydney acted like two teenage girls who'd scored tickets to a boy band concert. They jumped up and down, shouted, and laughed, celebrating the leap their business was about to take.

When they finally settled down, Alexis brushed a hand over the bodice of her navy-blue, A-line maxi dress. "Well, I don't think any house could hope to get a more glowing endorsement than that."

Sydney pumped her fist in the air. "You're damn right. Krystal Kouture is on the map now, for sure."

"Thanks for sending the samples out. If you hadn't done that, we wouldn't be getting all this free, positive press."

Sydney shrugged. "That's what I'm here for, Lex. But it's your vision as a designer that keeps this place afloat."

Alexis smiled and captured her friend and business partner in a tight hug.

The love fest was cut short by the shrill ringing of phones. Alexis listened to the cacophony for a few moments before she realized that *all* the phones were ringing. Her cell phone. Sydney's cell phone. The office line at Krystal Kouture. Every phone line coming into their first-floor office suite was lit up like the city skyline at night.

Her fingertips on Sydney's forearms, she smiled. "Looks like we're in demand."

All their hard work in creating their debut line was about to pay off, big time.

Dawn, the receptionist and office manager, stuck her head around the doorframe. "Y'all. The buyer for Lane Bryant is on line one. Chico's is on line two. And fricking Target is on line three."

Dawn, who'd been with the design house since it opened, hailed from the Midwest. At twenty-seven, she was a single mother of a five-year-old daughter. She had blue eyes and olive skin and wore her brown hair in a low ponytail. Wearing her uniform of black slacks and a white button-down shirt emblazoned with the design house logo, she stood just outside the door, waiting for instruction.

"Well, damn." Sydney's comment broke the silence.

Dawn's expression conveyed a mixture of amazement and uncertainty. "Which one do you want me to put through first?"

Alexis drew a deep breath, drinking in this embarrassment of riches. "Take the contact info for the Target rep. I'll talk to Lane Bryant. Syd, will you handle Chico's?"

Sydney nodded. "I'm on it. Transfer line two to my office, Dawn."

"Got it." The receptionist disappeared into the hallway.

Back behind her desk, Alexis grabbed a napkin from her top drawer and mopped up the puddle of herbal tea she'd spilled. Once she'd settled comfortably into her seat, she took another slow, deep breath. It was turning out to be one hell of an eventful morning.

Lifting the receiver of her desk phone, she tapped the

blinking button next to line one. "This is Alexis Devers at Krystal Kouture. What can I do for you?"

"Good morning, Ms. Devers. I'm Adam McCall, senior buyer at Lane Bryant. We saw the segment on the *Today* show this morning, and we'd love to speak with you about the possibility of selling your fashion line in our stores."

Inside, she felt giddy, but she kept her professional demeanor intact. "I'm flattered, Mr. McCall. If you'd send over an information package, my partner and I will be glad to take a look at it. Would you like our information?"

"Yes, certainly."

She recited her email and physical addresses to him and gave him a few moments to transcribe the information.

"Thank you very much, Ms. Devers. We'll definitely be in touch with you again soon."

"I look forward to it."

As she replaced the receiver, she released a sigh of contentment. This morning's turn of events would mean so much to her as a designer and as a business owner, and she couldn't wait to see where it all would lead.

Before she could get her breath, the phone began to ring again.

Closing the offer document she'd been reading on her computer screen, Alexis settled into her seat. If the past half hour had been any indication, she could expect to spend the entire workday fielding phone calls and emails. In any other instance, that thought would have annoyed her.

But since today's barrage of calls could ultimately

lead to massive success for her very first fashion line, she didn't mind it at all.

Picking up the phone again, she answered line one for the second time. "Alexis Devers of Krystal Kouture. Can I help you?"

Bryan's soothing baritone filled her ear. "Good morning, Ms. Devers You're doing big things, I see."

A smile lifted the corners of her mouth. "Good morning, Bryan. I guess you saw the segment."

"I did, and Angela was right to wear that dress. She looked amazing. You have immense talent."

She could feel the heat rushing to redden her cheeks. "Flattery will get you everywhere."

"Let's hope so."

The invitation in his tone sent a tingle down her spine. "Is there something you wanted? Our phones are ringing off the hook, as you can probably guess."

"Yes. I wanted to invite you to the Royal headquarters tomorrow. We've arranged for you to tour the facilities where your line will be manufactured. That is, if you're free."

She laced her fingers with the spiral cord attached to the receiver. "What time?"

"I'll work around your schedule. After all, you're the client. I work for you, Alexis."

A naughty thought entered her mind, about the type of *work* she might enjoy him doing for her. Pushing the errant thought away, she glanced at her desk calendar. "Syd and I can swing by around one thirty, after lunch."

"Sounds good. I'll let my team know."

"See you then, Bryan."

"I'll see you in my dreams tonight." He disconnected the call.

Untangling the cord from her hand, Alexis returned her receiver to the cradle. Unable to keep the grin from spreading over her face, she tried to set her thoughts back on work.

This man is just too much.

———∿∿∿———

At one o'clock Thursday afternoon, Bryan rose from his desk. He'd taken his simple lunch of chicken noodle soup and a garden salad there so he could catch up on some work. Now, as the time for Alexis and Sydney's arrival at Royal approached, he shrugged back into his gray sport coat.

Crossing his office, he stopped by the mirror on the wall near his bookcase. The mirror was tall enough to show his reflection from the waist up, and he checked to make sure he'd cleaned up well enough from his meal. Retightening the Windsor knot of his necktie, he turned to the side. Reaching for the boar bristle brush he kept on his top shelf, he ran it over his hair.

The sound of someone clearing their throat pulled his attention away from his reflection and toward his office door.

There, framed by the doorway, stood his father. Oscar wore a suspicious look on his face. "Bryan, what are you doing?"

"I just had lunch, so I'm making sure I look present-able for our newest client."

"I've never seen you do this for any other client."

He shrugged. "Most don't ask to meet right after

lunch, but this is about her convenience, not mine." He set the brush back on the shelf.

Oscar shook his head. "Whatever you say, Son."

A look passed between them, and Bryan could feel his father's scrutiny. Oscar's eyes said he sensed something more and challenged his son to tell him the whole story. Bryan didn't bite. He hadn't intended for his father to see him taking extra care with his appearance. Now that it had happened this way, Bryan would use it to his advantage. When the news of his and Alexis's "engagement" came out, this little encounter would only play into the story they planned to spin for the media.

"I'll see you downstairs, Pop."

"Okay, Son."

He watched his father walk away, then waited to hear the elevator chime. He waited a few beats more to avoid sharing an elevator car with his suspicious old man. Smiling to himself, Bryan grabbed his briefcase and headed out of the office toward the first floor.

In the lobby, he took a seat in one of the burgundy plush chairs. He didn't see his father around, so he assumed Oscar had already gone down to the factory floor. Now, the only other people in the lobby were the two receptionists, working behind the long silver desk that centered the room. Both women were presently engaged in work; one spoke to someone on her headset while the other typed at her computer.

Bryan settled into his seat, though he didn't think he'd be waiting there for very long. Everything about Alexis Devers led him to believe her to be prompt, especially when business was involved. Setting his briefcase at his feet, he glanced at his wristwatch. *1:13.* He directed his eyes toward the main entrance, expecting her to appear there at any moment.

The frosted glass door swung open, and Sydney entered. Wearing a red pantsuit and gold jewelry, she looked professional and put-together. She waved as she caught his eye. He waved back, gathered his briefcase, and stood, knowing Alexis couldn't be far behind her partner.

Sydney held the door open and stepped back.

Bryan inhaled as Alexis stepped inside the building, dressed in a black leather skirt and a leopard-print top with long, bell-cuffed sleeves. The outfit hugged her figure closely, and her legs were encased in thigh-high black boots. Her glossy hair was tucked into a low bun. As the door swung shut behind her, she removed the large pair of dark sunglasses she wore, tucking them into her bag. The action revealed the full beauty of her face, and he couldn't tear his eyes away from her. She wore very little makeup, but her lips were painted an irresistible shade of deep red.

Strolling in his direction, she smiled. "Bryan. Good to see you again." She stuck out her hand.

He knew he should shake it, but propriety be damned, he wanted more. So he captured her hand in his, brought it to his lips, and kissed the back. "The pleasure is all mine, Alexis."

The dark fringe of lashes framing her eyes fluttered in time with her rapid blinking. "Bryan, honestly." Her cheeks darkened, becoming almost as red as her lips.

He released her hand, sensing her embarrassment. Amusement touched his insides, but he managed to hold back his chuckle. *I wonder how she'll react when I start treating her as if she's mine.*

Sydney laughed, shaking her head. "Hello again, Bryan. A handshake will suffice for me, thanks."

Sensing the teasing in her tone, he smiled her way. "Welcome, Ms. Greer." Offering her the handshake as she'd requested, he then gestured toward the elevator bank. "If you ladies are ready, we can go down to the factory floor."

Alexis nodded, and the three of them began walking. He called an elevator car for them, and when it arrived, they stepped inside. He moved to the back, allowing Alexis and Sydney to stand forward of him. This time, he managed to keep his gaze high, purposely avoiding her backside. In truth, he didn't need to look again. The plump, firm curve of her behind had burned itself into his mind from the first time he'd seen it, and he imagined it would always be there.

The doors opened, and they stepped out of the car into the vestibule of the factory floor. The familiar sounds of the machinery and the conversations of the workers filled his ears. To him, the sounds were relaxing, but he wondered how his guests might perceive them.

Moving between the ladies, Bryan gestured toward the myriad activity happening before them. "Welcome to the Royal Textiles production department. It can be a little loud down here, so let me know if you need headphones." He gestured to the corkboard on the wall, where several sets of noise-canceling headsets were kept.

Alexis waved him off. "I'm fine."

Sydney, however, grimaced. "I'll take some."

Reaching for a pair, he gave them to her and waited while she secured them.

Keeping in mind that he'd need to gesture to Sydney

when he wanted her attention, he waved the two of them toward the side of the factory floor where their fashion line would be produced. "This way, ladies."

He led them over to the desk of Ron Harper, the production manager for the nondenim apparel floor. Ron, who'd been poring over a production report, stood when he saw them approach. "Hey, boss man. I'm guessing these are our new clients?"

"Yes, they are. Ladies, this is Ron Harper, the production manager who will oversee the manufacture of your clothes. Ron, this is Alexis Devers, the designer for Krystal Kouture, and Sydney Greer, her business partner."

Handshakes and greetings were shared among the group, and when they began walking again, Ron joined them. A twenty-year veteran of the company, Ron was a Charlotte native who'd started out on the machinery and worked his way up to management.

"As a designer, I'm sure you have a good understanding of the manufacturing process and the machinery we use." Ron directed the statement at Alexis.

She nodded. "Yes, sir, I do."

"So my main goal today is to let you know about the things we'll be doing that are unique to your line. At Royal, we focus on 'tailoring' our process to each individual apparel line." Ron winked.

Sydney chuckled. "Nice."

"Just a little textiles humor for you." Ron looked to Bryan.

Bryan smirked. "You're a regular stand-up comedian, Ron."

The four of them moved around the floor, with Ron and Bryan alternating the task of explaining the processes to their new clients. They also stopped to introduce the ladies to the folks on the floor who would play key roles in the production of the Krystal Kouture line. By the time Bryan led the ladies back to the elevator bank to go upstairs, they were chattering excitedly.

He stood at the back of the car again, listening to them without infringing on their conversation. He enjoyed hearing them express their excitement for the launch of their clothing line, and he especially loved the way Alexis's face lit up when she talked about her designs. He could tell she had a lot of passion for her work. He suspected she would bring that same level of passion to a romantic relationship, and it occurred to him that he didn't want to think of her feeling that way about any other man.

As they exited the car on the first floor, Sydney's voice broke into his thoughts. "Is there any way I could visit the sales department? I'm interested in learning how things work over there."

"Sure. I'll escort you there."

Sydney shook her head. "Nah. Just tell me where it is, and I'll go myself. Alexis hates that side of the business. She's a creative, and I wouldn't dare burden her with this kind of stuff. Right, Lex?"

Alexis rolled her eyes. "Right. Thanks for sparing me the torture."

Amused, Bryan pointed toward the west corridor. "Just follow that hall, and go through the double doors on the right. You can't miss it."

"Thanks." Sydney walked away.

Left alone with Alexis, Bryan turned her way. "Would you mind coming upstairs with me? There's one place on the contract you missed that I need you to initial."

She nodded. "Lead the way."

He extended his arm, and when she looped her arm through his, he guided her back toward the elevators.

Chapter 9

THE INSIDE OF THE ELEVATOR CAR SEEMED TO HAVE shrunk since they'd last ridden it. Or at least, that was the conclusion Alonis drew as she and Bryan stepped back into it, alone. Once the doors slid shut behind them, she could swear it had also grown considerably warmer. If she were honest with herself, she knew the warmth wasn't coming from the building's climate-control system. Rather, what she felt was the heat rolling off the large, sturdy body of the man standing next to her.

She glanced to her right, letting her gaze travel from his smiling profile down the rest of his body. He wore a gray suit that had obviously been cut for the express purpose of fitting his muscular frame. The dark-blue shirt and blue-and-gray-striped tie coordinated perfectly with the suit, as did the gray dress shoes with blue panels covering his feet.

Damn. How is it legal for him to look this good?

She inhaled, hoping the infusion of air would help her get her bearings. Instead, she got a healthy whiff of his cologne. His scent flooded her nostrils like a rising vapor. It was woodsy but not overly so, citrusy and fresh. It was also utterly masculine. She exhaled, letting the tip of her tongue moisten her bottom lip.

The longer she looked at him, the harder it became to look away. This man was fine, the kind of fine that made you want to reach out and…

"My office is on the third floor."

He must have noticed me staring at him. She averted her eyes. His remark had broken the silence but did nothing to lower her rising body temperature.

Resisting the urge to fan herself, Alexis closed her eyes for a moment. Even without the benefit of seeing him, her body prickled with awareness of Bryan's presence in the confines of the car. Since blocking out the sight of him didn't help, she opened her eyes again and focused on the doors, thinking she'd keep her gaze there until they reached the right floor.

When the doors opened, he extended his hand to hold them open. "After you."

She walked out into the carpeted hallway, waiting for him to join her. The corridor had many doors, and she had no idea which one was his office. When he walked ahead of her, she followed him.

He entered the far door on the left side of the hall, gesturing for her to come in. When she entered, she looked around his private office.

The floors beneath her feet were comprised of large planks of teak. Dark wood bookcases lined one wall, their patina a direct contrast with the light color of the flooring. Sheer curtains lined the back wall, which was comprised of floor-to-ceiling windows. The large rectangular desk, fashioned of the same dark wood as the bookcases, dominated the rear center of the room. It was situated in front of the windows, and the sunlight streaming through the curtains illuminated the surface of the desk.

"Have a seat." He sat down behind the desk, gesturing her toward the beige armchair opposite where he sat.

She took a seat, then watched as he reached into a drawer to extract her contract pages. He flipped through them in silence for a few moments before sliding one page across the desk to her. "My assistant put a little flag where we need your initials. Oh, here's a pen." He extracted a gold-plated pen from an inner pocket of his sport coat, placed it next to the page.

After a quick perusal, she located the flagged spot and wrote her initials there. When she finished, she slid the pen and the page back to him.

He tucked both items away. "Thanks for taking care of that."

"No problem." She laid her hands in her lap, awaiting whatever came next. Even though she'd done what he'd asked, she sensed he had something more to say.

"Alexis, I know it's not related to business, but I have to say this. You look stunning today."

She crossed one leg over the other. "Thank you, Bryan."

He got up from his seat, moving around to her side of the desk. There, he perched on the edge of his desk, right in front of her. "I know we're still in the early stages of our little game, but there's something I'd like to address."

Her brow hitched, curiosity getting the better of her. "What would that be?"

He leaned his upper body toward her until his face was level with her own.

Her heart pounded in her ears like a drum machine. A silent moment passed between them as he waited for her to respond. She knew what he was doing, but she made no move to stop him.

"May I?" He didn't specify what he was asking for.

He didn't need to. She knew. With every fiber of her being, she knew.

"Yes." Her soft response left her lips on a sigh.

A beat later, his lips touched hers. Her eyes closed right away. His kiss was gentle and soft and yet possessed an urgency, a desire that swept through her like flames licking at kindling. His large hand cupped her cheek while her hand rested on his forearm as the kiss deepened. His tongue swept over the curve of her lower lip, just once. Then he broke the kiss, moved away from her.

She opened her eyes, blinking. He was upright again, still perched on the edge of the desk. He watched her as if awaiting her reaction.

"How was that?" He asked the question so matter-of-factly, she was somewhat taken aback.

"I...it felt...real." It was the truth and the only answer she could formulate.

He smiled, showing off two rows of perfect, pearlescent teeth. "Good. It's supposed to."

Her eyes widened. She didn't know what to think. Had he kissed her the way he would kiss any woman he was romantically involved with? Or had he just been testing the waters to see if he could convince the world that they were truly an item?

"Listen. I don't want to start monopolizing your time, but I'd really like to spend some time with you...outside of work."

She searched his face. "Are you...asking me out?"

He chuckled at her question. "Yes, I am. You're my fiancée now, right? So we should be getting to know each other."

She nodded. Her lips were still tingling from his

dazzling kiss. Shaking off those thoughts as best she could, she addressed him. "I agree."

"We're not going to do that here, so can you meet me at the carousel at Pullen Park, tomorrow around one? I'm only working a half day."

"Sounds doable. We usually wrap things up a little early on Fridays, too." The anticipation she felt at spending more one on one time with him made her lips tilt into a smile. "I'll be there."

"Great." He winked, extended his hand toward hers. "Are you ready to go? I'm sure Sydney will be looking for you before long."

She stood, trying to shake off the last vestiges of his kiss. When she stumbled, his strong arm braced her, steadying her. "Thank you."

"For the kiss? Or for holding you up?"

She tilted her head up to look into his dark eyes. "Both."

—◦◦◦—

Around one thirty Friday afternoon, Alexis stood on the sidewalk in front of the carousel at Pullen Park. The park, located next to the campus of North Carolina State University, was a fixture in the lives of Raleigh residents. The oldest park in the state of North Carolina, Pullen had been established in 1887, as the sign hanging above the entrance reminded each visitor entering the grounds. Its central location, as well as the carousel, the miniature train, and the pedal boats that could be rented to ride around Lake Howell, made it a popular destination during temperate weather. The area's mild climate meant the park could be enjoyed year-round.

Today was a perfect day to be at the park. The temperature was a balmy sixty-seven degrees, and the sun shone down from an azure-blue sky punctuated by puffy white clouds. Alexis loved days like this, and she looked forward to exploring the park with Bryan. Anticipating being on her feet most of the afternoon, she'd dressed comfortably in a mint-green sweater set, light-blue jeans, and white sneakers.

Behind her, the music from the carousel filled the air. She'd spent many an afternoon riding the carousel with her brother and sister. She turned slightly, watching as the menagerie of painted animals revolved around its mirrored axis. A few adults and small children were aboard the carousel, and a few walked the paved paths that ran through the park. Alexis knew that as the afternoon wore on and area schools released for the day, there would be more people visiting the park.

She was so busy watching the carousel that she jumped when someone tapped her on the shoulder.

"Sorry. Didn't mean to scare you, Alexis." Bryan smiled, taking a step back. "You okay?"

Turning his way, she took in the beauty of his pearly white teeth before meeting his smile with one of her own. "Hi. It's okay. I guess I was just a little spaced-out there."

"Hypnotized by the carousel, eh? Happens to the best of us." He chuckled. "Do you want to go for a ride? I stopped by the welcome center and grabbed a few tickets, just in case." Reaching into his pants pocket, he produced a fistful of them.

She looked him over then. He wore a white polo and a pair of khaki pants, along with a pair of loafers the color of wheat. The short sleeves of the polo revealed the muscled strength of his forearms, while the pants clung to his powerful hips and thighs just enough to reveal their shape but not enough to be considered tight. Her eyes eventually rose back up to his handsome face, and she found him eyeing her expectantly. "I'm sorry, didn't you just ask me something?"

Another deep, rumbling chuckle left his lips. "I asked if you wanted to ride the carousel."

"Yes. Sounds like fun." She felt a little embarrassed to be caught staring at him that way, but he seemed to take it in stride. If his expression was any indication, he might even have been a little amused by her scrutiny.

He extended his hand to her. "Let's go for a ride, then."

She took his hand and walked with him to the gate.

A few minutes later, they were seated in one of the two chariots on the carousel. Painted in a shade of tan, accented by scrolls in greens and reds, the chariot had three benches of ascending height. Bryan eased onto the back bench, the tallest of the three, and Alexis scooted in next to him. The bench was somewhat narrow, which meant she had no choice but to ease close to him, so close that their thighs touched. Her skin burned where their bodies met, as if the fabric of their clothes wasn't even there.

As the carousel began to turn, Alexis tuned out the cheery organ music and focused on Bryan's voice as he spoke.

"I know you're busy getting ready for the festival, but do you think you could stop by the youth center and talk to some of the kids about fashion design? We've got about ten or eleven of them who want to hear from you."

She blinked, somewhat surprised by his request. "I

don't mind. So some of them have mentioned being interested in fashion design?"

He nodded. "Yes. And we try to get as many local businesspeople in to speak to them as possible. These are high schoolers, and it's important that they start thinking about careers."

"When do you want me there?"

"Next week, Monday night around six. Can you make it?"

She made a quick mental assessment of her schedule. "I'll be there."

"Thanks. I appreciate it, and I know Xavier will as well."

She smiled. She didn't know if she'd be able to keep the attention of a group of high schoolers, but she'd do her best. With any luck, she might inspire one of them.

"I spent the morning in meetings. Dad's on the warpath about production numbers this week." He ran a hand over his hair. "I love him, but I swear he's never been satisfied."

Watching the way his face crinkled up as he spoke about work, Alexis gave his upper arm a squeeze. "You said yourself that Royal is your grandfather's legacy. That probably means a lot of pressure for your father."

"It means a lot of pressure for me, too. I'm just as interested in Royal's success as Dad is, and so are the rest of the team and the board."

"Try to remember that he's probably just worried about making the company as profitable as possible. I'm sure he doesn't mean to put so much pressure on you." She couldn't imagine Oscar James enjoyed stressing his son out. It seemed more likely that the older man simply didn't realize what effect his demands had on his son.

"Logically, I know that. But when he brought in my cousin Wesley and started talking about how I might need his help, it just triggered something in me." Bryan looked away then, seeming to focus his attention on the mirrors in the center of the carousel.

Alexis could feel a frown creasing her brow. He was a handsome, intelligent man, and up until now, he'd exuded nothing but confidence in her presence. Hearing him speak this way threw her for a loop. "What is it about your cousin being here that's gotten under your skin?"

"Wesley and my uncle Otis run a car dealership in Asheville. My dad thinks that his sales expertise there might translate to more contracts for Royal." His back was straight and stiff as a board, and he kept his arms at his sides, his fists slightly clenched as he spoke. "Wesley agrees, since he thinks so highly of himself."

Her frown deepened, because she didn't see much of a connection between the two industries. "Um, selling cars isn't anything like working in the fashion industry."

He chuckled ruefully. "I said the same thing to my dad. But Wesley stayed anyway, so here we are. I never really cared for my cousin, because he's just not that pleasant a person. Even though I wish we could be closer, since neither of us has any siblings, I just don't think it's ever going to happen. Wesley is who he is."

She nodded. "I get it. I can tell you don't care for him. But don't let him distract you from your work. If you can keep your focus, I'm sure your dad will eventually see the light and send your cousin back where he came from." She could sense the tension rolling off him, and she hoped her words might help to ease his mind. In a way, it refreshed her to know that his confidence could be tested. She'd known far too many men who were sure of themselves to the point of arrogance. Bryan didn't seem to have that problem.

He turned back toward her then. "You really think so?"

"Yes, I do. You've been doing this job your whole adult life, and you're the one with valuable experience in the industry. You're the one with the connections. Your cousin may think he's hot stuff, but knowing how to sell cars isn't necessarily going to translate to textiles."

He watched her silently, seeming to turn her words over in his mind. "Thank you for saying that, Alexis."

She let her hand rest on his thigh. "I meant it. Don't let someone come in and distract you or make you doubt your skills. You know what you're doing, Bryan. If I didn't believe that, there's no way I'd have given you the contract for my fashion line."

His shoulders dropped as he relaxed, and he raised his arm to drape it behind her shoulders. "I appreciate the vote of confidence."

Feeling him relax next to her made her smile, because she knew she'd succeeded in calming him. "You're welcome."

He leaned over then, placed a kiss against her cheek. The contact was brief, but it left a tingle of warmth that quickly spread through her body. She looked up into his eyes, wanting more of his kisses. Before she could pursue them, though, the carousel came to a stop, indicating the end of their ride.

After they disembarked and returned to the sidewalk

hand in hand, he asked, "What next? Want to take one of the pedal boats out on the water? I've still got a few tickets left."

"Sounds great." On a beautiful, blue-sky day like this one, the trip was bound to be enjoyable.

After stopping off at the dock to pay the six tickets required for a half-hour boat rental, the two of them guided their small vessel out onto Lake Howell. Only a couple of other boats were on the water at this time of day, and as they both used their feet to turn the pedals powering the boat, Bryan handled the steering.

"Man, it's beautiful out today." His eyes were on some distant point as he spoke.

"It really is. We couldn't have asked for better weather."

He rested his large arm behind her, atop the blue plastic seat she sat in. Without slowing the motions of her feet, she leaned in closer to him, enjoying the warmth and strength rolling off his body. Her eyes scanned the rippling surface of the water, and a sense of peace washed over her.

Being with him felt so natural, as if they'd been together for years. She searched her memory, and it didn't take long to realize she'd never felt this comfortable with any other man. What was it about him? What was this quality he possessed that made her want to drop her guard and show him her most authentic self? "Thanks for meeting me here, Bryan. After a crazy week, this is just what I needed."

He smiled. "I think it's what we both needed."

As she settled into his embrace for the rest of the ride, she had to agree.

Chapter 10

STANDING IN THE FRONT WINDOW OF HER CONDO, Alexis looked down at the street below. The afternoon sunshine flooded her living room, warming her bare feet. She couldn't remember the last time she'd stood by the window like this, waiting for anyone, least of all a man.

Probably college. She thought that a safe assumption, though she didn't remember the guy's name.

Today, though, she was fully aware of whom she awaited. Bryan James, a man unlike any other she'd ever encountered. She'd planned to spend her Saturday hanging out on her sofa, watching movies and decompressing from the week. That all changed when Bryan asked her out.

Spending time with him at the park yesterday had been fun and relaxing. Conversation had flowed easily between them, as if they'd known each other forever. She'd enjoyed herself so much that she hadn't hesitated to accept his invitation for today, even though she had no idea what they'd be doing. She'd been turning over the myriad possibilities of their date in her mind all morning.

In a few hours, her curiosity about what Bryan had planned for her would finally be allayed.

She gazed out on the passing cars and pedestrians for a few moments more, then let the sheers fall back into place. Walking over to her bedroom door, she checked her reflection one more time in the full-length mirror mounted on the back. Unsure of what activities the day might hold, she'd chosen a pair of slim, dark denim jeans and a flowing pink top with a shark-bite hem. Diamond studs glittered in her ears, and a silver chain hung around her neck. With a pair of pink ballet flats on her feet and her hair left to fall around her shoulders, she felt comfortable and well put-together.

The buzzer sounded, and she grabbed her purse and went to the intercom. "Yes?"

"Hey, Alexis. It's Bryan. Are you ready?"

"I'll be down in a second." She'd let the doorman know when she moved into the building that visitors were to wait for her in the lobby rather than be allowed up. The round-the-clock security, along with the location, had been her primary reasons for purchasing the condo. Once she'd locked up, she crossed the hallway and rode the elevator down.

When the doors opened in the sunlit lobby, she saw him, standing in the center of the room. His casual dress did little to distract from his handsomeness. He wore jeans as well, though his were black. He'd paired them with a long-sleeved green tee bearing the Theta Delta Theta fraternity crest and motto. A gold Cuban-link chain with a lion's-head pendant hung from his neck.

Crossing the lobby to where he stood, she offered him a smile. "Hey, Bryan. Looks like I'm dressed okay for our little outing."

He smiled back, taking her hand. "You look beautiful."

"Thank you." She willed the warm blood away from her face. When he strode toward the door, still holding her hand, she followed. Once they were outside on the sidewalk, she asked, "What are we doing today?"

"I told you it was a surprise."

"I know. But curiosity is getting the better of me." She walked alongside him, moving north up the street, away from her building. When they passed the parking garage, she looked his way. "I assume we're going on foot?"

He nodded. "We are."

She'd lived in the downtown Raleigh area for several years now. The area was home to a plethora of museums, restaurants, and shops. There were so many things nearby that the knowledge they were walking to their destination didn't even narrow it down. "So are you going to tell me where we're headed?"

He chuckled, glancing her way. "I can see the suspense is killing you, so yes. We're going to Brandt."

She blinked a few times, confused. "Brandt. The jewelry store?"

"Yep."

They walked on in silence for a few moments while she tried to figure out what he was up to. By the time she spoke again, the black-and-white-striped awning above the door of Brandt Fine Jewelry was within view. "Why?"

He shrugged. "If you're going to be my fiancée, you should have an engagement ring."

The statement caught her so off guard, her brain couldn't formulate a response. Her jaw dropped, and she could feel her mouth hanging open.

Shaking his head, he used his free hand to gently close her mouth. "Don't look so shocked." He stopped walking, pointing at the storefront. "We're here. Let's go inside."

She stood, her feet rooted to the spot on the sidewalk. "You're serious?"

"Yes. Why wouldn't I be?" His tone held no evidence of humor.

She leaned closer to him, lowering her voice. "Considering what we're doing, do you really want to spend money on a ring?"

He met her gaze. "Yes. Because as far as I'm concerned, until you decide to end this little arrangement"—he leaned down, let his lips graze against hers—"you're mine."

The kiss, while brief, still made her see stars. She wanted another kiss, wanted more of his lips against her own. But since they were standing on a public sidewalk, in the middle of the day no less, she tucked the desire away. Sensing that arguing with him would be fruitless, she gave him a subtle nod to indicate her intention to go with it.

He held open the door for her, and she entered the store with him following close behind.

Her eyes swept over the store's interior. Muted wallpaper and carpeting served as the backdrop for the dozens of glass cases scattered around the space. Inside the cases, bright white lights illuminated the highly polished gold, silver, and platinum, as well as the sparkling facets of various precious gemstones.

Bryan strolled to the counter where a young man in a dark suit awaited. "Good afternoon, sir. I'd like to purchase an engagement ring for my beautiful fiancée."

Alexis swallowed the lump forming in her throat. *He's really laying it on thick.* From his tone and the way he tightened his grip on her hand, he seemed to be enjoying himself.

The man behind the counter offered a bright smile in

response to Bryan's declaration. "That's wonderful, sir. Congratulations on your engagement."

Lacing his arm around her waist, Bryan smiled back. "Thank you. We're very excited."

She offered a grin of her own, even though her brain was still trying to process the situation. If he could play the game, so could she.

"Is there any particular style of ring you're interested in?"

"Something that lets any man who looks at her know that she's taken." Drawing her body close to his, Bryan gave her a wink. "My budget is around ten thousand dollars."

Her hand flew to her mouth to cover a sudden coughing fit.

"You okay?" Bryan tilted her chin, looked into her eyes.

Regaining her composure and catching her breath, she nodded.

The store clerk's smile widened. "Excellent. We at Brandt's pride ourselves on our fine selection of diamonds. Let me show you a few things."

Inwardly, she shook her head. The clerk wore the anticipation of his commission all over his face. As the three of them moved around the store, looking at various rings in the cases, she decided she may as well get with the program. *If Bryan wants to spend his money, I'm going to get something I like.*

While they stood by a case, waiting for the clerk to remove a tray filled with diamond solitaires, Bryan leaned close to her ear. "Pick out your fantasy ring, Alexis."

She offered him a soft smile. No matter the

circumstances, his offer was more than generous, and she appreciated it. Turning her attention to the rings the clerk had set out, she picked up one that caught her eye. The cushion-cut diamond appealed to her visually, as did the platinum band. "This is beautiful."

"Ah, the lady has an eye for design. An excellent choice. It's one and three-quarter karats and won't overwhelm her delicate hand." The clerk clapped his hands together. "By all means, try it on."

Bryan took the ring from her, capturing her left hand in his.

He held her gaze as he slipped the sparkler onto her finger.

Their eyes held for a few long moments. Her senses were on alert, and she took in the feeling of his hand around hers and of the coolness of the band and the weight of the stone against her finger. When she finally managed to drag her eyes away from him to look at the ring, she smiled. If this were the real thing, if Bryan were the man she craved like air, this would be what she'd choose. An unexpected tear scurried down her cheek. In an emotional voice, she whispered, "This is it. This is the one I want."

Bryan nodded, brushed his lips against her forehead. "Then it's yours." He turned his attention to the clerk. "I don't think we'll be needing a box."

"As you wish, sir. How will you be paying?"

He reached into the hip pocket of his jeans, extracted his wallet. A few seconds later, Bryan handed off his gold card, but his focus remained on her. "How do you feel?"

Still staring at the ring, she wiggled her fingers. The

overhead lighting made the facets shimmer in time with her movements. "Like I'm dreaming. This is incredibly generous, Bryan. Thank you."

"You're welcome." He was silent for a moment, and when he spoke again, his tone held tenderness. "I'm just glad you like it."

She looked to him then, tried to read his thoughts by looking into the depths of his dark eyes. "What's happening between us, Bryan?"

He didn't hesitate. "Whatever you want to happen."

She didn't respond, didn't know how. When she'd presented her plan to Bryan, she'd been convinced that she could keep this farcical relationship casual, surface level, and most of all, free from emotional entanglements. That was what she'd wanted.

But as they left the jewelry store, Alexis realized she wasn't so sure of what she wanted anymore.

Bryan settled back into the couch at Maxwell's house on Sunday afternoon. He, along with Xavier, had come over to chill and to brainstorm the next round of activities and outings for the teens they mentored.

He looked at Maxwell, reclining on the opposite end of the sofa with a copy of *Car and Driver*. Maxwell looked relaxed, as a man should in his castle. Bryan couldn't help wondering how Maxwell would react when he found out what was going on between his best friend and his baby sister.

Xavier appeared from the kitchen with three tall boy cans of beer in his grasp. "Max, why don't you have any beer I recognize? What's with all this craft brewery stuff?"

"I have refined tastes."

"He means he's bougie." Bryan smirked on the tail of his smart remark.

Maxwell rolled his eyes. "No, it means I'd rather my beer taste good, instead of that gym-sock-tasting mess y'all like."

A chuckling Xavier tossed beers to his two friends, then flopped down in the minim half hour the sofa. "Whatever you say, man."

Popping the tab on his can, Bryan took a drink. The beer tasted pretty good, and even though he liked it, he decided not to tell Maxwell that. It was an understanding he and his fraternity brothers had. *Never tell Max he's right, because it only makes him insufferable.*

Maxwell set his magazine aside. "So, what are we going to do with our mentees for the summer quarter? They'll have way too much free time on their hands when school lets out."

"That's true." Xavier tossed his leg over the arm of the chair. "I do have a few seniors who'll be graduating high school, but those kids are aging out of the program. Most have internships or summer classes to keep them busy."

"Then our main focus will be on keeping the younger ones engaged." Bryan turned that over in his mind. "The eighth through eleventh graders, I'm guessing?"

Xavier nodded. "Yep. Aside from the fact that they'll be out of school, the kids that fall in that age group are the most impressionable as far as peer pressure goes. That means if we don't do this right, they're the ones we're most likely to lose."

Hearing that made Bryan think of Peter. He cared

about all his mentees but felt a deeper connection with Peter, who in many ways represented a younger version of himself. Peter was obviously smart but didn't like to show it. He'd been in a bit of trouble, but Bryan believed that with the right guidance, Peter could excel in life.

"What are we thinking? Field trips? Classes? Community service projects?" Maxwell's question brought Bryan's attention back to the present moment.

"I think we should plan for a combination of all of those things." Xavier grabbed his phone from the pocket of his track pants. "Y'all call out a few places you'd be willing to take them or things you want to do, and I'll jot them down in a note."

Bryan stretched his arms above his head, running through a list of places in his mind. He remembered well what it was like to be a boy of Peter's age, so he knew museums and the like were probably out. He had no desire to spend his time leading a group of sullen, disengaged teenagers around a place they didn't want to be. "No offense, Xavier, but there aren't going to be too many educational places that the kids will actually want to go."

"I know. But I was thinking we'd incentivize the educational stuff."

"How?" Maxwell drank from his can of fancy beer. "You'll need a pretty awesome prize to get them to do that kind of stuff over their summer break."

Xavier nodded. "Yeah, Max. I know that. So I figured we can offer them the opportunity to earn something they want at the end of the summer if they participate in all the activities we set up for them. Concert tickets, a gift card, something like that."

Bryan was impressed with the idea. "Might work. There is one of those teenybopper music festivals coming to the arena in September, with quite a few of the popular rappers and singers in it."

"Right. And I bet the lure of front-row tickets to the show will get the kids on the bus for the activities that aren't quite as entertaining." Xavier typed something into his phone, looking rather pleased with himself.

The three of them spent a few moments coming up with a list of possible locations to visit with the mentees as well as activities to set up for them.

The vibrating of Bryan's phone against his hip caught his attention. He excused himself from the conversation and went out Maxwell's open front door. Standing on the covered porch, he answered the call.

"Yo, Mr. J. Are you busy?" Peter's voice filled his ear.

"Not really. What's up, Peter?"

"Remember when you said I could call you if I needed something?"

"I remember. Do you need something now?"

"I wanted to ask you a favor."

"What do you need?" Leaning against one of the columns holding up the roof above him, Bryan waited.

Peter seemed to hesitate for a moment, then spoke. "My school is having career day, and my dad can't take time off from work. So I thought, if you had time, maybe you could come. If you have time."

Bryan felt his lips tilt up into a smile. It flattered him that Peter would ask him to do this. "When is it?"

"Wednesday after next." Peter paused again, letting out a long breath. "I hope that's enough notice. Do you think you can make it?"

"Yeah. I can do it. I'll tell my assistant to clear my schedule for that date."

"Really?" Peter's voice conveyed his surprise.

"Yes, really. I can spare a day to help you out. Besides, with this much notice, I have time to take care of things that need my personal attention and put someone in place to handle things that arise in my absence."

"Okay. Great. I appreciate this, Mr. J."

"No problem. I'm glad I could help."

"Okay. I'll let you go. Thanks again."

"It's cool. Later, Peter."

"Later."

After the call ended, Bryan tucked his phone back into his pocket. As he reentered the house, he thought about what he might say to a group of high school kids about his job as a textiles executive. It wasn't the most glamourous job in the world and would probably be unfamiliar to most of them. Figuring he'd just stick pretty close to the things he told his mentees on a regular basis, he went back into the living room and returned to his seat on the couch.

Settling into the thick cushions, Bryan noted that the conversation between his friends had taken a turn. The new topic on the table: women.

Xavier, with a broad grin on his face, praised the virtues of marriage. "Listen, Max. You just don't know the joy of waking up to a beautiful woman every morning."

Maxwell's brow hitched. "I beg to differ. I have plenty of experience with that."

"No. This is different, man. I mean a beautiful woman who loves you, who's always down for you and has your back no matter what. A woman whose very presence enriches your life." Xavier clasped his hands together. "It's priceless. There's nothing in the world like it."

In response, Maxwell rolled his eyes. "Spoken like a man that's whupped. Bryan, can you believe how far over the deep end our boy has gone?"

Bryan shrugged. Listening to Xavier wax sentimental had conjured up a mental image of Alexis and the teary eyed smile she'd given him when he slid the engagement ring on her finger the previous day. "I don't know, Max. I can see the value in having a good woman in my life."

Maxwell shook his head, wearing a look of pity. "And what woman has got your head messed up to make you say shit like that?"

He turned up his lips. "I'm not about to tell you. Regardless, you need to admit that it's possible to be happily married. Look at your parents."

"Yeah!" Xavier chimed in. "They've been married, what, forty years?"

"Yeah. That's different, though." Maxwell drained the last of his beer. "But I'm not going to argue with y'all."

Bryan shook his head. *Typical Max. Bailing out before we can tell him why he's wrong.*

They spent the rest of the afternoon finalizing their list for the summer mentoring program. Bryan contributed as much as he could, but whenever there was a lull in the conversation, his mind drifted to Alexis. He'd enjoyed their day together, especially the way she'd reacted to the ring.

Now, he needed to find out when she was free to go out again.

Because when it came to spending time with her, he couldn't seem to get enough.

———

Monday evening, Bryan sat in one of the desks in an upstairs room of the Revels Youth Outreach Center. All around him, the other desks were filled with students who used the services at the YOC. They ranged in age from thirteen to seventeen and were high schoolers from various schools around the district. They had come to hear Alexis talk about careers in fashion, and Bryan was pleased with the turnout. In all, sixteen of the kids had elected to hear Alexis speak. The din of their conversations and the music playing on their various electronic devices filled the room, creating a lively atmosphere.

Xavier entered then, carrying three stacked chairs, and Bryan stood, intending to meet his friend halfway. Xavier was a few steps into the room when Alexis appeared behind him, smiling.

Dressed in a pair of dark denim jeans that hugged her hips like a second skin and a bedazzled black T-shirt, she looked casual yet beautiful. She'd placed a crystal headband around her hair, which held back her glossy curls and allowed him a full view of the graceful lines of her face.

Bryan grabbed a chair from Xavier, and once the three chairs had been set up near the front of the classroom, Bryan turned his attention back to Alexis. "Hey, Lex. Thanks for coming."

Xavier chimed in, gesturing to the chair he'd centered in front of the students. "Yes, Alexis. Thank you so much for taking time out to talk to the kids. My staff and I really appreciate it."

Alexis smiled. "It's no problem. I don't do a lot of public speaking, so I'll try not to bore them."

Looking at her hands, Bryan frowned when he noticed something missing. Easing closer to her, he whispered, "Where is your ring?"

She leaned up to whisper her response. "At home. I didn't want to draw attention to it."

He frowned, unsure of what she meant by that. "What? Why?"

"Think about it. Don't you think one of the kids would notice the ring and ask about it? At that point, the conversation could go places we aren't prepared for it to go." She looked into his eyes. "Do you understand what I mean?"

He nodded. He hadn't really thought about what it might mean if one of the kids wanted to ask about Alexis's personal life. But now that she'd mentioned it, he could see that she was right. No one knew about the ring, not even Xavier. Her cautious approach would probably be best in a situation like this, so he didn't press her any further.

Xavier clapped his hands together then, as he did when he wanted to get the kids' attention. After a few moments, the room fell into relative silence. "Okay, folks. Today, we are honored to have a wonderful guest speaker. Ms. Devers is a local fashion designer, and she's taken time out of her busy schedule to be here with you. So I want you to give her your full attention and be respectful. Let's welcome Ms. Devers with a round of applause."

With varying degrees of enthusiasm, the students clapped for Alexis as they'd been asked to do.

Glancing at Bryan, Alexis quipped, "I guess I'm on."

Bryan sat down next to Xavier in the chairs positioned

off to the side of the classroom and watched Alexis sit down in front of her audience.

"Hi. My name is Alexis Devers, and I design women's sportswear. That includes the basics of a woman's professional wardrobe—blouses, slacks, skirts, dresses."

From her tone and the way her leg bounced as she sat in the chair, Bryan could tell Alexis was nervous. He hoped her nerves would wear off as she continued to speak and built rapport with the kids.

She sat a little straighter, stilled her bouncing leg. "I started my career studying fashion and textiles at North Carolina Central University."

As Alexis continued to talk about her education, Bryan learned about her past right along with everyone else in the room. He knew about her internship with Tracy Reese, because she'd told him about it the first time they'd gone out for coffee to get their origin story straight. But he didn't know about how she'd met Sydney during those days or how she'd saved her money and found an angel investor to help her start her own design house. The more he listened, the more impressed he became. Alexis had worked hard to get where she was. Nothing had been handed to her, and while she'd achieved a lot in her field for someone still so young, he didn't detect a hint of arrogance or conceit in her. Her attitude about her work and the passion she exhibited for it only made her more attractive.

"There's an old adage that says, 'If you do what you love, you never work a day in your life.' I've found that to be true. I love what I do, and going to work each day is a joy." Alexis paused, took a deep breath. "I think I've rambled on long enough. So I'll be happy to take your questions now."

A young girl near the front of the room raised her hand.

Alexis acknowledged her. "Go ahead."

Dropping her hand, the young girl asked, "What do you do in a typical day?"

"Good question, Lisa," Xavier commented.

Alexis smiled. "That is a good question. Let's see, I spend a good portion of my day at my table, working on my flat sketches. Those are the images from which the clothes are made. I also have to do other things, like meetings with my staff. I have a seamstress and a few fit models I work with, as well as a business partner. The seamstress makes up the samples, and the fit models try on the clothes. I also spend time talking to retailers and manufacturers."

"Sounds like you're pretty busy." Lisa sat back in her desk.

"I am. Any other questions?" Alexis scanned the room for other raised hands. "Right there, in the middle. What's your question?"

A young man called out his question. "What's the hardest thing about being a fashion designer?"

Bryan found his own curiosity piqued by that question as he wondered how Alexis would answer it.

She looked thoughtful for a moment. "I guess the hardest part is deciding which designs to pursue first. I have so many ideas and sketchbooks full of clothes I've drawn over the years. Some of them may never get made, because I have to think about what fits with the line I'm currently working on. Does that make sense?"

The young man nodded. "Sure. I get it."

Bryan listened, intrigued. As a very left-brain

person, he was led by logic and practicality. His personality fit his career as an executive, and to be honest, he couldn't imagine doing anything else for a living. His days were filled with paperwork, meetings, and all manner of seriousness and rigidity. Because of that, hearing Alexis describe her predicament of creative overload sounded completely foreign to him. He couldn't imagine being burdened with so many ideas that he couldn't pursue them all. But like everything else he'd discovered about Alexis so far, he noted that she seemed to take it in stride, handling it with grace and a positive attitude.

He watched as she took question after question from the kids, answering them with a smile. All signs of nervousness had faded away, replaced with quiet confidence. Even when one of the kids asked her how much money she made, she remained patient. Her response, diplomatic and measured, answered the question without revealing too much of her personal business. The kids seemed very engaged in the conversation, and Bryan thought Alexis was doing well, especially considering how nervous she'd been in the beginning.

After the last question, Xavier stood. "Okay, folks. Let's thank Ms. Devers again for coming."

Another round of applause filled the room, this one much more enthusiastic than the first. Bryan joined in as a grinning Alexis stood and took a bow.

After the applause died down, Xavier began directing the students out of the room. They'd be returning downstairs to await their parents, since the center would soon be closing for the day. Bryan wanted to go over to Alexis, but a few of the students crowded around her.

Standing back, he watched her talk to them and was again struck by his admiration for her.

The more time he spent with her, the more she amazed him. And that was why, for as long as she would allow it, he planned to treat her as if she were his...for real. If fate smiled on him, before this was all over, their fake engagement would become the real thing.

Chapter 11

Tuesday night, Alexis stepped out of the Performing Arts Center with her arm looped through Bryan's. "Wow. That show was fantastic."

"It was, wasn't it?" He smiled her way. "I knew I was taking a chance when I bought the tickets, but I'm glad you liked it."

"Jill's vocals were amazing. She has so much range." She glanced over her shoulder at the giant poster in the window advertising the show they'd just seen. It was a long-overdue revival of the 1981 Broadway play, *Sophisticated Ladies*. The show, which was a revue of Duke Ellington's greatest hits, featured talented dancers and musicians as well as vocal talent. The standout performance, though, had come from Jill Scott, who'd filled the starring role previously played by late R&B singer Phyllis Hyman.

"You're right. She doesn't get enough shine. I really enjoy her music, and when I saw that she was starring in this, I knew I wanted to see it." He stopped at the curb, watching for traffic before they crossed the street toward the parking deck.

"I've never done something like this in the middle of the week." She took in the city lights twinkling around her as they strolled along. Considering the short amount of time she'd known him, it surprised her how comfortable she felt being with him. Over the past few days, she'd even become accustomed to wearing his ring on her hand.

"Why not?"

"Too busy working on one project or another." That was the disadvantage of being self-employed. While she loved being able to make a living fulfilling her artistic desires, sometimes she felt like she never clocked out. No matter how she occupied herself during her free time, there always seemed to be another design idea in the back of her mind, waiting to be drawn and developed.

"Hopefully, the time you spend with me will change that." He glanced her way as they approached his car, parked on the lower level. He unlocked the car, held open the passenger door so she could climb in, then closed it behind her.

Once he was inside and the drive got underway, she directed her attention at the passing scenery. Focusing on the skyline of the City of Oaks kept her from openly staring at Bryan. He looked so handsome in his coal-black suit, crisp white shirt, and bright-green tie.

When he moved his right hand away from the steering wheel and let it rest on her thigh, she felt the wave of electricity roll through her.

"Is this okay?" He asked the question without taking his eyes off the road.

"Yes." She would be lying if she said she didn't enjoy his touch. The warmth of his large hand penetrated the fabric of her gold charmeuse cocktail dress, radiating through her. She imagined what it would be like to let him touch her fully, to bare her body to his hands, his lips...

"I thought we'd go out for dessert. That is, unless you want to go right home." His voice cut into her reverie.

Dessert. Just what I was thinking of. Although she knew he meant something sugary and edible, not the carnal sweetness that had flooded her mind the moment he'd touched her. Keeping her tone light, she responded. "Sounds good. Where are we going?"

"A little place called Carmine's."

"The Italian restaurant?"

"Oh, so you know the place. Good."

She nodded. "I've gone there for lunch with Sydney a few times." The family-owned establishment served authentic cuisine, and the staff was friendly and attentive.

"They have a fantastic tiramisu. I thought we'd have that and some coffee."

She smiled. "Great." She'd sampled many of their pasta dishes but had never had the dessert. Tonight was as good a time as any to try it, and she couldn't ask for better company.

They arrived at Carmine's several minutes later, and Bryan parked the car and escorted her inside. The interior was dim, mainly lit by the lanterns on the white-clothed tables. After a brief stop at the hostess stand to confirm their reservation, they were whisked off to a table for two. The table, positioned near the side entrance, was tucked away from the front of the house, where those who hadn't made reservations were waiting for a table.

While they waited for a server, she looked out the window to her right. It was just past nine, and the city was still bustling with activity at this hour.

"I hope I'm not keeping you out too late," he commented.

She turned his way. "No. I'm fine as long as I get my

eight hours. Since I don't generally take any meetings or make any big decisions before ten a.m., we're good."

He reached across the table, taking her hand in his. He said nothing, seeming content to look in her eyes.

The moment he touched her, she felt it again—that wondrous sensation that swept through her body whenever they connected physically. If she reacted like this to a simple display of affection, she couldn't imagine how she'd react if she ever let him…

"Are you okay, Alexis?"

"Huh?" She snapped back to the moment at hand when she heard him speak.

His dark eyes held concern and were squarely focused on her face. "I asked if you were okay. For a few moments there, you were breathing pretty heavily."

She blinked a few times, tamping down her embarrassment as she tried to come up with a suitable reply. "I'm fine. Just remembering how I felt during the play. Did you hear that high note Jill hit during 'In a Sentimental Mood'?"

His expression changed, the concern replaced by a smile. "It was really impressive. That sister's got pipes."

"I mean, it gave me chills." And it had. Jill's vocals were nothing short of spectacular. Alexis chose to leave out the fact that she also got chills every time he touched her. After all, she was attempting to keep things casual and non-awkward.

A waiter approached the table then with menus in hand. "Good evening, Mr. James. Good to see you again."

Bryan turned his way. "Same here, Neil. My companion and I won't need menus tonight. Could we just have the deluxe tiramisu and some coffee, please?"

Alexis raised her hand to get Neil's attention. "Decaf, please."

Neil nodded. "Not a problem."

Once they were alone again, Bryan looked her way. "I hope you don't mind sharing with me. The tiramisu here is pretty large."

She shook her head. "I don't mind." The idea of sharing things with him seemed…natural. Since she was still figuring out what exactly was happening between them, she didn't give voice to her thoughts.

He reached across the tabletop, captured her left hand. "You know, that ring looks great on you."

She could feel the heat rising into her cheeks. She'd already thanked him profusely, so she didn't want to repeat the sentiment for the hundredth time. "I don't know what to say."

"You don't have to say anything."

A long, silent moment passed, with him holding her hand.

The waiter returned then, bearing a tray with their coffee and dessert. Bryan released her hand, and they both sat back to make room on the table for their order.

Neil arranged the items on the table, then placed two forks on the plate with the tiramisu. "Enjoy it."

Bryan thanked Neil, who then made himself scarce.

While she doctored her coffee with a touch of sugar and cream, he grabbed one of the forks. When the coffee was to her liking, she picked up the other fork. Each of them cut off a small portion of the espresso-soaked ladyfingers.

Before she could lift her fork, she found Bryan's fork hovering near her mouth.

She looked at him over the fork. "Really?"

He winked. "Open wide, baby."

Ignoring the tingle that went through her when he called her by the endearment, she did as he asked. He gently placed the soft, sweet dessert between her parted lips, then slipped the fork out.

Her eyes slid closed as she chewed. The sweetness of the ladyfingers, set off by the slight bitterness of the espresso and the creaminess of the chocolate filling, created a delicious flavor combination. She'd had tiramisu before, but none had ever been this good. She wondered if it was the recipe or the fact that Bryan had fed it to her so sensually that made it taste so heavenly.

When she opened her eyes again, she found him watching her. "How is it?"

As she answered, she knew she was speaking about both the dessert and the man who'd delivered it to her mouth. "It's magnificent."

He smiled.

She offered up her forkful. "Now, you open up."

With a chuckle, he obeyed.

They finished the dessert in convivial silence, feeding each other until the plate was empty. As she set aside the fork and drained the last of her coffee, she sighed contentedly. "I'm going to sleep so good after that richness."

"Let's hope so." He slid back from the table.

A wave of impulsiveness washed over her, and before she could stop herself, she rose and rounded the table. There, she leaned down and kissed him on the lips. "Thank you for this, Bryan. I really appreciate all this, the way you've been treating me."

"I'm just treating you the way you deserve to be treated. Like a queen. Any man who doesn't know that isn't worthy of you." He reached up, ran his knuckle over her cheek.

She leaned in and kissed him again. And this time, she allowed the kiss to deepen naturally, doing nothing to stop it or temper it.

～～～

Bryan loosened the blue necktie around his neck, opening his collar against the steamy air. Of all the days for a working lunch outdoors, his father would choose today. The forecast had called for record humidity, and unfortunately, the weatherman had been correct. Even though the calendar indicated early September, today's weather seemed more appropriate for the middle of July.

Oscar sat to his right at the square table in the outdoor dining section of the Steel Drum, a local eatery specializing in Caribbean food. The old man had abandoned his sport coat, tossing it over the back of his chair, and currently mopped his damp forehead with a red linen napkin. Across from Bryan sat Wes, perusing the menu and wearing the same annoying, self-indulgent smirk he wore most of the time. He seemed completely oblivious to Vernon, the waiter standing silently next to the table. Having already taken Bryan's and Oscar's orders, Vernon exhibited remarkable patience considering the five or six minutes he'd been waiting.

Bryan fought the urge to roll his eyes. "Wes, we do have to get back to the office sometime today. Are you going to order or what?"

Wes cut him a look.

Undeterred, Bryan folded his arms over his chest, stared right back, and waited.

Wes turned his attention to Vernon. "I'll have the picante de pollo, please."

Vernon started to say something, but Bryan's gesture stopped him. He jotted down the order on his pad. "Your order will be up shortly, gentlemen."

"Thank you." Bryan watched the ever-patient waiter walk away and reenter the restaurant.

As if sensing the tension between his son and his nephew, Oscar spoke up. "So, boys. We need to talk about our plans for the Krystal Kouture line. Now that we've secured the contract, we should establish our road map."

Bryan nodded. "I agree. Ms. Devers and Ms. Greer have very high expectations, but I'm sure we can meet them with proper planning and execution."

"Word around the office is that you're already trying to fulfill Ms. Devers's needs, B." Wes's expression was one of a man who considered himself extremely witty.

Bryan begged to differ. "I wouldn't know. I don't participate in office gossip, Wes. Maybe your time would be better spent in the secretarial pool with the rest of the hens?"

Wes's face scrunched up in disgust, but he said nothing more.

Bryan pushed away his growing irritation with his cousin's smart-ass remark. What he did with Alexis was none of anybody's business until the two of them decided otherwise. They were both consenting adults. Aside from that, he didn't like the way Wes characterized their dealings. He'd spoken of them like they were two teenagers necking in a parked car.

I'm done with him for the day.

Turning his attention toward Oscar, he asked, "What do you think is a realistic drop date for the first few pieces?"

Oscar scratched his chin. "If we're just starting with a few pieces for the festival, I think we can get it done in the next seven business days."

Pulling his phone from his hip pocket, Bryan noted that in the calendar app. "I'll reach out to Ms. Devers, but I think that should work. That will give her another few days to get the pieces fitted to her models."

Wes clapped his hands together. "What about a street date for the line? Didn't you say the buyers are champing at the bit for the clothes?"

Bryan nodded, glad Wes's attention seemed to be back on business. "Yes. She's had offers from several major retailers, and I'm sure there will only be more once her models hit the runway."

Oscar, appearing thoughtful, took a long drink from his water glass. "Let's aim for three weeks until we can produce the first fifteen thousand units. Sound good?"

Both Bryan and Wes communicated their agreement.

"So now we can work backwards and determine everything we need to do to make this happen." True to his old-school sensibilities, Oscar extracted a pen and small legal pad from an inner pocket of his sport coat and laid them on the table. Even as chief executive, he didn't balk at the tasks most men in his position would pass off to an assistant.

For the next several minutes, the three of them tossed ideas back and forth, with Oscar noting them on his pad. When the food arrived, the men set their work aside for a bit to make room.

Bryan inhaled the spicy, enticing aroma of his curry chicken, rice, and mixed vegetables. Rather than dig in, he waited with his eyes on his cousin. As Wes lifted a forkful of picante de pollo to his lips, Bryan could feel the smile spreading across his face.

Once he closed his mouth around the food, Wes chewed for only a few seconds before his eyes enlarged to three times their normal size. He reached for his water glass while his free hand flew to his throat. Tipping the glass, he drank the three tablespoons of water left in the bottom, then grunted in Bryan's direction.

Sitting back in his chair, Bryan asked, "Need a refill, Cuz?"

Wes's wide eyes grew angry, but it was obvious he couldn't speak.

Oscar looked up from his own plate of jerk chicken. "Good Lord, Wes. I forgot what a lightweight you are when it comes to spicy food."

Shaking his head and holding back his chuckle, Bryan raised his hand to signal Vernon. Making a gesture of water being poured into an invisible glass, he then dropped his hands. It took all he had not to burst out laughing as he watched his cousin's bulging eyes and flailing hands.

"Man up, Wes." The comment came from Oscar.

At that point, it became painful to stifle his laughter, so Bryan let a small chuckle slip.

Vernon delivered a tall glass of ice water to Wes, who snatched it from his hand and immediately downed the entire contents.

After Vernon left, Wes turned red, watery eyes on his cousin. "Really, B? You just gonna let me damn near choke to death like that?"

Bryan shook his head. "Nah. I wasn't going to let anything happen to you. I was just illustrating a point."

Confusion crinkled his face. "What the hell are you talking about?"

"See how that spice snuck up on you?" Bryan leaned in close to be sure Wes could hear him. "If you think you're going to come into Royal and interfere with my work in any way, that's exactly how I'm gonna get you. You won't see it coming until you're already burned."

Wes blinked a few times but said nothing.

That was fine by Bryan. Picking up his own fork, he went back to his food.

Oscar shook his head. "You two."

Bryan was glad his father didn't ask him to apologize, because he had no intention of doing so. Wes needed to know what he was walking into, so he'd provided his cousin with fair warning.

Now he just hoped Wes would have enough sense to heed it.

Chapter 12

ALEXIS CURLED UP ON THE SOFA IN MAXWELL'S living room, holding her mug of peach white tea. She'd come to her brother's house in the middle of the week, something she rarely did. She preferred to catch up on work on Wednesdays, to keep office minutiae from haunting her weekends. But she'd eschewed her routine in favor of coming over so she and her big brother could have an important, long-overdue discussion.

Looking around her brother's house, she thought about how much it resembled the stereotypical bachelor pad. With the money Maxwell earned as an architect and business owner, she'd wager it was much larger than the digs of the average single man. Still, he had most of the expected trappings: the wet bar in his kitchen, the ginormous flat-screen television, black leather furniture, and plain black curtains. His wealth showed in his décor, but so did the lack of a woman's touch.

She could hear Maxwell rifling around in the kitchen as he fixed himself a drink. Sitting there alone, she thought back on Sydney's words when she'd told her about the little scheme she and Bryan planned to undertake. *Maxwell is going to freak the hell out*.

At present, Maxwell had no idea of what was going on between his best friend and his baby sister, and Alexis planned to keep it that way as long as possible. To that end, she'd left her beautiful new ring safely at home. Knowing Maxwell, Sydney might well have been correct in her prediction of his reaction. With everything else going on in her life right now, Alexis didn't want to deal with that potential drama.

He appeared then, rounding the corner from the kitchen. Instead of a mug, Maxwell had his hands wrapped around a short, cut-crystal glass, partially filled with some clear liquid and ice cubes. He slid onto the couch next to her, taking a drink from the glass as he settled in.

She cocked a brow, because she knew it wasn't water. "What are you drinking?"

"Patrón." He lifted the glass in her direction before taking another sip.

She folded her arms over her chest. "Really, Max? In the middle of the week?"

He shrugged. "It's after five. I'm over twenty-one. And I'll have you know that tequila is a probiotic. Don't be mad at me for protecting my digestive system."

She rolled her eyes. "Sure, that's why you're drinking it."

He chuckled. "Stop hassling me, *Mom*, and let's deal with the issue on the table. What are we going to do about Kelsey?"

She sighed at the mention of her sister's name. "I don't know. But we have to be really careful, whatever we do."

"When did she call you?"

She shook her head. "She didn't call. She texted. But it was yesterday." Taking her phone out of the pocket of her jeans, she opened her messaging app, pulled up the conversation with Kelsey, and passed it to him. "Part of me feels relieved that she's finally ready to leave him. But the other part…"

Maxwell finished where she left off, his tone grim. "You're worried that we won't be able to get her and the kid out safely. It's a valid worry. We're her family, not a SWAT team."

She nodded, unsure of what else to say. After all this time waiting for Kelsey to finally let go of the illusion of a healthy relationship with Scott, things were finally changing. But now that Kelsey felt ready, Alexis realized just how wholly unprepared she was.

"Listen, I've been waiting a long time to get Kelsey out of there, and I'll do whatever it takes." The hard set of Maxwell's jaw showed his determination.

"She doesn't want to involve the police, at least not until she and Naji are a safe distance away." She understood Kelsey's concern. Scott had shown himself to be impulsive, hot-tempered, and mentally unstable. If he got any indication that law enforcement was nearby, he could snap and seriously hurt—or kill—her sister and the innocent little boy caught up in this very adult drama.

"I'll honor her wish, but I'm sure my frat brothers won't mind tagging along."

She crinkled her brow. "Maxie, we're trying to do this peacefully."

"Nah. I said I'd get Kelsey and Naji out peacefully. After that, all bets are off."

She pursed her lips.

"Don't give me that look. I'm not gonna start anything with him." He cracked his knuckles. "But if Scott tries to break bad with me, he'd better hope the cops show up fast. If not, he's gonna get a healthy dose of these hands." He held up his fists.

She shook her head but didn't protest. She wouldn't pass up the opportunity to lay into Scott, either, so she couldn't judge her brother for voicing a desire she was sure many of her family members shared. Scott had spent the last few years making Kelsey's life a living hell, and Alexis couldn't wait to see him pay the price for his misdeeds.

Draining the last of the liquor, Maxwell set the glass aside. "The last message says she'll text us when he's out of the house. I guess whoever is closer at the time will just haul ass over there."

"Yeah. I'm more than willing to stop whatever I'm doing. And I'm going to pull Syd and Dawn in on this, too, in case one of them is closer." As her closest friend, Sydney was well aware of Kelsey's situation, and Alexis felt sure Dawn, their office manager, wouldn't mind helping if she was needed.

"I'll do the same with my frat brothers." He passed her phone back to her. "Where is she sending Naji? I didn't see it in her messages."

"She's been communicating with Scott's sister and brother-in-law. When the time comes, they've agreed to take Naji with them until things settle out, and permanently if needed." Even though she had no blood ties to the child, she still felt sympathy for him. He was faultless in all this but would have his life uprooted and turned upside down anyway.

"Then we're good. Now, I guess we just wait for her to reach out." He cast a glance toward his hallway. "Where is she going to stay? She's welcome to use one of my extra bedrooms."

"I don't know if she'll go for that, considering how overprotective you were when we were growing up. She can use the spare bed in my office at the condo, too."

He shook his head. "I'm not so sure she'll want to cozy up to your drafting table and your dress forms. Maybe she'll stay in the mother-in-law suite at Mom and Dad's."

She blew out a breath. "It doesn't matter to me. We're all waiting to take her in, so she can stay wherever she wants. I just want her safe."

"Me, too."

They settled into silence then, each of them entertaining their own thoughts. Sipping her now tepid tea, Alexis sent up a silent plea to the heavens for when the time came to bring Kelsey home.

Please let this go smoothly.

⸺ ❊ ⸺

Maxwell straightened his tie as he stood by the open doors of the YOC's van, watching the kids climb out. The van idled at the curb on Edenton Street, which ran between the grounds of the State Capitol and two of the state's museums. It was a Thursday afternoon, and the kids were about to tour the North Carolina Museum of History. As something of a closet history nerd, Maxwell had volunteered to leave work at his architectural firm early so he and Bryan could escort the students through the museum. It was a small group, only eight students, but Maxwell didn't mind. As far as he was concerned, having so few of the kids made it easier to transport and keep up with them.

Bryan, in the driver's seat of the van, called out to

Maxwell. "Yo, Max. Wait with them by the entrance while I park."

"I got it." Maxwell shut the doors and watched the van pull away from the curb. Downtown Raleigh had experienced so much growth over the past decade that parking on the street was a very rare occurrence. In most cases, drivers had no choice but to park in one of the city's many parking decks. Since there was no street parking near the museum, Bryan would have to navigate the youth center's passenger van into one of the decks.

With the five young men and three young women in tow, Maxwell led them to the steps in the front of the Museum of History. "While Mr. James is parking the van, let's talk about the three statues here on the steps. Can anyone tell me who they are without reading the plaques?" The three bronze figures, representing North Carolinians who'd played important roles in state history, were the first thing to greet visitors to the museum.

One of the girls raised her hand. "I know that one is Thomas Day, the famous cabinetmaker. We talked about him in my social studies class."

Maxwell smiled. "That's right. You just got yourself a point, Lisa."

She pumped her fist in the air.

Maxwell turned to the other students. "Now, remember what Mr. James and I told you before we left the center. Your participation in this outing can earn you points toward winning a front-row ticket to the SuperFest. How many of you want to be at that concert?"

All eight hands shot up.

Chuckling, Maxwell quipped, "That's what I thought. So remember to pay attention today and to ask questions.

You're not going to get points for just standing around looking bored, all right?"

Nods and murmurs of agreement rose from the group.

Bryan walked up then, tucking the van keys into his pockets. "How were they?"

"They were no trouble at all." Maxwell started up the steps. "Okay, you all. Let's get this tour started."

Inside the museum, Maxwell and Bryan took the students around the building's interior. Their assigned curator, a short woman with brown hair, led them through a variety of exhibits featuring artifacts from the state's history. In the 1920s Drugstore exhibit, the kids were fascinated by the patent medicines that were once prescribed for various ailments.

As they worked their way through the Story of North Carolina exhibit, Maxwell watched the students' eyes light up with interest. The exhibit was like a life-sized timeline of the state's fourteen-thousand-year history, tracing life from its earliest inhabitants through modern times. As they rounded the corner leading to the civil rights section of the timeline, Maxwell saw the glass-enclosed section of a Woolworth's counter from a Greensboro store where a sit-in had been staged.

Seeing the lunch counter did something to him. He'd read about the incident as a student in Raleigh's public schools, and it was easy for him to imagine the humiliation those young people who staged the sit-in had suffered. He didn't consider himself an expert by any stretch, but he felt compelled to say something while he had the kids in front of the lunch counter.

So Maxwell raised his hand to get the attention of the curator. "Miss, do you mind if I say something?"

"Not at all." The curator stepped aside, surrendering the floor to Maxwell.

Ignoring Bryan's questioning look, Maxwell stood in front of the group of students. "I'm sure most of you know about the sit-ins, because it's a big part of the curriculum when you all study state history. Am I right?"

The kids agreed.

"But I want you to really look at this exhibit and think about what it all means. The people who staged the sit-in were not that much older than you. How do you think they felt as they sat at the lunch counter, having food and condiments dumped on their heads and being heckled by an angry crowd?"

Their expressions changed, and Maxwell thought the kids must be considering his words.

Finally, one of the boys said, "They were probably scared."

"And angry themselves that they were being treated so badly," added another student.

"Right." Maxwell clasped his hands together. "And they probably knew going into the place that they would be treated that way. But that didn't stop them from doing what they felt was right. Remember that the next time you have to do something you think is hard."

The kids started to talk quietly among themselves, and Maxwell noted that even Bryan looked impressed. Maxwell stepped aside then, turning the floor back over to the curator. He was no teacher or anything, but he'd joined in Xavier's mentoring program because he genuinely cared about the kids. So when the opportunity to make a point to them arose, he'd take it. Hopefully, they'd been listening and would recall his advice when life presented them with an opportunity to make a hard choice.

Later that evening, when he and Bryan were leaving the youth center, Bryan stopped Maxwell by the front door.

"That was pretty cool, what you said to the kids today, Max."

Maxwell winked. "Thanks, brotha, I have my moments."

"I'm glad you decided to come along. I think you really reached them." Bryan fished in his pocket for his keys. "Usually Xavier's the one to say something inspiring, but you stepped right into that role today."

He shrugged. "I just felt compelled. I think I might come along on the next field trip, too." He'd enjoyed himself, not just because of the things he'd learned at the museum, but because of the kids. They were a bright group, and he could easily see the untapped potential in them.

"Who knows? You might even make a decent father one day." Bryan chuckled as he approached his car, unlocking the driver's side door.

"Maybe. See you later, B." Maxwell waved as he walked away, returning to his own car. As he drove home, he thought of his friend's comment about his potential as a father. He'd never thought much about what it would be like to have kids. In a way, he felt as if he'd had a hand in raising Alexis and Kelsey. But he had to assume actual fatherhood would involve way more responsibility than he'd taken on in protecting his two younger sisters.

Seeing no need to dwell on any of that now, he put his focus back on driving.

If and when the time came for him to raise a child of his own, he supposed he'd figure it out then.

Seated in one of the gray plastic folding seats at O'Kelly-Riddick Stadium, Bryan shifted a bit to his right. The move didn't do much to change the comfort level of the hard seat beneath him, but it did allow him better access to Alexis. As he draped his arm around her shoulders, she glanced his way and gifted him with one of her beautiful smiles.

"So do you think you'll be ready for this interview on Tuesday?"

He shrugged. "I'll do my best. Tell me again what we're doing?"

She giggled. "We're going on *Morning Buzz*, remember? They're interviewing us about the line and about our engagement. I'm doing it as a favor for a local reporter I know."

He nodded. *Maybe I'll run a web search on us later, just to see what they're saying.* "Okay. I can take the time off from work. I know my dad isn't going to make a fuss, not when free publicity is involved."

"Great. The show films in New York, but I was already going up there to get together with Tracy Reese. I'm going to fly out Monday afternoon, since it's an early taping."

"Sounds good. I don't foresee any problem grabbing a flight."

A few moments passed between them in silence, and he contemplated what they were about to do. In a way, they'd already gone public with their relationship by not making any effort to hide it. Talking about it on television would seal the deal. When they returned from New York, they'd have to deal with all the repercussions of their announcement.

She yawned, covering her mouth with a small, graceful hand.

"Are you good? Do you need anything?" He knew she wasn't the biggest sports fan and wanted to make her time in the stadium as enjoyable as possible.

When he'd asked her to accompany him to the game, he'd been surprised by how quickly she said yes. He didn't know if she'd come because she wanted to see the game or because she just wanted to spend time with him. Either way, he felt grateful she'd agreed.

She shook her head. "Nah, I'm good. You already got me a drink and some popcorn." She gestured to the tray that held her snacks in the empty seat to her right.

He nodded. "Well, just let me know if you change your mind."

She snuggled closer to him. "You're really spoiling me, Bryan."

"That's the plan." He winked.

All around him, the seats were filled with folks who'd come to enjoy the game and the beautiful weather. The buzz of a dozen or more random conversations, as well as the cheers coming from the squad running through a routine on the field, filled his ears.

He inhaled a deep breath of the crisp fall air, which carried with it the scents of freshly popped popcorn, hot dogs, and other concessions being sold for the game. The temperature was chilly for early September, but he wasn't too concerned. He'd donned his maroon Eagles windbreaker to stave off the cool air, just in case. He'd also advised Alexis to wear something warm, and she'd taken his advice. She wore a black tracksuit with a white stripe running down the sides of the sleeves and legs, with the jacket zipped up to her throat. As an extra precaution, he'd brought along his oversized fleece throw, emblazoned with the mighty Eagle. The throw was folded neatly and tucked into the seat to his left.

It felt good to be back at his alma mater, looking out on the field he'd played on more than a decade ago. Being there with Alexis made it even better. He glanced at his gold wristwatch, which showed twenty minutes until the four o'clock kickoff.

"I haven't been back here for a game in ages." Alexis took a sip of her soda as she made the comment. "Even when I was in school, I only went to one or two games every season."

He chuckled. "I spent a lot of time here, since I was on the team for two years." He'd played on the team his freshman and sophomore years. A slipped disc in his back had brought his football playing days to an end, and he'd accepted his fate for what it was. As his parents' only child, it had been a foregone conclusion that he'd go to work at Royal. He'd gone into playing with his eyes wide open and without any expectations of ever playing professionally.

"Oh, this is hilarious." She turned his way, a wry smile on her face. "All through college, I wanted to date a guy on the football team. None of them ever fit the bill…and here we are."

He couldn't help chuckling at her expression and her tone. A small voice in the back of his mind reminded him that this relationship wasn't supposed to be real. He pushed that voice away. *I don't need my conscience killing my fun right now.*

"Here come the teams."

Alexis's words drew him out of his thoughts. He turned his gaze on the field in time to see the last few members of the opposing team, from Duke, run out on the field. The Blue Devil fans in the stadium roared with applause, the sound mixing with the jeers and boos of the Eagles fans. Moments later, the scenario was reversed as the Eagles took the field. Home field advantage kicked in big time, with the cheers far outweighing the jeers as the players took their positions. With everyone in place, the game got under way.

As the game and the afternoon wore on, clouds rolled in, blocking out some of the sun's warmth. Bryan felt it, but the thick lining of his windbreaker kept him warm. When he looked to Alexis, though, he could tell she was getting cold.

Running her palms up and down her forearms, she spoke. "I'm starting to get a little chilly." She then drew a deep breath between her slightly parted, cherry-red-painted lips.

He grabbed his throw, opening it up. Spreading it over both of their laps, he dragged a section of it up and tucked it behind her right shoulder. "How's that?"

She pulled the thick fabric close, snuggling into it and into the crook of his arm. "Much better."

The absence of armrests on the seats meant there was no physical barrier between them, so as she edged close to him, their lower bodies touched. Warmth radiated from the spot where his right thigh pressed against the

softness of her left hip. He took a deep breath, reminding himself of where they were, to keep his hand from
traveling to places he suddenly longed to caress.

An Eagles touchdown on the field drew raucous
cheers and celebration from the crowd as the game
entered the second quarter. That made the score fourteen
to nothing in favor of the home team. He raised his hand
in the air, joining in. When the cheers died down, he
looked back at Alexis. She was watching the field, a soft
smile on her face.

Beneath the throw, however, her small hand was on
the move.

He jumped slightly when he felt her hand come to
rest on his thigh. She applied just enough pressure to let
him know she was touching him, no more and no less.

She glanced his way, shot him a wicked little smile,
then turned her attention back to the game.

He felt his own lips tilting into a smile. Confident she
wouldn't protest, he matched her gesture, letting his open
palm rest on her firm, full thigh. When he felt the muscle
twitch beneath his touch, he felt certain she wasn't cold
anymore. There was a heat building between them, and
he knew she could feel it. It was real, palpable, and had
nothing to do with the temperature.

They remained that way, snuggled together beneath
the throw, until the half. She got up then to go to the
restroom, and he couldn't help admiring the sway of her
hips when she walked away.

When she returned, she slipped back beneath the throw,
pressing her body close to his again. Many of the seats
around them were empty as people visited the restrooms
and concession stand during the lull in action on the field.

He draped his arm around her, enjoying the closeness. "I'm really enjoying your company, Alexis."

She looked up at him, her dark eyes sparkling. "I'm enjoying this, too. Probably more than I should, considering."

Hearing her statement, he relished what she'd said. There was still the matter of what she *hadn't* said, though. The specter of their agreement to maintain a fake relationship still hung between them, like a transparent film separating him from her. "I've been considering this arrangement a lot lately, if I'm honest."

She blinked a few times, her eyes widening. "What do you mean?"

"I think you know. When we first discussed it, I told you up front that I was attracted to you. And you admitted your attraction to me. I'm sure you haven't forgotten."

She shook her head. "No, I haven't."

He watched her, taking in the way the sunlight played over her beautiful face. "The more time I spend with you, the more real this becomes to me. I care about you, Alexis." He didn't say the three words women loved to hear to solidify commitment, because he didn't feel ready for that. No matter how she reacted, he would feel secure in the knowledge that he'd respected her enough to be honest with her.

Her next words came on the wings of a sigh. "God, Bryan. I feel it, too."

Reaching out to her, he tilted her chin and pressed his lips to hers. Ignoring the people around them, he kept his sole focus on exploring the sweet cavern of her mouth. Their tongues mated, and while she held back at first, she soon gave in to the magic sparking between them.

When the announcer indicated the start of the second half, she broke the kiss. As her eyes slowly opened, she grazed her fingertips over his cheek.

"Bryan James, you are nothing but trouble."

He turned back to the game, not bothering to hide his smile. "And you love every minute of it."

Chapter 13

ALEXIS WATCHED THE BUSTLING SCENERY OF MID-town Manhattan roll by through the tinted window of the hired town car. It was late Monday afternoon, just before five, and the heavy foot and vehicle traffic flowing around the car reflected that.

For the life of her, she couldn't figure out how people drove in New York City. Between careless pedestrians, distracted tourists, bicycle rickshaws, and horse-drawn carriages, the roads were a complete circus. Add in the influx of drivers who seemed solely focused on reaching their destination five minutes ago, and she knew she would never get behind the wheel of a vehicle here.

Bryan, seated to her left on the black leather seat, seemed more interested in his phone than in taking in the sights. He had the phone resting on his leg, scrolling through his social media feed with one hand. His other hand had made its home on her skirt-clad thigh, and he'd been touching her that way since the moment they'd climbed into the car at LaGuardia. That was after he'd spent the entire hour-long flight from RDU with his arm draped around her shoulder.

She glanced at his large, strong hand where it rested and was struck by how accustomed she'd become to having him touch her.

The town car made a right onto Madison Avenue from Thirty-Ninth, and Alexis ran a hand over her hair.

The strands hung loose because she'd had to take off her metal hair clip at the airport and hadn't put it back on yet. Rifling through her handbag, she dug out the clip and reached up to secure her hair just as the car pulled up at the curb in front of the Library Hotel. A smile tipped the corners of her mouth. She'd stayed there once before and found the accommodations charming, unique, and well worth their elevated price.

The driver got out of the car, opening the door for Bryan on his way to the trunk. While the driver handled their baggage, Bryan came around to her side and opened the door for her. Taking his extended hand, she let him help her out onto the sidewalk. As they passed beneath the beige stone archway over the entrance, he held open the door for her with his free hand.

Inside, she took in the familiar warmth of the Library's lobby. Soft beige tile floors mimicked the soft hue of the smooth ceiling above, where recessed lighting lit the space. Warm, dark wood paneling gave unique character to the walls, and the camel-colored furniture, with soft, tufted cushions, welcomed visitors to sit down. Her favorite elements were the bookshelves, bursting with selections beckoning to be read. The colorful spines drew her eye right away, just as they had the first time she'd entered the place.

"Nice place," Bryan commented as he led her toward the front desk. "You can check in first."

She nodded and stepped up to the desk.

The smiling clerk spoke then. "Welcome to the Library Hotel. Are you checking in today?"

"Yes." Alexis handed over her driver's license and credit card. "My assistant made the arrangements for me."

The clerk took the two cards, then accessed the computer behind the desk. "Ah, I see your reservation here, Miss Devers. You'll be staying in our Love room on the eleventh floor for two nights. Do you have identification, Mr. James?"

Bryan's thick brow cocked. "I do, but you can take care of me after Miss Devers is squared away."

A look of confusion on her face, the clerk said, "I'm showing you and Miss Devers sharing a room. Has there been a mistake?"

Alexis's eyes widened, and she swiveled her head to look at Bryan.

He shrugged.

She blinked a few times, wondering what was going on with the reservation. Then it occurred to her what had happened. Offering the clerk an apologetic smile, she asked, "Can you excuse me for just a second?"

"No problem, ma'am."

Stepping away from the desk, Alexis grabbed Bryan's hand. With a gentle tug, she moved him to the sitting area to the right of the desk. She spoke in a hushed whisper. "This is obviously Sydney's doing. I'm sure Dawn wouldn't have booked us in the same room on her own." She couldn't wait to pop Sydney upside the head when she returned home.

His answering chuckle rumbled forth. "I agree about who's likely responsible. But I'm not going to lie and say I'm upset."

She stared up at him.

He smiled. "We're engaged, remember? Why wouldn't we be sharing a room?"

She drew a deep breath. *Damn it*. He was right, and

she knew it. She also knew that any plans she had on avoiding him during this trip were now dashed on the jagged rocks of reality. Fixing her face into a soft smile, she nodded. "You're right. Let's just check in."

They returned to the desk, hand in hand.

"Sorry about that." Bryan handed over his driver's license.

"The one room is correct, then?" The clerk's tone was cautious as she posed the question.

Alexis smiled. "Yes, it is."

After a little more typing, the clerk presented them with two plastic key cards inside of an envelope displaying the room number. "Enjoy your stay."

"Thank you." Bryan accepted the cards and tucked them into his back pocket.

They strolled away from the desk together, and when they arrived at the elevator bank, the bellhop awaited. Next to him stood the cart laden with their baggage.

Upstairs, they tipped the bellhop and watched him depart with the empty cart. Bryan stood back, holding his one bag and all three of Alexis's, while she opened the door.

The interior of the room was cozy and welcoming. Done in soft shades of ecru and mother-of-pearl, it featured a king-size bed centering the space. A long desk with a built-in bookshelf occupied one wall. Several windows filtered light into the room, and tasteful pieces of framed art graced the walls. Directly across from them was a door bearing a glass panel covered by a set of Venetian blinds.

Alexis moved into the room with Bryan close behind her. He stopped to set the bags down, but she continued, curiosity compelling her to open the door.

When she did, she found herself on a private terrace that looked out over Madison Avenue. The sounds of the traffic, as well as the myriad activities taking place in the city on a beautiful evening, filled her ears. She smiled as she took in the sight of the tall buildings surrounding the hotel. Two armless iron chairs faced each other on the terrace, a short-legged wooden table between them. A pair of matching planters, home to vibrant orange mums, sat between the chairs and the terrace railing. Window boxes beyond the railing also brimmed with colorful blooms, making the terrace seem like a garden retreat in the heart of an urban metropolis.

He stepped out of the room then, and she felt his presence immediately.

He draped his strong arms loosely around her waist. "What a view."

"You're telling me." She let herself enjoy his embrace. "I don't know if I'll be able to muster much anger at Sydney now. This room is fantastic."

"I know I'm not mad at her." He pressed a soft kiss to the side of her throat. "So what do you want to do now?"

She inhaled, keeping the intake of air slow and long. She was not about to fall down the rabbit hole with this man. Yes, he was fine. Yes, she was attracted to him, and yes, they were ensconced in a beautiful room in the heart of the city…

"What do you say, Alexis? What we do is up to you."

Before she could answer, her stomach growled, reminding her that she hadn't eaten since the small salad she'd had before she'd left her condo for the airport. The sound was loud, and she knew he'd heard it.

He laughed. "Sounds like your stomach has made the

decision for you. I'm hungry, too, so why don't we get something to eat?"

She swiveled around in his embrace until she faced him. Embarrassment heating her cheeks, she nodded. "Yes, let's."

"Do you want to go up to the restaurant? It's on the rooftop." Bryan had seen a pamphlet about the place, called Madison and Vine, when they were in the lobby.

She shook her head. "I'm kind of tired from the traveling. Something about running around the airport just takes it out of me."

"I feel you. How about I order us some room service, then?"

"Sounds great." She smiled up at him. "Can you order me the chopped salad with grilled salmon? I had it the last time I stayed here, and it was delicious."

"You got it." He released his grip on her, reentering the room. He took a few minutes to look over the menu that had been left on the desk before calling to place their order.

Later, Bryan sat with Alexis on the terrace, overlooking the city. The hustle and bustle of the city hadn't slowed or ceased, despite the approaching night. Sitting in the wrought-iron chair across from her, he found himself ignoring the spectacular view of the city in favor of watching her. The expression of peace that had settled over her beautiful face touched him in a way he hadn't expected. She looked as carefree as he'd ever seen her, as if the burdens of life and adulthood had been lifted from her shoulders. He wanted to give her that gift, the gift of letting go, for as long as she would let him.

"How long did they say it would be before they brought up our food?" She asked the question without taking her eyes off the city skyline.

"About forty-five minutes. Shouldn't be too much longer."

A few minutes passed quietly between them, with her admiring the view of the city and him admiring her serene profile.

A knock sounded on the door of the room, followed by a voice announcing, "Room service."

She poised to get up.

Rising from his seat, he stayed her by laying a hand on her arm. "Sit. I'll take care of it."

Her soft smile melted his heart. "Okay."

He slipped into the room, answered the door. Once the food had been brought in, he sent the room service attendant away with a twenty-dollar tip. Grasping the handles of the large tray holding their food, he returned to the terrace.

"Mmm. Smells great," she commented as he set the tray down on the small table between them.

"It does. I can't wait to dig in."

Once they'd both taken their plates, silverware, and napkins into their laps, they did just that.

She groaned in delight as she chewed the first bite of her salad. "It's just as good as I remember."

Sitting across from her with his well-done New York strip steak, loaded baked potato, and sautéed spinach, he shook his head. "You're such a dainty eater."

She giggled, gesturing to his plate. "I can see you're not."

"I rarely eat like this at home. While I'm traveling, I eat whatever I want. Then I just burn it off in the gym when I get back."

They continued that way for the rest of their meal, laughing and talking like two old friends. By the time he gathered their empty dishes onto the tray and set it out in the hallway for the hotel staff to collect, the sun had gone down.

Escaping the chill hanging in the night air, Alexis came inside and shut the door to the terrace. She kicked off the black kitten heels she'd been wearing all day and seemed relieved to be free of them. Plopping down near the head of the bed, she tucked her legs beneath her. "What a day."

"You're telling me."

He sat down on the opposite end of the bed. He wasn't the biggest fan of traveling, especially by air, but in his line of work, it couldn't be avoided.

She sighed. "Did my brother tell you about what's going on with Kelsey?"

He nodded, giving her ample space as he sat down on the side of the bed. Removing his loafers, he set them aside. "Yes. And I want you to know that if you guys need me, I'm there."

She smiled again. "I really appreciate that. We've been waiting a long time for the day when she would be ready to leave."

He could see the emotion playing across her features. "She's lucky to have siblings who care so much about her. I'm an only child, so I have no idea what that's like." Wes was the closest thing he had to a sibling, which was pretty pitiful, seeing as he didn't like his cousin very much. *We should be close, Wes and I. But he works overtime at being a jackass.*

"That makes me think. It sounds like you wanted siblings, but there were times when I wished to be the only child."

In a surprised tone, he asked, "Really?"

She nodded. "Yes, really. I'm the baby of the family. Someone was always standing over me, or at least it seemed that way."

"I never thought about it that way."

"Don't get me wrong, I love Max and Kelsey. It's just that sometimes I wanted to be able to do my own thing without someone looking over my shoulder, you know?"

He nodded. "I can understand that. I only had Mom and Dad for that, so when I wasn't with them, I was pretty much left to my own devices."

She chuckled. "I wish. When I was in high school, a lot of boys wouldn't even talk to me because of Maxwell's overprotectiveness. And when I actually did go on dates, Mom would send Kelsey as a chaperone." Alexis remembered sitting through movies with her sister sitting behind her and her hapless date.

"I guess it's like they say. We want what we can't have." Bryan scratched his chin. "In a way, I got the siblings I always wanted when I pledged TDT."

She smiled. "That's good. I never said it before, but I really respect the way you guys always have each other's backs. It's awesome to see men who share such a close bond."

"Thanks." His gaze locked with hers.

A few silent moments passed as they looked into each

other's eyes. When she leaned in for his kiss, he gave her exactly what she sought.

She pulled away a few hot moments later, her chest heaving in time with her heavy breaths. Eyes aglow with desire, she spoke. "I'd really love a hot shower. Would you care to join me?"

His body reacted right away, his blood warming and rushing south. "Alexis, you know what this means, don't you? Once we go down this path…there won't be any going back." He was more than willing to make love to her, but he needed to know that she was absolutely sure.

She let her tongue dart out to wet her bottom lip as she held his gaze. "I have no intentions of going back. Only forward." She got up then, and once she was on her feet, she tugged his hand.

He stood and let her lead him toward the bathroom.

Chapter 14

ALEXIS COULD FEEL HER BREATH COMING HARDER AS SHE and Bryan entered the bathroom. Her mind raced, and one of the many questions in it was: *Is this right?*

She wasn't one for sleeping around, though she firmly believed in a woman's right to sexual autonomy. It had been several months since she'd had any romantic involvements, and in many ways, she felt as nervous as a virgin faced with a man of experience.

When he placed his hand on her shoulder, then slipped it around to the back of her neck to lift her face to his kiss, her doubts melted away like snow in the spring sunshine. Her body reacted to his nearness, his touch, and the magic of desire flowing between them. She leaned into the kiss and into his embrace, draping her arms around his neck.

He swept his tongue over her bottom lip before breaking the seal of their lips. "We're both overdressed."

She agreed. Running her open palms down his arms, she could feel the powerful muscles beneath the thin fabric of his dove-gray button-down shirt. She inhaled deeply, taking in the intoxicating scent of his cologne while her hands drifted to his chest, where she began undoing his buttons.

She pushed the shirt off his shoulders, and he shrugged out of it. Then he stripped out of the white tank he'd been wearing underneath, baring his torso above the waistband of his black slacks. Again, she touched him, a tremor running through her as she felt his smooth, dark skin and rippling muscles beneath her hands for the first time. He was solidly built, and she took her time to enjoy the fortress that was his body, languidly running her fingertips over his arms, his chest, his shoulders, his back.

He groaned low in his throat, kissed her again. His large hands went to her waist, and he dragged her silk blouse and camisole up and over her head. Clad in only her black lace bra and matching panties, along with her wool-blend pencil skirt, she could feel the warmth of his breath as it touched her bared skin. He leaned forward to kiss her throat, her collarbone, and the valley between her breasts. His large hands cupped her breasts, his palms grazing over her already taut nipples. When he gave her breasts a gentle yet insistent squeeze, she died a little inside.

Between the torrid kisses he laid on the tops of her breasts, he undid the zipper on the back of her skirt. After he'd worked it down her hips, it pooled at her feet, and she kicked it away. Before it could slide across the tiled floor, he slid his hand inside one of the lacy cups of her bra. Lifting out her breast, he dipped his head and captured the dark nipple in his mouth.

Her knees buckled, but his free arm braced her, steadying her. If not for his support, she would have crashed to the floor. The sensation of his hot mouth and damp tongue caressing her nipple shot through her like flames devouring dry brush.

"Mmm." He made the sound of delight low in his throat, as if he were savoring some decadent dessert.

When he transferred his attention to her other breast, her knees buckled again. Once again, he rescued her from what would have been an inevitable fall. His dedicated suckling continued until her eyes rolled back in her head. Then he blew his warm breath over her dampened skin, and she yelped with delight.

He reached around her, freed her of the bra. "If we don't get in the shower soon, we're going to be making love on the floor."

Having no desire to end up naked on the cool tile beneath her feet, she eased away from him and went to the white porcelain tub. There, she started the water and adjusted the temperature before switching on the overhead sprayer.

She turned around, intending to return to him.

He was already there and had stripped out of his socks and slacks. Now nothing remained between them but her panties and his boxer briefs. Her eyes drifted downward, just past his waist...

He smiled. "I'm ready. Don't worry."

She could feel embarrassment heating her cheeks. She hadn't meant to ogle him so openly, but what he had in store for her looked so impressive, she couldn't help herself. "Sorry."

He shook his head. "Don't apologize. I'm staring at you, too. And I definitely like what I see." He reached out, grasped the waistband of her lace panties, and whisked them away from her. She lifted her feet to facilitate his efforts. As she stood before him, nude and trembling, she watched him hook his thumbs beneath the waistband of his boxers and slide them down.

Her eyes widened. He was...in a word, *thick*. His

aroused state let her see his girth, and the pounding heat between her legs liquefied into a pool of molten lava at the sight.

Steam now filled the room, and as she stepped into the shower with him, she thought the steam might be rolling off their bodies instead of the hot water. She barely had a moment to snatch the shower curtain closed before he descended on her. Beneath the stream of water, she let herself be swept away by his kisses and his skillful caress. She gave no thought to her drenched hair or the water streaming down her face. All that mattered in the world was his body, pressed so intimately against hers.

His need throbbed against her stomach, and she felt a tremor go through her. Putting a bit of space between their bodies, he groaned. "Alexis. Can I…"

"Yes…" A breathless sigh carried her answer to his ears. She had no idea what he meant to do, but she knew it would be wonderfully sensual, and she was beyond ready to give herself over to him.

His large hand cupped her buttock, then slipped down to the back of her thigh. Gently, he guided her to rest her back against the shower wall. Lifting her leg, he knelt, placed her leg on his strong shoulder. Using his fingertips, he slowly opened her like the delicate petals of a flower.

She had only a single, wide-eyed moment of realization before the first lick.

He gave her no quarter as he kissed and licked her, and her body shook with pleasure. Her soft cries of ecstasy rose over the sound of the running water, and she could do nothing to stop them or lower the volume. His hands grasped her buttocks, keeping her in place so that he could enjoy her at his leisure.

Her back arched off the shower wall as the delicious sensations built, her head falling back. Her hands found the back of his head, and she splayed her fingers over his close-trimmed hair. Her eyes were closed tightly, but a glow of white heat spread across her field of vision. She felt light, as if she were floating, and yet a steady, pleasurable pressure pressed down on her body like a weight. She cried out again, loud and long, as the glow exploded and the weight suddenly lifted, her body shattering into brilliance.

She became aware of him carrying her, but her senses were swimming and bleary. Eventually, she came to rest atop something soft. Something else soft began to sweep over her skin. It took her a few moments to come back into herself, and when she did, she realized he was toweling her off. She didn't hear the water running, so she assumed he'd turned it off.

She lay there on the bed, smiling up at him as he whisked the droplets of water away from her skin. He went about the task in such a patient, caring way that she felt her heart turn over in her chest. He'd already brought her pleasure like no other man ever had, and the night had just begun.

When Bryan thought Alexis's body sufficiently dry, he leaned down to brush a kiss across her forehead. "I'll be right back."

She nodded, her soft smile visible in the dim lamplight.

He strode away, hating to leave her stunning nudity even for a moment. Back in the bathroom, he dried himself in record time, mindful of the lovemaking that lay ahead. As he dashed away the droplets of water, he reveled in the remembered tastes of her and the sound of her pleasure. She'd been deliciously sweet, both to his mouth and to his ears. His dick twitched, demanding to be treated to the wonders of her soft, nubile body.

He moved to the closet, bending to retrieve a handful of condoms from his overnight bag. He had the feeling he would need more than one, and he didn't want to have to leave her again to retrieve it. For the rest of the night, or at least for as long as she could stand it, she would have his full and complete attention.

Returning to the bed, he found her lying on her back in the center of the comforter. Her legs were just slightly spread, her upper body propped on a pillow. He took in the sight of her, finding it enticing and altogether erotic. He stashed all but one of the condoms on the small table next to the bed, opening the one he kept. The bed gave as he climbed in with her, kneeling near her feet. There, he sheathed himself with protection.

She looked up at him with fire in her eyes. "Hurry, Bryan."

Taking a deep breath to calm his raging desire, he smiled. "Don't worry, baby. I'll make it better."

He slid his hands over the length of her legs, starting at her ankles and working upward. By the time he moved them around to cup her lush ass, she lifted her hips and parted her legs. Moving between her thighs, he lowered himself over her body and entered her.

He took his time, not wanting to hurt her. It only took a few seconds for him to be overcome by her marvelous tightness. Her body gripped his, drawing him inside. Going slow became difficult, but he intended to follow her lead. So he gritted his teeth and eased inside a bit more.

Her hips rose to meet him, and he entered her fully. In that moment, he stayed completely still, giving her a moment to adjust. He hadn't assumed she was a virgin, but the way her body molded to his made it difficult to tell. All he knew was that she felt like pure heaven.

As if growing impatient, she began to move beneath him. As her hips rocked, he forgot about his pledge to take things slow. She'd shown herself ready for him, so he joined her in the age-old dance. He drove into her, each stroke punctuated by a moan passing her lips. Soon, the moans began to meld together, lengthening and intensifying.

Hands filled with her hips, he sped up, giving himself over to the cravings of his body. The more he got of her, the more he seemed to want. He leaned down, placing his kisses over her mouth, her face, her throat, never breaking his rhythm. Then his kisses moved lower, to the tempting mounds of her breasts. Her nipples stood up, the buds tightening before his eyes.

She mewled as he flicked his tongue over one chocolate nipple, then the other. Doing as his body demanded, he rose above her, giving his full attention to the joining of their bodies. Lifting her legs up behind him, he hooked them around his waist.

"Yes…"

Fueled by her enjoyment, he used the new positioning to his advantage and picked up his pace again. Now he could love her the way he wanted, taking his strokes longer and deeper. Her moans rose again, climbing an octave as she drew closer and closer to completion.

He could feel orgasm building within him and knew that he couldn't last much longer. Not in the face of her body gripping him so tightly and of her musical moans filling his ears.

She went over the edge again, a scream escaping her lips. "Oh, Bryan!"

Moments later, he joined her in ecstasy, growling and thrusting and holding her hips.

When he slipped out of her, he rolled over onto his back. She turned on her side, cuddling into his chest. Taking her warm, sweat-dampened form into his arms felt natural, right. Holding her like this filled him with a strange sensation, a feeling he couldn't name. He realized he never wanted to let her go, never wanted to return to the time before she'd entered his life.

Is that what love is? Am I falling for her?

The thought gave him pause. When he'd decided to take her up on her offer, he'd also agreed to her terms. A casual relationship, strictly for publicity. They could enjoy each other's company and even indulge their mutual physical attraction. But no romantic entanglements were supposed to come from it. No strings, no emotional declarations, and certainly no commitments.

Her soft snores began rising in the silence, and he smiled at the sound. She'd fallen asleep in his arms, and that struck him as a sign of her level of comfort in his presence. He felt honored that she'd trusted him with the gift of her body and touched by the way she clung to him even in sleep.

His body stirred, and the temptation to awaken her rose

along with that part of his anatomy. She'd granted him access to her private paradise, and he was hooked. He sensed he'd want to return there as often as she'd allow.

The peaceful expression on her face and the evenness of her light snores deterred him from pursuing another round of lovemaking. He couldn't bring himself to disturb her, so instead, he closed his eyes, waiting for sleep to claim him.

As the night deepened, her movements awakened him.

When he opened his eyes, he found her hovering over him in the darkness.

"Alexis, I…" He stopped when he realized what she was doing.

Rolling a condom down over his hardness, she spoke, never looking away from her task. "Shh. I want to go for a midnight ride."

And before he could draw a deep breath, she climbed aboard and settled in.

Chapter 15

TUESDAY MORNING, ALEXIS WALKED HAND IN HAND
with Bryan into the television studio where their interview would be filmed. She'd dressed in a cobalt-blue
crepe pantsuit. The shark-bite hem, roomy sleeves, and
wide pant legs left her plenty of room to move around,
but she knew she looked good in it. She'd swept her hair
back off her face and fashioned it into a French braid.
Anticipating time in the makeup chair in the studio, she'd
left her face free of cosmetics. She felt earthy and comfortable but still glamourous enough for the occasion.

She looked at Bryan, offered up a smile. He looked
incredibly handsome in his navy slacks, light-blue shirt,
and striped tie. They'd talked about what they would
wear, so their semimatching outfits weren't a surprise to
her. The surprise had come last night, when she'd invited
him to take things to the next level. And they had, several
times over. Looking at him now, she had to force away
her memories of this morning, when he'd come up behind
her as she was getting dressed and taken her again…

As they moved down the corridor in the back of the
studio, a woman stepped into their path. She wore a
pair of drab black slacks and a green button-down shirt,
and a headset with a mic rested atop her blond hair.
Pushing the mic away from her face, she addressed
them. "Good morning, Miss Devers, Mr. James. I'm
Meg, one of the producers. We need to get you in

makeup right away." She waved them into a room on the right side of the corridor.

Inside the small room, they sat in chairs opposite each other while the makeup artists prepared them for their appearance. Whenever her eyes were open, Alexis stole glances at Bryan and, in most cases, found him watching her as well.

The woman with the headset returned when their makeup was done. "You look great. Now the two of you can just hang out in the green room, and someone will come for you when it's time."

Alexis walked behind Bryan and the producer, following them into another room farther up the corridor. Meg left the two of them alone there, and after she left, Alexis sat down on the brown leather couch. "This has already been an eventful morning, and we haven't even done the interview yet."

He smiled, sat down next to her. "You look worried."

"Not worried. Just a little nervous. Aren't you?"

"Nothing to be nervous about. I'm just going out there to tell them how talented you are as a designer and how wonderful you are, right?"

Her cheeks warmed, and she looked away. "Smooth talker."

He reached out, his fingertips applying gentle pressure to her chin until she turned back to face him. "Maybe. But I'm telling the truth. You are wonderful, Alexis."

She knew she'd broken into a rather goofy grin but was powerless to change that. Instead, she leaned up to his kiss.

"Oh, my bad." A velvety male voice broke through her delight.

She broke the kiss and looked over Bryan's shoulder toward the door as he swiveled around to look as well.

In the doorway stood R&B singer Miguel, his eyes hidden behind a pair of dark sunglasses. A burly guard, dressed all in black, stood close behind him. "Sorry, y'all. Carry on." Flashing a bright smile, he moved on.

Alexis turned wide eyes back on Bryan. "That was Miguel!"

He chuckled. "I know who it was. I guess he's on the show today, too."

She jumped up. "I'll be right back." She jogged over to the door, stuck her head out, and looked in each direction until she saw the guard's back.

"Where are you going?" Bryan called as she dashed out.

"To get an autograph!" By then, she was already halfway down the corridor.

After a brief and very pleasant encounter with Miguel and his bodyguard, she returned and showed Bryan where he had signed her purse.

He made a face at her. "I didn't think you were the fangirl type."

She rolled her eyes. "I'm not, but I like his music."

Bryan chuckled. "I can see that."

Meg appeared in the doorway then. "We're ready for you two on set. Right this way."

Taking a deep breath, Alexis joined hands with Bryan. "You ready?"

"Of course."

After following Meg onto the set, the two of them were escorted to a bright white love seat. Next to the love seat sat the show's host, Verna McCoy, in a matching armchair.

Once they were seated, Verna reached out and shook both their hands. "So nice to meet you both. We'll talk about your fashion line and all the interest it's generated, and then just a little about your engagement. Sound good?"

Alexis nodded. "Yes, that sounds fine."

Bryan echoed her sentiment as he slipped his arm around her shoulders.

"Great. We'll go on in a couple of minutes. The camera you should speak toward will have a green light above it, so look for that once we go on. Until then, just relax." Verna settled back into her chair, her eyes scanning over a small notebook.

Just as the music announcing the show's return from the commercial break started, Verna tucked away the notebook.

Alexis let her gaze wander the bevy of cameras trained on them before settling on the one with the green light above it. She sensed Bryan doing the same thing next to her.

Verna smiled brightly, then launched into her introduction. "On this segment of *Morning Buzz*, we're happy to welcome fashion designer Alexis Devers and her fiancé, Bryan James. We're going to hear more about her hotly anticipated Krystal Kouture One line— that's Kouture with a *K*—and her engagement to the handsome Mr. James. Welcome to the show, you two."

With smiles and nods, they accepted her welcome.

"So let's start with the Krystal Kouture One line. We saw Angela Bassett wearing one of your dresses on the

Today show last week, and it's created quite a buzz. You're going to debut the line toward the end of this month during the Carolina Fashion and Music Festival, as I understand. Tell us about your pieces."

As often happened when Alexis spoke about her designs, the words tumbled forth like water from a faucet turned on full blast. "I really wanted a line that would be a nice cross between ready-to-wear and haute couture. I feel that the everyday woman should have the option to dress up without going bankrupt. So the collection includes a lot of classic silhouettes with a modern, edgy update. Think of the peplum Ms. Bassett wore last week. The peplum has been around for a while, but I added the two-tone effect, the contrast trim, changed the fabric. Doing those things leads to a whole new look."

"I see. And it's obvious from the way you speak about it that you're very passionate about fashion. So when the line goes out for sale, what retailers will be carrying it?" Verna leaned forward as she asked the question, conveying her concern.

"We're looking at several options right now. As you mentioned, there's a lot of interest, but the strategy I've adopted with my business partner is to get the line into at least one high-end department store and one mass-market retailer."

"You just mentioned your partner, and that's Sydney Greer. We asked Ms. Greer to appear with you, but she declined. Can you elaborate on that?"

Alexis smiled. "Syd is terribly camera shy and more of a behind-the-scenes person. I'm pretty sure she'd rather light her hair on fire than appear on television."

Verna laughed. "What an answer. Any idea when we can expect the line to be available to consumers?"

"Our goal is to roll it out in late November or early December. I invite people to keep an eye on our website, Krystal Kouture dot com, for updates."

"Sounds great. Now, let's move on to you, Mr. James. You are Alexis's fiancé, right?"

He nodded. "Yes, I am. And I'm honored and blessed to have her in my life."

When Alexis met his eyes, she could swear she saw emotion there.

Verna placed her open palm on her chest. "Well, I'm sold. Alexis, where did you find a man this handsome and this romantic?"

She chuckled. "Actually, he's a friend of my older brother."

"Juicy, indeed. So tell us about how you met, Bryan. I've already bugged Alexis with enough questions." Verna smiled his way.

Alexis realized she didn't care for the doe-eyed look the host gave Bryan but knew better than to let that show. She didn't want to come across as catty or petty on live television.

Bryan's voice cut into her thoughts as he began to answer Verna's question. "We've known each other in passing for years. But when I ran into her a while back at a step show, I just knew I couldn't let the opportunity pass to talk to her. We hit it off, and the rest is history."

"Wow. You two are a gorgeous couple. And I understand that you are an executive at the textiles company that will make the clothing for Alexis's line?"

He nodded. "Yes. And every piece will be made to her exacting standards, I can assure you."

Verna clapped her hands together. "There you have it, folks. Talk about a match made in heaven. Alexis, hold that ring up for us to see."

Blushing, Alexis did as she was asked, turning her cushion-cut sparkler toward the appropriate camera.

"You heard it here first on *Morning Buzz*. We'll check back with these two over the coming months, because I want an invite to the wedding!" She turned to them, shook their hands again. "Thank you for coming on to the show today."

"No problem."

"Thanks for having us." Bryan tipped an imaginary hat in her direction.

Verna turned back to the camera. "We're headed to a break. But don't go away, because when we return, alternative R&B star Miguel will be performing and talking about his latest album. We'll be right back with more *Morning Buzz*."

"And clear!" A voice from behind one of the cameras shouted out, letting them know they were no longer live.

⁓

At the hotel that afternoon, Bryan sat on the terrace of their room with a cup of coffee.

When he'd returned to the hotel from the television studio, Alexis had gone out to lunch with her mentor. After returning from the meal, she'd declared herself exhausted and fallen into bed. He'd come outside in part to keep from disturbing her nap. She'd been asleep before he could close the terrace door. Thinking of her lying there, a few feet away from him, made him wonder if she was still tired from their night of lovemaking and this morning's encore. He couldn't remember ever having a woman affect him that way; something about her made him insatiable.

He took a deep breath and redirected his thoughts, lest he go in there and awaken her for another round. The weather was temperate, and he found the thick cacophony of city noise fascinating. Downtown Raleigh was a busy place, especially during rush hour or when popular shows and concerts played at the Performing Arts Center. But even on its busiest day, the City of Oaks couldn't hold a candle to the activity level of a typical Tuesday in the Big Apple.

I can see why this place is so popular with tourists. But I couldn't live here. Too much going on.

The buzzing of his phone against his hip caught his attention. He set the cup down on the table, pondering whether to answer the call. It had been ringing all day, ever since the segment of *Morning Buzz* had aired, and he knew why. He envied Alexis, whose current peaceful sleep was due in part to her decision to turn off the ringer on her phone.

Sighing, he pulled the phone from his pocket and looked at the screen. Sliding his finger across it, he placed it to his ear. "Hey, Pop."

"Don't you 'Hey, Pop' me, boy! What the hell is this I hear about you getting married to Alexis Devers?"

"So you saw us on TV this morning, I'm guessing."

"No, I didn't. Don't be such a smart-ass. Wes told me about it."

He rolled his eyes. Once again, Wes had come

through to make his life more difficult. "We're engaged, Pop. I thought you'd be happy that I'm finally settling down."

"Damn it, Bryan. You know I want to you to marry and raise me some grandsons. But you also have enough sense to know how this looks. You close a business deal with her and, five minutes later, announce to the world that you're getting married? Without even a word to your family first?"

Bryan sighed, touched his fingertips to his temple. "Pop, you've got to chill. Everything is going to be fine. We'll talk more about this when I get back home."

"Bryan, I—"

Rather than listen to his father's tirade, he interjected a quick "I love you, Pop" before disconnecting the call. He looked at the time displayed on the screen of the phone. It was just past one, and though they'd opted for late checkout, it was getting close to the time they'd have to vacate the room.

Before he could pocket the phone, it went off again. This time it was a text alert. Reading the screen, he frowned. The all caps message was from Maxwell.

I SAW THE INTERVIEW. WHAT THE HELL?

As Bryan watched the screen, more messages came through, each as "loud" as the first one.

DUDE, I CAN'T BELIEVE THIS.

I SHOULD HAVE SOCKED YOU THAT DAY AT THE STEP SHOW.

YOU HAVEN'T KNOWN HER LONG ENOUGH
TO BE IN LOVE.

He chuckled at that one. A few weeks ago, he would
have thought the same thing. Spending time with Alexis,
however, had changed his views on a lot of things.

IF YOU ARE TOYING WITH MY BABY SISTER,
EXPECT AN ASS WHUPPING, BRO.

Shaking his head, he stuck the phone back in his
pocket. First, his dad had yelled in his ear, and now, his
best friend was doing it by text message. He'd expected
to catch a little crap for the stunt he and Alexis had
pulled, but he'd at least thought it would wait until they
returned to North Carolina.

He settled back in the chair, retrieving his cup and
taking a sip of the dark brew. He supposed his father's
worry was just a sign of his concern. After all, Oscar
had spent the last several years mourning the loss of his
soul mate and took the institution of marriage very seriously. Bryan didn't necessarily share his father's views,
but he did think there was something serious happening between him and Alexis. What had started out as a
clever ruse had now turned into something else entirely,
something far more complicated.

I love her, don't I?

The silent question echoed in his mind, and deep
inside, he knew the answer. Deep down, he knew she'd
taken over his heart, leaving him no way to resist her.
After what they'd shared last night, he wasn't sure he
wanted to resist anymore.

He was pretty sure she'd want to know how he felt. He felt far less sure that she shared his feelings. Yes, she'd admitted to their growing attraction and to enjoying spending time with him. She'd also been the one to initiate last night's epic lovemaking session. But none of that meant anything if she didn't come out and say that she was in love with him. If he told her how he felt and she didn't feel the same way, both his heart and his pride would be crushed like an anthill annihilated by a steamroller.

He blew out a breath. *This is a fine mess.*

The sound of the terrace door opening made him turn his head.

She stood just inside the doorway, stifling a yawn. Before she'd lain down, she'd taken off her pantsuit and put on a simple white tee and a pair of jogging pants. Dressed in the comfy outfit, her makeup-free face still showing remnants of sleep, she looked ravishing.

Their eyes connected, and she smiled. "Has your phone been blowing up?"

He nodded. "Pop thinks I've gone crazy, and your brother threatened to whip my ass."

A musical laugh left her lips, complete with a little snort. "Now you see why I turned mine off."

He shrugged.

"Did either of them scare you off? Because now that we've gone public, we're in this thing for the long haul."

He looked directly into her eyes. "Nope. There isn't a damn thing on earth that's going to keep me away from you at this point." He watched her standing there, with her hands resting on her shapely hips, and decided she was the most beautiful woman he'd ever seen. Just looking at her made his body temperature rise.

"This may sound really naughty, but we have to be out of the room pretty soon."

He stood, entered her space, and draped his arms loosely around her waist. "And let me guess. You want to put our remaining time to good use."

She winked.

Not needing any further encouragement, he followed her inside and slid the terrace door shut behind them.

Chapter 16

THAT NIGHT, ALEXIS STEPPED OUT OF THE SHOWER IN HER condo and toweled off. Putting on a pair of panties and an oversized tee bearing the face of Dorothy Dandridge as Carmen, she padded barefoot toward her bed.

The last two days in New York with Bryan had been eventful, to say the least. Now that they'd slept together, she knew he was in her system. The feelings she'd been having ever since she ran into him at the step show that day had been growing. It seemed they'd finally reached their full bloom, because she was falling for him. For real.

Still, she was a big girl. She'd made this arrangement with Bryan; she'd decided the parameters and gone into it with her eyes wide open. This was about business first and foremost, so whatever feelings she'd developed for Bryan would have to be set aside. Krystal Kouture One was her first fashion line, and everything she did for the rest of her career would be affected by its success or failure. After the hard work she, Sydney, and their team had put in, she wouldn't ruin things for them by letting emotions distract her from the goal.

Just as she lay down, a knock sounded at her door. Confusion knit her brow as she wondered who would be paying her a visit this late on a Tuesday night. It was almost ten, and she was ready to catch up on the sleep she'd missed the previous night when Bryan had...kept her up.

It has to be Max. Who else would the doorman let up this time of night?

When she reached the door, she asked in an abundance of caution, "Who is it?"

"Lex, it's me. Let me in."

Recognizing her brother's voice, she opened the door.

He barged right in, his face twisted into a frown. "I've been trying to call you all day. Why didn't you answer?"

"I turned off my ringer."

His eyes bulged. "Why the hell would you do that?"

She gestured to him. "Look at how you're acting, Max. This is precisely why I would do that. I wasn't in the mood to hear you lecturing me then, and I'm not in the mood now, either."

"You're my baby sister, and I'm trying to protect you."

She edged around him to close the door. "What you're trying to do is wake up all my neighbors. Jeez. Lower your voice."

"Oh, I'm sorry I'm too loud for you. I tend to get upset when I see someone I love making a terrible mistake."

She couldn't help rolling her eyes. "Seriously, Max. Chill."

"I can't." His eyes softened as he placed his palms on her forearms. "I already failed to protect Kelsey from getting hurt. I can't fail with you, too."

She sighed. "Max, this isn't the same thing. It isn't even close."

"Maybe you're not in actual physical danger like Kelsey. But your heart is in danger, Lex."

She frowned, moving over to the couch to sit down. As much as she wanted to crawl into bed, she sensed her brother had no intention of leaving anytime soon. "What are you talking about?"

He joined her on the couch. "Don't you know what kind of reputation he has?"

She shook her head. It wasn't something they'd discussed when they were building their backstory, and up until now, she hadn't given it much thought. "No, so why don't you enlighten me?"

"Listen. You know I love Bryan like a brother. But he's a playboy. He's never been in a relationship with a woman that lasted longer than a few months."

She cringed. *Why didn't I ask him more questions about his past relationships?* Despite how she felt, she refused to let Maxwell see it. She raised and lowered her shoulders in a halfhearted shrug.

"In college, when he played ball, he was with a different cheerleader every month. He has more notches on his bedpost than you have hairs on your head."

"What's your point?" She kept her tone and her expression flat.

He pursed his lips. "Lex, don't even try it. You really think he can commit to you, when he's never committed to anyone or anything before in his entire life? Y'all have been sneaking around for, what, a few weeks? And you think he's ready to get married, just like that?"

"Max, you've got this all wrong. I'm not expecting anything from Bryan, except for him to honor the deal we made."

Maxwell's brow hitched. "Deal? What deal?"

She sat back, sinking into the cushions to brace herself against his oncoming reaction. "I don't want you to tell anybody this, but we're not really engaged.

We're just doing it as a PR stunt until my line gets off the ground."

He appeared confused. "What?"

She gave him a brief rundown of the story Sydney had shared with the reporter and the plan she and Bryan had cooked up to corroborate it.

"Lex, this has got to be the dumbest thing you've ever done."

She folded her arms over her chest. "Well, it's a good thing I didn't ask your opinion. No matter what you think, what's done is done. We've announced our engagement, so it's out there." She hated the way he sometimes came down on her, sounding more like her father than her brother. She didn't care whether he agreed with her choices, because she was a grown woman. That didn't mean she'd let him sit here and insult her intelligence.

"Fine. Go ahead and keep the foolery going if you want. But I have a question. What are you going to do when this ruse is over?"

She looked away from him, squirming a bit under his assessing stare. "We'll announce our amicable separation, and then we'll each go on with our separate lives."

He laughed, but the sound lacked humor. "It's cute that you think it will be that easy. You're not cut out for this kind of thing, Lex. Mark my words. Your feelings *will* get involved, and you *will* end up getting hurt. But you won't be able to say I didn't warn you."

She opened her mouth to respond, but a yawn came out instead. She stifled it with her hand. "I appreciate the warning, but I'm a big girl, Max. I can handle myself."

He rose from the couch, started toward the door. "If you say so."

"I do. Now go home and let me get some sleep."

He shook his head as he swung open the front door. "Good night, Lex."

"Night, Maxie."

With a final, sidelong glance, he left, closing the door behind him.

Stifling another yawn, she locked up and returned to her room. Climbing into bed, she lay in the dark for a few long moments with Maxwell's words echoing in her mind.

Your feelings will get involved.

You will end up getting hurt.

Little did he know, her feelings were already involved. But at this point, she didn't think there was much she could do about it.

Bryan entered the main hall of Stonecrest High School Wednesday morning and headed straight to the main office. There, the principal greeted him and, after a brief chat, referred him to the receptionist for a visitor's pass. With the sticker proclaiming him as "Mr. James" stuck to the lapel of his black sport jacket, he got directions to Peter's classroom and turned his steps that way.

While walking the quiet halls, his mind flashed back to his own days in high school. The pranks, the silliness, the all-nighters spent studying for chemistry and Spanish exams. He didn't really miss any of that, but what he did miss was the carefree way life had been back then. Back then, he'd had no clue what awaited him in the adulthood he'd been so eager to reach. A small sigh escaped him as he rounded a corner, then found the classroom.

The door stood open, but someone was speaking. He assumed the man in front of the class was either the teacher or one of the other speakers. Not wanting to interrupt, he stood back, waiting for the person to finish.

The man wrapped up his remarks in the next few minutes, then glanced toward the door. Seeing Bryan there, he gestured him inside.

Bryan walked into the classroom, extending his hand. "Hi. I'm Bryan James, Royal Textiles."

"Welcome to Stonecrest, Mr. James. I'm Alvin Myers, and this is my business and economics class." Mr. Myers gave him a hearty handshake.

"Thanks. Glad I could come." Bryan turned his gaze on the class. There were twenty-three teenagers of all different races seated at the metal-and-laminate desks. A quick assessment told him there were fourteen girls and nine boys, each displaying varying levels of disinterest. He gave them a smile, wondering if any of them would even be listening to his talk.

Two rows back from the front, his eyes landed on Peter, who gave him a sheepish grin.

Looking out on the group of students, sitting where he once sat, he took a deep breath. "Good morning. My name is Bryan James, and I'm the chief marketing officer of Royal Textiles. I'm the third generation of my family to be an executive in the company, which manufactures clothing and leather goods."

Silence met his words. One student in the front yawned. Two or three of them up front looked semi-interested, so Bryan continued.

"I understand what it's like to be a kid and have some old guy come in and talk at you. So I'm not going to do that. I've told you who I am and what I do, and now the discussion falls to you. Ask me questions. Make comments. Because if I just stand up here and talk, half of you will fall asleep, and the other half won't learn anything."

A few chuckles came from the students, and Mr. Myers looked amused as well.

A smiling Bryan clapped his hands together. "Okay, then. What do you all want to know?"

A young girl, wearing her blond hair in a ponytail and sitting near the back, raised her hand.

Bryan pointed to her. "Go ahead…"

"Amy. I just wanted to ask, what does a chief marketing officer do, exactly?"

"Great question. My job is to be the lead salesperson for the company. I secure accounts with design houses for Royal to produce their clothes, give final approval of our brochures and marketing materials, do interviews and press for the company, that kind of thing. Does that answer your question?"

Amy nodded.

Another hand shot up. "Do you get to travel?"

Bryan chuckled. "It's more like I have to travel. When I'm trying to lock down an account, a lot of times that means flying to New York or LA or Paris to meet with the designer and their staff. I rack up plenty of frequent flyer miles."

The young man, his eyes partially hidden by long strands of black hair, seemed impressed. "Doesn't sound like a bad gig."

"It's not. I love what I do, and knowing that I'm preserving my grandfather's legacy by working for his

company just makes it better." It was true. As much
as his father rode him about getting new accounts and
meeting sales goals, he couldn't imagine himself doing
anything else for a living.

Another girl, this one with two afro puffs and a
Chance the Rapper T-shirt, stuck up her hand. "Peter
says you know J. Cole. Is that true?"

He laughed, shook his head. "In a way, yes. I met him
several weeks ago when we signed a contract to produce
his clothing line."

The girl's eyes widened. "What's he like?"

He shrugged. "I only spent about three hours with
him, but he seems like a pretty cool dude. He was nice
enough to sign his CD for me."

The girl leaned over to another girl sitting to her left,
the two joining hands and releasing the kind of squeal
that could only come from teenage fangirls.

Bryan laughed. "I'm glad I've said at least one exciting thing."

Most of the class giggled at that.

"Any other questions for me?"

For the next twenty minutes, he took more questions from Peter's classmates. While answering them,
he explained parts of the textiles process for producing
clothes. The kids were particularly interested in how
jeans were made, and he gave them as much insight as
he could without overwhelming them. He also divulged
the street date for J. Cole Jeans, leading to more squeal-
ing from the girls in the class.

After the class was dismissed, Peter strolled up to the
front with his hand extended. "Thanks for coming, Mr. J.
I really appreciate it."

He shook his mentee's hand. "No problem, Peter. Glad I could help. So what's your next class?"

"Actually, this is my lunch period." He tossed his black backpack over his right shoulder.

Bryan thought for a moment. "Look, I took the day off. So why don't I stay for lunch? Is that cool with you?"

The crooked grin on Peter's face gave away his answer before his words did. "Yeah, that's cool. It's on you, right? I mean, since you're ballin' outta control, meeting celebrities and stuff." He winked.

Bryan smiled. "Yeah, kid. It's on me." Giving Peter's shoulder a pat, he followed him out of the classroom.

A short time later, the two of them were sitting at a table in the cafeteria with burgers, fries, and sodas. Bryan couldn't remember the last time he'd eaten in a high school cafeteria, though he knew he'd done it a couple of times since he graduated from one. "You know, cafeteria food has really improved since I was a kid."

"You mean back when y'all rode a horse to school?" Peter's tone was laced with teasing as he popped a fry into his mouth.

Bryan snorted. "Okay, youngster. You got jokes. But let me ask you something."

"What's up, Mr. J?"

"What do you plan on doing when you leave here? You're, what, a junior now?" He took a bite of his burger.

Peter nodded. "Yeah. I can't wait for senior year."

"I'm glad you're excited about it, but you really should be thinking about what comes next for you. Will it be college? Trade school? The military?"

Peter rolled his eyes as he tipped up his soda can. "Definitely not the military."

Bryan shrugged. "Don't knock it, man. One of my frat brothers was in ROTC, and if you do join up, they'll pay for your education."

Looking contemplative for a moment, Peter swallowed. "I'll think about it."

"That's all I ask." That said, he went back to his food. Having been Peter's age himself once, he knew better than to force the issue. The more an adult insisted on something, the more a teen would rebel. All Bryan wanted was for his mentee to start considering his future and all the places it might take him.

And if he could get him to do that and to act accordingly, Bryan felt his job as a mentor would be done.

Chapter 17

By Thursday, more good news arrived at the Krystal Kouture Design House. As Alexis and Sydney sat in her office, participating in their morning ritual of watching the *Today* show over coffee, they chatted about what was ahead.

"So do you think we're finally decided on the retailers?" Sydney asked the question from her seat in the armchair by the desk. Her open laptop was on her lap.

"Yes. I've already started making calls." Sitting at her desk in front of her own computer, Alexis opened the contact file she'd been keeping with the names and phone numbers of retail buyers.

"What about the boutiques? Our request list from them is, like, a mile long." Sydney used her laptop's touchpad to scroll.

"We'll start with the three local ones. Threads, A Queen's Closet, and Masquerade. I figure we'll roll the line out to the other small boutiques over the next quarter or so." Alexis drew a deep breath, looking through the file for that section of buyers. In most cases, the buyer and owner of a small boutique were the same person.

"Oh my GOD!"

"What?" Alexis looked up from her screen in response to Sydney's squeal.

"Girl, look at the TV!"

She did, and when she saw the screen, she broke out in a broad grin. "Holy shit. I can't even."

On screen were Tamron Hall and Kerry Washington. Tamron was interviewing Kerry about her upcoming role as Fanny Jackson Coppin in the Anna Julia Cooper biopic.

Both women were wearing their Krystal Kouture sample dresses.

"Am I a genius, or am I a genius?" Sydney set her laptop aside and got to her feet, breaking out in a celebratory tootsie roll.

"Not always, Syd. But sending those sample dresses out was genius, though." Alexis felt the tears welling in her eyes as she saw her designs so elegantly displayed on the bodies of two women she admired so much. She was aware of the ongoing interview, but her focus was on the wardrobe. Tamron wore her Sunrise dress, a sleeveless, A-line creation in a taffeta blend. It was soft yellow at the top, with rings of muted peach, orange, and lavender forming the skirt, mimicking the horizon at dawn. "Tamron looks amazing."

"Right? And look at Kerry. I knew that Midnight dress would be perfect for her."

Still staring at the screen, Alexis had to agree. Kerry's cap-sleeved dress was navy-blue charmeuse and fell just past her knees. Tiny crystals embedded in the bodice of the dress represented stars, and a crescent moon fashioned of silver sequins embellished the dress's right shoulder.

The tears that had gathered in Alexis's eyes started to fall, and she tried to brush them away but found herself unable to keep up with them.

Sydney rushed over, like any best friend worth her salt. She grabbed Alexis's shoulders, showing her a broad smile. "Don't cry, Lex. This is what we've worked so hard for."

"I know," Alexis admitted in a voice quaking with emotion. "That's why I'm crying!"

Sydney dropped down, planting her bare knees in the soft carpet to embrace her.

"I just never knew it would feel like this...to see my designs this way." Alexis returned the hug, and the two of them stayed there for a few long moments, crying and celebrating. She had no words to express the sheer joy of seeing her work displayed so beautifully.

In the end, Alexis's ringing cell phone drew her out of her celebratory snuggle with Sydney. Once she'd composed herself enough to answer, she picked it up. "Hello?"

"Miss Devers, this is Oscar James." The voice on the other end sounded gruff, almost demanding.

Confusion furrowed her brow, but she kept her voice even. "Good morning, Mr. James. What can I do for you?"

"You can explain to me this so-called relationship you're having with my son."

She sighed. She'd already gone through this with Maxwell, and she wasn't in any mood to do it again. "There's not much to explain, Mr. James. Your son and I are engaged, and we plan to get married."

He didn't sound the least bit convinced. "Oh yeah? And just when is this blessed event going to take place?"

"We haven't set a date yet."

"Really. I've never known a woman in love to drag her feet when it comes to choosing her wedding date."

She picked up a note of hostility in his tone, and

despite what she and Bryan had originally set out to do, things had changed. Either way, she didn't like how Oscar was speaking to her. Her raising dictated that she remain respectful to him, because he was her elder. "Things have been extremely busy lately, but we'll get around to it."

"That's utter crap, but whatever."

Alexis laid her open palm over her face. "I'm sorry, Mr. James, but I have things I need to take care of. So unless you want to speak about a business-related manner…"

"Tsk, tsk. I'm well aware of how business-related this whole thing is."

She froze, said nothing. *What exactly did Bryan say to his father?*

"If you're wondering, my son told me basically the same thing you did. I appreciate you all getting your lie straight, but I'm from the old school. I'll believe it when I see it."

Not knowing what to say to that, she cleared her throat. "Fine."

"There is something I need, though. I need your word that the contract you've given to Royal to produce your fashion line will be exclusive."

She frowned. "There was no exclusivity clause in the contract."

"I know that, Miss Devers. But if you're going to use my son this way, then this company ought to get something out of it."

Taken aback by his cool manner, she asked, "And if I don't agree?"

"There isn't any 'if' involved. It's an either/or. Either you sign an addendum of exclusivity, or your line doesn't go into production."

She wanted to curse. "Now, wait a minute. The contract is legally binding, and you are obligated to produce…"

"Within ninety days of the date you signed. I know what the contract says, dear. I helped write it. But without your signature, I'm afraid we won't be able to produce your line in time for the festival."

Alexis cursed under her breath. She'd had very little personal interaction with Oscar James, but at the moment, she found him decidedly unlikeable. "I don't appreciate you threatening me this way, Mr. James. But I'm willing to sign the addendum, under one condition."

"I don't think you're in the position to be making conditions."

She gritted her teeth. "I'm making one anyway. The condition is this: if you ever insult me as a business woman this way again, I will forget that you are my elder, and this whole respect thing will go out the window. Trust and believe that I will defame your name and your company wherever I go."

"So you've got claws." He seemed surprised.

She was as serious as sin. "Call it what you want, as long as we understand each other."

He let a few beats pass in silence before he spoke again. "Deal."

"Good. I'll drop by your office tomorrow. Have your document drawn up and ready, because you won't be wasting any more of my time. Good day, sir." And she disconnected the call.

A wide-eyed Sydney stood near the desk. "What was that all about?"

"My future father-in-law has absolutely no couth.

Calls here saying he knows I'm trying to scam him by pretending to be engaged to his son, and making demands about altering our contract."

Syd frowned. "Did Bryan tell him that?"

She shook her head. "No. I guess he's just perceptive."

"Good thing he's not going to really be your father in-law." Syd flopped down in the armchair and reopened her laptop. "Unless…"

"Unless what?" Alexis looked her way.

"I mean, if what I saw is any indication, you're developing real feelings for Bryan. You know what that means."

Alexis shook her head, placed her focus back on her computer screen. "Come on, Syd. Don't be ridiculous."

Sydney chuckled. "Okay, whatever you say, Lex. But I'm not blind, and neither are any of the other people who've seen you together. And everybody in the office noticed how different you've been acting since you came back from New York."

She sighed. "Whatever, Syd. We have too much work to do to be talking nonsense."

"Mmm-hmm." Syd didn't bother to look up from her laptop.

Alexis retreated into her work, attempting to push away the one thought that kept echoing in her mind.

This fake engagement doesn't feel so fake anymore.

━━━◆◆◆━━━

Bryan left his office shortly after ten on Friday morning and headed for the elevator. Alone inside the car, he pressed the button for the basement. Today, the first pieces of Krystal Kouture fashion would come off the production line, and he wanted to be there. Quality control wasn't part of his job description as a marketing executive. It was, however, in his job description as someone concerned with the success of the family business.

When the car delivered him to the production floor, he stepped off and made his way to Ron Harper's desk. He found the production manager seated there, filling in the top portion of one of his quality control forms.

"How are things looking, Ron?"

He looked up. "Morning, Bryan. Things are right on schedule. We're running quality checks on the fabrics now, and we expect to hand them over to the pattern cutters within the next hour or so."

"No problems so far?"

He shook his head. "None that I've seen, and I'm always watching."

He patted Ron on the back. "Great. I'll be hanging around for a while, so come find me when the cutters start on the fabric."

"Will do."

Bryan then strolled away to observe the other preparations that were already under way. Royal's machinists were performing maintenance on the machines that would soon turn out Krystal Kouture pieces en masse, the fabric cutters were sharpening and lubricating their shears, and the seamstresses were readying thread and fresh needles for the more intricate pieces that would require embroidery. He stopped at each station to speak to the employees and offer encouragement for the busy day ahead, as well as his thanks for their hard work.

By then, he noticed Ron calling his name, so he returned to the cutting station.

"So we're going to hand cut some of the more delicate fabrics, like the silk," Ron said, gesturing to the cutters seated at their short tables. They'd already begun the task of attaching the silks to the appropriate pattern pieces for cutting.

"Good. I don't want to leave fabric that expensive and fragile to the machines."

"With the hardier fabric, like the poly blends, cotton, et cetera, we are using the cutting device." The computer-controlled device allowed for the operator to scan in a pattern piece, place sections of fabric beneath its specialized cutting head, and produce several duplicates of the same pattern piece in the space of several minutes.

Bryan was pleased with what he saw and wanted to be there to see the first garment come out of production if possible. "Do we have an ETA on the first piece?"

Ron shrugged. "I'm thinking eleven thirty or so. Right before lunch."

"Gotcha. I'll try to swing back by here then." It was already fifteen minutes to eleven, but he needed to return to his office, if only for a little while. Once he tied up the loose ends there, he'd return to see the staff's work come to fruition.

He left the factory floor and returned to his office. When he stepped off the elevator on the third floor, he was surprised to see Alexis, walking out of his father's office.

She walked toward him, eyes on her phone. He watched the hypnotic sway of her hips in the pair of red jeans she wore with a long-sleeved white blouse. Tall black boots encased the lower part of her legs, and black pearl jewelry shone around her neck and in her ears.

What is she doing here? He wasn't unhappy to see her, just surprised.

As if finally sensing his presence, she looked up as she came abreast of him. A smile spread over her previously tight face. "Hi, Bryan."

"Alexis." He touched her cheek, then leaned down and kissed her ruby-red lips. "What brings you here? Did you come just to see me?"

She rolled her eyes in response to his question. "Unfortunately, no. Your father asked me to come. Or forced me, depending on your perspective."

He frowned. "What are you talking about?"

"Your father thinks we're playing at being engaged."

He tensed. "Lex, I never told him that."

"I know, but that's the conclusion he drew. He pretty much demanded I come over here and sign an exclusivity agreement."

Shaking his head, he gave her another brief peck on the lips. "I'll talk to him. I'm sorry he acted that way, and I hope you don't feel like he forced your hand."

She offered a dismissive wave. "In a way, he did. But it's not a big deal. I never intended to withdraw from the contract, regardless of what happens between us."

"Speaking of which..." He gathered her into his arms and pulled her close. "Let's talk about what's already happened between us."

She blushed, but her eyes sparkled with desire. "Bryan, we're in the hallway. Anybody who walks by can see us."

His answering smile was accompanied by a shrug. "So what? It only feeds into our little illusion, right?"

She said nothing, just looked up into his eyes with a soft smile.

"Alexis, making love to you in New York was wonderful. And you might call me greedy, but I want to do it again."

Her eyes closed. "Bryan..."

He ran his fingertips slowly along her jawline. "I know you're not going to act like you didn't enjoy it or like you don't want it as much as I do."

He kissed the side of her throat and heard her sharp intake of breath.

He leaned in, nibbled on the edge of her earlobe. His next words were whispered, so only she could hear. "I remember the way you moaned and screamed for me. And I can't wait to hear it again." He dragged his tongue over the delicate skin between her ear and her hairline, sampling her fragrant skin.

She went nearly limp in his arms. "Bryan, please..."

"Oh, I'll please you, baby." He continued to place humid kisses and licks around her ear, down the column of her throat. As he neared her collarbone, he spoke again. "All you have to do is say yes."

"Yes..." A breathy sigh carried her answer to his ears.

Feeling as though he'd made his point, he backed off, letting her get her bearings. "When are we getting together again, Lex? So I can give you everything you need and more?"

Her tongue darted out and swept across the red petal of her bottom lip. "As soon as possible." A flash of realization passed over her face. "Listen, would you mind doing another television interview?"

"When is it?"

"Monday."

He sucked in a breath. "That's kind of short notice for me to travel, Lex."

She shook her head. "We won't have to travel this time, because the show is sending a crew to my office. So can you do it?" She fixed him with her best set of doe eyes. "Please?"

He wasn't fond of doing interviews, but he was used to them because he worked in marketing. Still, he knew he'd do just about anything to make Alexis smile. "Sure. I'll be there."

"Great. I really appreciate it." She gave him a peck on the cheek. "Oh, and it's not a morning show, so you don't have to come over until about noon. Is that cool?"

He nodded. "Works for me."

She glanced at her phone. "Shoot. I really need to get back to the office so I can wrap things up for the weekend. I'll call you a little later, okay?"

"Gotcha."

She started to walk away, until Oscar appeared in the hallway. Seeing him, she eased back to Bryan and placed her hand to his jawline. She said nothing, just stared up at him as if he were a tall drink of water and she was dying of thirst.

Looking down into those sparkling eyes, something came over him. Laying his own hand atop hers, he spoke. "I love you, Lex."

Confusion danced in her eyes momentarily, only to be replaced by acceptance. "I love you, Bryan." She leaned up for his kiss.

He pressed his lips to hers and kissed her full on, not for his father's benefit but for his own.

Because he now knew that for as long as he lived, he could never get enough of her kisses or of her time.

She might have thought he'd spoken out of a desire to stick it to his father, but he'd never spoken truer words in his life than when he'd admitted to her—and himself—that he loved her.

He could only hope her response had been as sincere.

Chapter 18

ALEXIS RAN A COMB OVER HER HAIR FOR THE FINAL time, hoping it would cooperate and stay in place. She regarded her reflection in the small, oval hand mirror she kept in a desk drawer. She'd decided to wear her hair down for today's interview, and now it seemed determined to frizz up at the mere mention of water or humidity.

Sydney stood behind her, shaking her head. "Girl, stop fussing over your hair. I told you it looks fine."

"Says the girl who's going to run out of here like her tail's on fire to avoid being on camera." She took a moment to check her makeup. Since the showrunners for *The Tea* didn't have the budget for makeup artists, the task of beautifying for the camera had been left up to her. She slipped her mirror back into her desk drawer and spun her chair around. Then she stuck her tongue out at Sydney.

Sydney rolled her eyes. "I told you when we first partnered, I don't do cameras. I'm the business manager because I'm comfortable around numbers and paper-work, not an audience."

Alexis laughed. "Yeah, you did say that." Reaching for the ice-cold can of seltzer water on the edge of the desk, she sipped through the straw, careful of her lip-stick. The crew for the show was scheduled to arrive within the next hour or so. "Did you make sure the reception area is clean?"

"Everything is always clean here. This is an all-female outfit, so who's making messes?"

"But you double-checked, right? I mean, did Pam run the vacuum? Did somebody make sure there are enough coffee pods in the break room? Did you…"

Sydney laid a hand on her shoulder. "Lex. Chill. We made sure everything is in place, so stop freaking out. If you keep this up, you'll end up looking all crazy and bug-eyed on national television. Is that what you want?"

She shook her head. "Hell no."

"Then take a few deep breaths and find your Zen, girl."

With her friend's hands resting on her shoulders, Alexis took a few deep, slow breaths until she felt her racing heart slow down a bit.

Seemingly satisfied, Sydney dropped her hands. "There. Now, what time did you tell Bryan to be here?"

"Around noon, since we're filming at one."

Sydney sucked her teeth. "He's late."

Alexis cut a look in her direction. "He'll be here. Meanwhile, isn't it about time for you to scurry away before the crew gets here? I know you don't want to risk being photographed." She smiled, her tone laced with teasing.

Rolling her eyes, Sydney grabbed her purse from the floor and slung the leather strap over her shoulder. "You're wrong for that. But you're right. Bye, girl." And she strode out the door.

Alexis sank back into her chair, enjoying the quiet of her office. She could hear the distant sounds of Dawn, the receptionist, typing on her computer, and the whirring sound of the office's climate-control system running.

Then she heard someone enter the office. When she heard Dawn greet him, she knew he was here. Straightening up in her chair, she listened to the measured cadence of his footsteps as they approached her private office.

When he stepped through the door, she couldn't help letting her eyes rake appreciatively over his frame. He wore a chestnut-brown suit, custom cut to fit his tall, muscular frame. The beige shirt and the gold-and-brown-striped tie and pocket square showed off his good taste in fashion, as did the smart brown lace-up dress shoes. His handsome face bore a broad grin as his eyes met hers. "Hey, Lex. You look beautiful."

She stood, smoothing her hand over the off-white jersey wrap dress she wore. "Thank you. You don't look so bad yourself." She strolled over to where he stood. The closer she got to him, the stronger the aroma of his cologne became. She had no idea what brand it was, but he smelled like pure heaven.

He moved toward her, and they met in front of her desk. Wrapping his arms around her waist, he dropped his head to kiss her.

She lifted her arms around his neck and let the kiss carry her away. His tongue pressed against her lips, and she opened to him immediately, reveling in his attention. One of his large hands slipped down to cup her ass through the thin fabric of her dress, and white-hot desire shot through her like an electric charge.

"Knock, knock." An unfamiliar voice yanked them out of their private paradise and dropped them back in reality.

Alexis jerked her head toward the open door of her office.

There stood two women and one man. All of them wore T-shirts proclaiming them as staff from *The Tea*, and the man carried an impressive-looking camera as well as a box of other equipment.

Alexis hid her face in Bryan's shoulder momentarily before addressing them. "Sorry. I'm Alexis Devers. You must be from the show."

The raven haired, fair skinned woman holding the mic and wearing a knowing smile walked over, stuck out her hand. "I'm Lynn. I'll be interviewing you two."

"Nice to meet you," Bryan volunteered, shaking hands with her.

"Likewise. I see we can put an end to any speculation that the two of you aren't in love, then."

His hand still cupping Alexis's bottom, Bryan gave it a firm squeeze. "Yes, you can."

Alexis felt her face grow hot, and though part of her wanted to disappear, she couldn't hide her smile.

Within the next twenty minutes, the crew helped get Alexis and Bryan set up for their interview. They were positioned for the best lighting, and furniture was moved into that area. Two portable studio lights were then set up, with their bright white bulbs set to shine on them. After they were all seated, with Lynn off camera, microphones were plugged in and affixed to their collars.

"Okay, are you ready?" Lynn asked the question from the high stool she sat on, behind the camera and the lights the crew had set up. "We're going live in just a few moments. Bret will give us a countdown."

Bryan reached out, grabbed Alexis's hand. "We're ready."

Already hot from the lights beating down on her,

Alexis nodded. This was about as ready as she was going to get.

Bret, the camera guy, began his countdown. "We're live in five...four...three...two..."

Lynn launched into her voice-over. "Hey, people, this is Lynn with a *Tea* exclusive. We're here in Raleigh, North Carolina, with fashion phenom Alexis Devers and her too-handsome-for-words fiancé, textile executive Bryan James. Welcome to *The Tea*, you two."

Alexis smiled and waved at the camera with her free hand.

Bryan added, "We're glad to be here."

Lynn smiled and nodded from behind the camera. "So we've all heard about this hotly anticipated fashion line of yours, Alexis. Krystal Kouture One is expected to debut at the Carolina Fashion and Music Festival in just ten days, and then it's going to hit store shelves later this fall. We've already seen several celebs wearing your clothes, like Angela Bassett and Kerry Washington. What's next for you at Krystal Kouture Design House?"

Alexis cleared her throat. "We're working very hard in conjunction with our manufacturer to prepare not only for our fashion show at the festival, but for the larger launch to the public. We're hiring models for the runway, setting up agreements with retailers, and lining up our endorsements for an ad campaign. It's a very exciting time here, and I can't wait for people to get to see what my team and I have come up with."

"Sounds great. Now, let's get to the other burning question. We asked viewers of *The Tea* what they wanted to know about you. The overwhelming majority asked the same question. When are you and Bryan getting married?"

Alexis could feel her eyes widening as panic set in. *We never discussed that. What the hell do I say?*

While Alexis turned inward, Bryan offered an easy chuckle. "We think a winter wedding might be nice, so…"

Her brain kicked into gear then. "We haven't set a date yet, but we will soon."

Lynn looked confused. "Well, which is it? A winter wedding or no date?"

Alexis plastered on her best fake smile. "I like the winter idea. But we're not going to rush things, since we're both so swamped right now."

Bryan's hand tensed around hers. "Whatever Lex wants is what she's going to get." He was still smiling as well, but Alexis could tell some of the light had gone out of his eyes.

"Well, folks, you heard it here first. It's a winter wedding for Alexis and Bryan, but we're not sure if it'll be this winter. Now I'm gonna throw it back to Jess in our Charlotte studio. What's up, Jess?"

"We're clear." After shutting off the camera, Bret came around and turned off the bright lights.

Alexis felt her body temperature drop without the lights, and she couldn't remember feeling more relieved.

That relief slipped away the moment she saw the expression on Bryan's face.

———

Bryan said nothing and didn't move from his seat until after the television crew had packed up and left. Dawn swung by to tell Alexis she was leaving for the day to take her son to a doctor's appointment.

Alone in the office with Alexis, he watched her pace the floor for a few silent moments more.

"Where's the rest of your staff?"

"Pam's on vacation, and Sydney never hangs around when cameras are involved."

"So there's no one else here?"

"No." She continued pacing.

He watched her, waiting to see if she would wear a trench in the floor.

Finally, she turned his way. "Bryan, why are you looking at me like that? Just say what you gotta say."

He folded his arms over his chest. "What was that?"

"You're gonna have to be a little more specific."

"Why did you start acting crazy when she asked us if we'd set a date?" He fixed her with an intense stare. "This whole thing was your idea, and when someone asks you that, you don't know what to say?"

She sighed. "Bryan, we never discussed a wedding date."

"I know that."

She shook her head. "I was caught off guard."

"You didn't expect anybody to ever ask us when we're getting married?"

"Yes, but not this soon."

He felt his brow furrowing. This whole thing had become as confusing as hell. Just when he thought he knew what she wanted and he tried to give it to her, he turned out to be wrong. "Okay, then, let's keep it from happening again. Let's pick a date now."

She sighed again. "I can't."

"Why not?"

"I...just can't, Bryan."

"Just throw out a date. Since this is all supposed to be fake anyway, what does it matter?"

She looked away, her gaze dropping as if she were studying the carpet.

He stood, walked over to her. "Alexis, look at me."

She didn't look up.

He touched her chin, repeated himself. "Lex, look at me. Please."

She acquiesced then, and when their eyes met, he could see her tears.

Concern immediately flooded his mind, replacing his frustration. "Baby, what's wrong? Why are you crying?"

"You keep saying it's all fake."

"That's what you wanted, isn't it? That's how this all started, so why does it upset you now?"

A tear slipped down her cheek as she whispered her reply. Another tear soon followed. "It's not fake to me, not anymore."

His heart did a somersault in his chest. Using the pad of his thumb, he wiped away her tears. "Are you saying what I think you're saying?"

She closed her eyes as if hiding from something frightening. "Yes, Bryan. I love you. It may make me a total idiot, but I love you."

He enveloped her then, pulling her as close to his body as he could manage. "Baby, if that's the case, we're both idiots."

Her eyes popped open, and she stared at him.

"I love you, Alexis Devers." He held her gaze, hoped

she could see the truth in his words as she looked into his eyes.

A sob escaped her throat.

He covered it with his kiss. First, the sound became muffled, then it morphed into a moan as his hand circled over her hip. He kissed her possessively, because more than anything and more than ever, he wanted her to be his. No other man would touch her this way; no other man would kiss her soft, yielding lips. No. He needed her to be his, and his alone.

She started to move, stumbling backward.

Not wanting to break the connection of their bodies, he followed her movements until they came to rest against something solid. He broke the kiss, looked over her shoulder to see that her hips were pressed against the edge of her desk.

Her heavy breathing filled the silence.

He looked at all the things on the surface of the desk: the papers, her laptop, the framed pictures, and knick-knacks. Everything was so carefully arranged, the exact opposite of his own disastrous desktop. As much as he wanted to, he couldn't bring himself to sweep it all onto the floor.

She took the pressure off by doing it for him. Using her hand, she cleared half of the desktop and shimmied onto the surface. Her dress rode up her thighs in tandem with her movement.

His breath escaped in a whoosh when he saw the brown skin newly revealed to his eyes. Moving closer to her to stand between her parted legs, he grazed his fingertips over the bared portion of her lush thighs. "God, Alexis. I want you so much."

In response, she grabbed his tie with both hands. After loosening his Windsor knot, she tugged the two ends of the tie and dragged him to her waiting lips.

The kissing began anew then, with his hands touring the warm flesh of her thighs and her fingers digging into his shoulders. Passion sparked between them like a five-alarm blaze, hot and intense. Between their bodies, his body answered the call of desire, hardening like a length of steel.

When he broke the kiss this time, he looked down into her sparkling eyes. "Do you really want to do this here?"

"Yes, Bryan." She traced her fingertip over his jaw. "There's no one else here but us."

His entire body tingled with anticipation. Slowly, he peeled the slinky dress from her body, leaving her perched atop her desk in nothing but her white silk undergarments. The bikini panties were the only thing standing between him and the treasure between her thighs. She arched, thrusting her breasts forward. To his mind, she made the most beautiful, provocative sight he'd ever seen.

Her wicked gaze swept over his body before she met his eyes again. "Make love to me. Here. Now." She all but growled the words.

He didn't need to be asked twice. Shrugging out of his sport coat, he tossed it aside and began undoing the buttons running down the front of his shirt.

He planned on giving in to her every desire, for as long as she could stand it.

Chapter 19

ALEXIS FELT HER BREATH STACKING UP IN HER THROAT like traffic at a red light as she watched Bryan undress. Having been with him before, she knew his sexual prowess well. But she sensed an intensity in him now that she hadn't during their first encounter. Something told her this was a turning point, that their declaration of love for each other would fuel him to even higher levels.

He tossed away his shirt, then stripped off the tee beneath, baring his upper body to her eyes. Her tongue slid out to swipe over her bottom lip at the sight, her anticipation getting the better of her.

He noticed the gesture and smiled.

Laying his palms flat on his rippling abs, he slowly moved them down toward the waistband of his slacks, where he made slow work of undoing the button and zipper. All the while, he fixed her with a look that could only be described as sinful.

She bit her lip. *He's teasing me.* The insistent throbbing between her thighs now matched pace with her heartbeat. Her swollen core ached with wanting him, and she couldn't wait for him to make it all better.

He let the pants pool around his feet before kicking them away. Now, he wore nothing but a pair of red boxer briefs, the front of which did nothing to conceal the evidence of his desire for her. He took a step that brought him back into her space. Grasping her hips where they rested on the surface of the desk, he tugged her forward until his hardness pressed between her thighs.

She groaned, wanting to do away with the thin layers of fabric keeping their bodies from touching, from joining.

Moments later, he put something else between them—his hand. She found she wasn't upset at all. Rather, as his fingertips eased her panties aside and began plying her wetness, she dissolved into pleasure.

"Do you like that, baby?" His deep voice held the promise of so much more.

"Mmm." The sound was all she could manage as he circled his thumb over her swollen clitoris. A wave of bliss rose within, radiating out from his magical touch to reach every nerve ending in her body.

He slipped one long finger inside of her, aided by the liquid desire he'd inspired. Her hips rose off the desk of their own accord as he began a slow rhythm, moving his finger out, then back in, simulating what was to come. When he brought a second finger to the party, her back went into a full arch. A beat later, she shattered, a scream falling from her lips before she went limp on the wooden desktop.

She lost awareness for a few long moments, but part of her felt him whisk away her panties and re-center her on the desk. Before she could fully come down from the heights he'd delivered her to, she felt his condom-covered erection probing her. She was flat on her back on the desk, and he stood between her open thighs.

Locking her legs around him, she urged him forward. As he filled her, she released a long moan, the sound mingling with his own growl.

He began the lovemaking with a slow, skillful stroking that set her entire being on fire. His large hands cupped her hips, bracing her for the impact of each thrust of his powerful hips. The building heat made her hum low in her throat. The hum rose to a moan, climbing an octave as she sang his name in ecstasy.

Her body tensed around him, clenching his hardness. Her mind became consumed with him and the magic emanating from that part of him. *Deeper. Harder. More.*

He reacted to the flexing of her inner muscles around him by giving her everything her body craved and more. He lifted her hips, driving deeper, giving her more. His pace increased, and her eyes slammed shut against the rising tide of bliss.

"Alexis." He growled her name as he withdrew partially, only to drive into her again in one long, impassioned stroke.

The sound of her name on his lips and the delicious friction he created between her thighs conspired to undo her. Surrendering to the glory of his lovemaking, she cried out as orgasm flung her soul skyward.

Not long after, she heard him groan her name again as he met with his own completion. Giving her ass a firm squeeze, he stepped back and allowed their bodies to separate.

She lay there for a few moments, with the coolness of the desktop against her hot, damp skin. Her mind told her that it was Monday and that she still had plenty of work to do.

Her body told her that she wanted more of Bryan, as much as he would give her.

To that end, she sat upright and scooted off the desk.

Dressed in only her bra, she regarded Bryan's delectable nudity as he stood before her.

He smiled. "See something you like?"

"Yes, I do." She eased closer to him, slipped her hand around his dick, and closed it. Feeling him harden again beneath her touch made her smile.

He drew in a sharp breath. "You're a hell of woman, Alexis Devers." His words were just above a whisper.

She winked, placed a soft kiss against his full lips. "And don't you ever forget it." Releasing him, she grasped his hand and led him to the armchair by her desk.

———

Sitting back in the plush armchair, Bryan settled in as Alexis lifted her knee to climb into his lap. The wicked gleam in her eye let him know she was about to give him the ride of his life. She seemed able to match him in the game of passion, in pace and in stamina. As she straddled him, he added that to the list of things he loved about her.

I love her. He buried his fingers in the depths of her hair, massaging her scalp while pulling her close for his kiss. The moment their lips met, she opened her mouth to his seeking tongue.

A sound rang through the empty office. He ignored it.

She didn't. Jerking away from his kiss, she got up and scurried over to their discarded pile of clothing. Fishing around in it, she found her cell phone and answered in a panicked voice. "Kelsey?"

He sat up, remaining alert in case she needed him.

"He's gone? And his sister's there to pick up Naji?" She dressed as she spoke, balancing the phone between her shoulder and her face as she put on her panties and skirt. "Okay, okay. I'll let Max know. Give me fifteen minutes." She dropped the phone and shimmied her top on over her slightly disheveled bra.

He stood, willing his body to cooperate with this new reality. "It's your sister."

She nodded. "I'm sorry to break up the party, but I need to get over there, fast."

"Do you need me to come with you?"

She shook her head. "No. Max will meet me there. But if we do need you, we'll call." She grabbed her purse, stepped into her low-heeled pumps.

He began gathering his own clothes and getting dressed. By the time he'd gotten into his underwear and tee, she was headed out the door.

"I'll call you later. I love you, Bryan."

"I love you, too." He watched her disappear around the doorway.

From the hallway, he heard her call, "Lock the door behind you, please."

"I will."

After spending a few more minutes getting back into his suit, he grabbed his keys and left the office. As she'd requested, he turned the lock on the doorknob. Without the office key, he couldn't bolt the door, so he made his way to the parking garage and climbed into his truck.

A glance at the clock on his dash told him the time. It was just past three. *Too late to go back to work.* He'd told his assistant he didn't know if he'd return, because he hadn't known how long the interview would take. Beyond that, he certainly hadn't known he'd end up making sweet love to Alexis on top of her desk. The memory of her spread out before him made him smile, but he pushed the thought away before his body reacted and rendered him unable to sit comfortably.

Riding through the streets of downtown Raleigh, he watched the passing scenery and reveled in the familiarity of it. The last few weeks of his life had thrown him so many curves, he needed that comfort wherever he could find it.

Using his hands-free technology, he called Xavier. In general, Xavier was the most levelheaded of all his frat brothers. Bryan knew he could count on him to give straightforward, objective advice.

Xavier's voice came over the car speakers. "What's up, B?"

"You busy, man?"

He chuckled. "Nah. Just left the council chambers. We're done for the day. You need something?"

Bryan sighed. "Yeah. I need some advice."

"Oh, Lord. What kind of trouble are you in? Do we need to call Ty?"

He laughed despite his mood. "No, man. If I needed a lawyer, I would have called him myself. I got lady trouble."

"What's the problem? One of those models from the Paris trip after you for child support?"

He shook his head. "No, but I guess I deserve that crack. This is about Alexis."

Xavier's tone changed, sounding confused. "I was going to ask you about that. I saw the interview on that morning show last week. How did y'all even get together in the first place? And why didn't you say anything to your frats?"

Bryan gave Xavier a brief rundown of the arrangement he'd originally made with Alexis. He didn't bother lying to Xavier, because the brother had an A1-quality bullshit detector and would have immediately seen right through it. "So that's how this all started. But now, things have changed."

"You love her." Xavier stated it as fact.

"Yes," Bryan responded in kind. "How did you know?"

"Why else would you have called me? We all have our strengths. If you wanted to know how to break things off with her without getting sued, you would have called Ty. If you wanted to get out of town to avoid her, you'd have called Orion and asked to join him on tour. And if you wanted your ass kicked, you'd have called Maxwell."

"Ha, ha. Very funny." Bryan touched his fingertips to his temple as he sat at a red light. "But back to the lecture at hand, X. What am I supposed to do now? This isn't how things were supposed to go down."

"Obviously. The first question is, did you tell her how you feel?"

He nodded, even though he knew Xavier couldn't see him. "I told her. She told me she feels the same way."

"Then what's the problem?"

"I want to go through with this engagement. I want to marry her, for real."

Xavier sucked in an audible breath. "Whoa, dude. That's a pretty big leap from 'I love you' to 'Let's get married right now.'"

"I know it is." Even as he said the words, he realized how absurd it sounded. But when he thought about it, this whole agreement had been an exercise in absurdity from the very start. "But I want Alexis to be my wife. I've never been this sure of anything in my life. How do I approach her about it?"

"You know me. I always advocate for complete honesty when it comes to dealing with the ladies. Be straight with her, Bryan. But you have to realize she may be shocked and hesitant. Don't rush her. If she wants to wait, you're just going to have to suck it up, brotha."

By now, Bryan had made it home. Parking his truck in his driveway, he cut the engine but remained in his seat to finish the call. "Does this mean I have to do a real live proposal?"

"Yeah. I don't think there's any getting around that. But look on the bright side. You already bought her a ring, right?"

"True." He could clearly picture the way the ring sparkled on her finger and the way her eyes had glistened with tears when he'd given it to her. "All right, Xavier. I'll let you go. Thanks for the advice."

"Anytime, dude. You know TDT men will always hold each other down."

"Damn straight. Later."

"Later."

Turning the key ended the hands-free connection, and he slipped it from the ignition and climbed out of his truck.

Chapter 20

ALEXIS SCANNED THE SCENERY AS SHE TURNED ONTO Grover Street. The neighborhood was pretty typical of lower-middle-class areas of the capital city. Tall oaks, pines, and maples lined the roadway and towered over the neat, one-story homes. Most were made of brick or stone, but a few newer construction homes wore their soft pastel siding with pride. American flags, attached to porch columns and short poles in front yards, flapped in the breeze. More than a few of the cars parked in the paved driveways bore ichthys insignias, church bumper stickers, stick-figure families, or a combination of all of them. Having lived in Raleigh most of her life, the sights were familiar. But she was also old enough to realize that behind the idyllic facade, one could never truly know what went on inside these prim little homes. Her mere presence here was a reminder of that.

She gripped the steering wheel tightly, remaining alert as she approached the home that had been her sister's prison for far too long. She looked around to get the lay of the land and was relieved to see Maxwell's SUV parked in front of Scott's small, brick house. Scott's old pickup truck was noticeably absent from the driveway, and she was glad of that as well. She parked her car at the curb across the street from the house and cut the engine.

She got out of her car, and after a quick glance in each

direction for oncoming traffic, darted across the street. On the sidewalk, she picked up her pace in approaching the front porch.

She was on the bottom step when Kelsey emerged, holding little Naji by the hand. The youngster had a cartoon bookbag on his back and a stuffed bear tucked beneath his arm. Maxwell was close behind them, pulling along Kelsey's bright pink suitcase. As he exited the house, he shut the door behind him.

Tears stung Alexis's eyes as she laid eyes on her sister for the first time in eighteen months. A mixture of happiness at being reunited with her and frustration over what Kelsey had suffered flooded her heart.

Kelsey's watery eyes and smile revealed that she felt similarly.

Alexis skipped over the next two steps and ran to her sister. Naji stepped back as the two women collided in a tearful embrace. Alexis clung to her sister as if she'd never let her go, and truth be told, she never wanted to.

Kelsey finally backed up. "Okay, okay. I missed you, too, Lex. But we don't have a lot of time before Scott gets back."

Nodding, Alexis released her sister and dashed away her tears. "You're right. Where's Naji's aunt?"

Kelsey pointed. "She's sitting in that white sedan on the other side of the street. Right behind where you parked."

Alexis looked and waved at the woman when she saw her. Turning back to Kelsey, she asked, "She's not getting out of the car?"

Kelsey's eyes said it all. "She knows how her brother is."

Maxwell shook his head. "This guy is a class-A jerk, and I'm glad you're finally leaving."

Kelsey started moving toward the steps. "Me, too."

As Kelsey passed, still holding onto Naji, Maxwell leaned down to whisper in Alexis's ear. "Bryan and Xavier are waiting around the corner. Just in case."

Alexis felt a smile tug at her heart. "Good to know." She knew Maxwell's frat brothers wouldn't hesitate to step in if they were needed, and she felt especially grateful to Bryan. But for now, it looked as if they would get Kelsey and Naji out of Scott's house without too much fuss.

Alexis and Maxwell followed Kelsey as she strode down the sidewalk, crossing the street to where Naji's aunt was parked.

The woman rolled down the window. "I've got his booster seat back there. Just make sure he's buckled in."

Maxwell opened the rear driver-side door and lifted Naji into the seat. Kelsey leaned in and kissed him on the forehead while securing his seat belt. "Be good, Naji."

"Are you coming to see me, Mama Kelsey?" Naji's brown eyes sparkled with tears.

Nodding, Kelsey kissed him again. "Don't worry. I'll be over there as soon as I can, okay?"

That seemed to calm him, and he sat back in the seat with the stuffed animal in his lap.

After she shut the door, Kelsey leaned in to shake the woman's hand. "Thank you, Tammy."

She smiled. "I wasn't going to leave my nephew with my crazy-ass brother. Thank you for protecting him all this time."

Kelsey smiled. "What can I say? I love him."

Alexis looked on, and it became crystal clear to her why her sister had stayed under Scott's dictatorial hold as long as she had. Kelsey had a heart of gold, and it was obvious that little Naji had claimed a portion of it, even though he wasn't Kelsey's biological child.

The three of them stood back as Tammy started her car and pulled off with Naji safely ensconced in the backseat. Kelsey waved until the car turned a corner and disappeared from sight.

Alexis turned toward her car. "Do you want to ride with me or with Max?"

Kelsey turned her way to answer. Before she could speak, her eyes grew wide. Looking over Alexis's shoulder, she said, "Oh my God. There's Scott's truck."

A shaken Alexis turned in the direction Kelsey indicated. Sure enough, the beat-up old red pickup Scott drove rolled in their direction.

Maxwell pulled out his phone. Seconds later, he spoke into the receiver. "Mount up, boys." He then turned to Alexis. "Pop your trunk so I can toss Kelsey's bag in."

Using the remote on her key, she did as he asked. With one arm around Kelsey's trembling shoulder, she watched her brother hoist the large suitcase into the trunk and slam it shut.

"Get in the car. The boys are on the way." Maxwell opened the passenger door for Kelsey to slip in.

Alexis climbed in as well, sliding behind the wheel. Once her brother shut them in, she locked the doors.

Maxwell crossed the street, but rather than get into his SUV, he waited on the sidewalk in front of Scott's house. Even at a distance, Alexis could see the fire in her brother's eyes.

Scott's raggedy truck rattled by, then turned into the hilly driveway before coming to a stop.

Alexis frowned as Scott's face came into view. He was tall and tan, with dark hair and piercing blue eyes. If he weren't such a jackass, she would have considered him handsome.

When he climbed out of the truck and saw Maxwell standing there, he glowered. "What the hell is going on?"

Alexis could hear Scott shouting as she and Kelsey buckled their seat belts. Maxwell simply stood with his arms folded over his chest, calmly answering Scott's rude demands. She started her engine when she saw Scott turn and stalk in their direction. She put the car in drive and tried to pull out of the space but wasn't fast enough.

Scott pounded furiously on the closed passenger window. "Kelsey! Get out of that car and get your ass back in the house!"

Tears coursed down Kelsey's face as she looked at him and shook her head.

"Where's my son? You can't do this!"

Tired of Scott's crap, Alexis prepared to hit the gas. If she took off his foot, so be it, but she wasn't going to let her sister be subjected to any more trauma at his hands.

Just as she touched her foot to the gas, two tall, dark figures appeared behind Scott. The look of shock on Scott's face was priceless as Bryan and Xavier each grabbed him by an arm and roughly dragged him away from the car, still cursing and red-faced.

Alexis smiled as she guided the car away from the curb. *I hope they bust his ass.*

Kelsey released a long, slow breath. "Max's frat brothers?"

Alexis nodded, still smiling. "You know they stick together like glue. No worries, Kelsey. They'll set him straight."

As she drove her sister toward freedom and safety, Alexis thought of all the ways she would thank Bryan for what he'd done, the first chance she got.

Lying on the weight bench in his home gym Tuesday evening, Bryan lifted the one-hundred-pound barbell above him, then lowered it. When he'd completed the last set of ten reps, he brought the weight down slowly, letting it rest on his chest before sitting up and setting it aside. He'd performed three sets of ten reps, and while he felt good right now, he knew his arms and shoulders would be screaming tomorrow if he didn't take proper care to prevent it. He ran through his upper-body stretch routine to recondition the muscles he'd just punished.

He moved from the weight bench to his gray yoga mat. Once he'd gotten into the proper stance, he started his gluteal routine. After fifty squats, he flopped down on the weight bench again, wiping the sweat from his brow with the white towel he'd slung around his shoulders earlier.

Later, as he stood beneath the hot stream of his shower, Alexis came to mind. When he closed his eyes, he could still see her lying in front of him, taking everything he had to give. She'd been so responsive, and she'd felt like heaven wrapped around him. His body reacted to the memory of her warm tightness, and he willed the beast back to sleep, vowing to call her once he got out of the shower.

Dressed in a fresh pair of boxers and striped pajama

pants, he strode to his valet to retrieve his cell phone. He hadn't heard from Alexis since the previous day, and he wanted to check on her. He'd seen the satisfied smile on her face when he and Xavier carried away her sister's idiot boyfriend but hadn't spoken to her so far today. It was around seven in the evening, so he assumed she would be home from work by now. He strolled barefoot through the house, dialing her number as he reached the kitchen. There, he activated the speaker phone and set the device on the kitchen counter while he grabbed a sports drink from the fridge.

She picked up on the third ring. "Hey, Bryan."

He smiled as her voice filled the room, twisting the cap off the bottle. "Hey, baby. What are you up to?"

He could hear the smile in her voice as she answered him. "Not much. Just crashed on the couch in front of the TV. You?"

"Just worked out, took a shower. Will probably read the paper."

She laughed. "So why'd you call? You miss me already?"

"Yes. But I wanted to see how you are and how your sister is after what happened yesterday."

Her tone became more serious. "That's really sweet of you. I'm fine, really. As for Kelsey, she's staying in the mother-in-law suite at our parents' house until she decides what she wants to do next."

He exhaled. "I'm glad to hear that."

"Did Scott give you much trouble?"

"Not after you left. When we hauled his ass across the street, he tried to square up with your brother. Maxwell knocked him out."

She sounded shocked but pleased. "Seriously?"

"Yeah." He chuckled as he thought back on the encounter. "Maxwell made sure to tell him to stay away from your sister first. After Scott was out cold, we sat him in one of the chairs on his porch and bounced."

The next sound he heard could only be described as a guffaw. "Oh my God."

He smiled, picking up on her amusement. "You all right?"

Between chuckles, she answered. "Yeah. I just...I know I shouldn't laugh, but..."

"Don't feel bad. Did I mention Scott did a face-plant on the sidewalk after your brother whupped him?"

Peals of laughter erupted from her mouth. "Stop, stop!"

By now, Bryan was laughing, too. "I don't think you lose points with the good Lord for laughing at somebody who got what they deserved."

"I hope not, because I couldn't help it." She giggled one more time, then took a deep breath. "I never really thanked you for what you did. I'm so glad you and Xavier showed up to help us out."

He smiled at that. "You know Theta brothers always look out for each other. And since I knew you were there, I wasn't about to stand by and let anything crazy go down."

"So you were protecting me?"

"Of course. Why wouldn't I?" He answered without a second thought, and it occurred to him how much his perception had changed when it came to her. He'd gone from thinking of her as his best friend's baby sister to a client to a lover. He'd started wondering what it would be like to have her as his wife, but he wasn't ready to mention that to her yet.

"You're so sweet." Her tone indicated her rising emotions.

"Alexis, I told you I love you. And I meant what I said, baby."

There was a pause before her soft reply. "I love you, too, Bryan."

Hearing her words touched his heart. He didn't think he'd ever tire of it. "Listen. There are some things we should discuss, and I'd like to have a talk with you."

"We're talking now. So what's up?"

If only it were that simple. "No, baby. I want to talk to you in person. This is important." Inside, he kicked himself for not having this discussion with her from the beginning. He'd bet good money that everything he had to tell her would have been much easier for her to digest back then before their feelings were involved. Now he'd simply have to hope she could accept things as they were.

"Where do you want to meet? The coffee shop downtown? Dinner?"

He thought about it for a moment and concluded that he didn't want to discuss this with her in public. The conversation would likely go smoother without the prying eyes and listening ears of strangers surrounding them. "Why don't you come over to my place? I'll make something great."

"You cook?"

He chuckled. "I dabble a little."

"Oh, I gotta see this. It's a deal."

"Can you come over on Friday?"

"No, I'm going out with Sydney that night. What about Saturday?"

"That'll work. So I'll see you Saturday at seven."

"That seems so far away. But I'll be there."

After he disconnected the call, he leaned against the counter to finish his sports drink. When he thought of the night he had in store for Alexis, his lips flexed into a broad grin.

It's time to seal the deal and make her mine.

———

With the large plastic tote balanced in his arms, Maxwell walked up the narrow stairway that led to the mother-in-law suite above his parents' garage. Kelsey walked ahead of him, carrying her purse and a large stuffed animal.

He watched his sister as she stopped at the door, using the key their mother had given her to unlock it. Once she swung the door open and walked inside, Maxwell followed her. He had to do a bit of maneuvering to get the wide plastic tote through the door, but he finally made it in and set the tote on the floor by the long buffet table. The buffet was loaded down with their mother's dust collectors and old family photos, and he was careful to avoid knocking anything over as he used his foot to scoot the tote out of the way.

Kelsey set her purse down on the short-legged coffee table and tucked the giant, pink stuffed rabbit against the arm of the sofa. Turning to him, she asked, "Are you going to let me help bring the rest of my stuff up here?"

He shook his head. "Do you need to ask? Have yourself a seat, and let me bring in the rest of your things."

She pursed her lips. "Maxie, I'm not helpless. I can at least help you—"

He put up his hand, effectively cutting her off mid-sentence. "Kelsey, I know you're not helpless. But will you just humor me? Now go sit down, relax, and let your big bro take care of you, okay?"

She sighed, but it was accompanied by a smile. "If you insist." Apparently resigned to her fate, she plopped down on the couch and tugged the stuffed rabbit into her arms.

"Thank you." A satisfied Maxwell turned and went back down the stairs. Taking a turn in the hallway at the bottom, he passed through the door into the three-car garage where he'd parked his SUV.

While he grabbed another of Kelsey's plastic totes from the open hatch, he thought about the events of the past few days. Monday had been the day he, Alexis, and his fraternity brothers extricated Kelsey from Scott's control, and Maxwell was relieved to have her home. Now, on this balmy Wednesday morning, he'd come over to their parents' house to help Kelsey move her things into her temporary space. Doing this now would mean going in to work at his architectural firm about an hour later than normal, but since he was the boss, no one was going to check him about it. As far as he was concerned, the rest of his day would simply have to wait. His first priority was making sure that Kelsey was comfortably settled in.

Wrestling the tote up the stairs and tucking it inside Kelsey's suite, he made several more trips up and down the stairs, lugging her totes and cardboard boxes. They varied in weight, filled with clothing, shoes, and other personal items, and by the time he'd brought up the last box, he could feel a sheen of sweat beginning to form on his brow. Since he'd be heading straight to his office after this, he'd donned his usual business attire—a gray suit with a white shirt and red tie. He'd had the good sense to taken off his sport jacket before he started hauling Kelsey's things and left it in the passenger seat of his truck.

"Whew." He flopped down on the couch next to his sister, taking a moment to catch his breath. He grabbed a tissue from the box on the side table and wiped his brow. "That's everything."

"Thanks, Maxie. Bet you wish you'd let me help now, huh?" She playfully punched him in the shoulder.

He chuckled, shook his head. "Nah. I'm a little winded, but I don't mind it at all." He paused, looking at the pile of boxes and totes. As he realized they'd need unpacking, he grimaced. "You will have Mom and Lex help you put all this stuff away, right?"

She nodded. "Yeah. Mom hates for things to be out of place, so I'm sure she'll be up here before the day is out to help with that." Her eyes swept over the space. "I can't believe how much crap I have. I just hope I can find places to put it all."

"You know what they say. You never realize how much you have until you have to move it." He clasped his hands together in front of him.

She looked away then, and for a moment, she seemed to be studying her stuffed rabbit.

Maxwell watched his sister intently, sensing the sudden change in her mood. "Kelsey? What's wrong?"

She blew out a breath. "I'm just...frustrated, I

guess. Here I've put you and Alexis through all this inconvenience the last few days, to help me move my stuff and all."

He reached out, touched her shoulder. "Come on, Kelsey. It's not an inconvenience. We love you, and we're just glad to have you safe and back home."

She sniffled, her arms tightening around the rabbit. "I know, and I love you guys, too. I just wish I'd left sooner. I shouldn't have let you and Lex and Mom and Dad worry about me for so long. I'm really sorry."

He scooted closer to his sister, gathering her and her stuffed friend into his arms. "Kelsey, there's no need to apologize. What happened to you wasn't your fault. It was Scott's. That dude is an asshole of the highest order."

Tears were streaming down her cheeks, but her lips turned up into a smile. "You're right about that. Thanks for punching him, by the way."

Maxwell shook his head. "I'm not proud of that, but he squared up. I'm not saying he didn't deserve the business end of my fist, but I didn't go over there looking for a fight." He gave her shoulders a squeeze. "But I would have done anything, and I do mean anything, to get you out of there."

She brushed away her tears with the back of her hand and turned to look into his face. "Thank you, Maxie. Thank you so much, for everything."

He could feel his chest tighten with all the love he felt for her. "Hey, that's what big brothers are for. Who knows what kind of shenanigans you and Lex would get into if you didn't have me to look out for you?"

Her teary smile brightened. "You're right. We do need you to have our backs."

"You're a smart girl, Kelsey. Now if I could just get Lex to admit that, I'd be golden." He winked.

She snuggled close to him. "You know Lex is too stubborn to ever say that."

He chuckled. "Keep hope alive, Kelsey. Keep hope alive."

He sat there with his sister in his arms, determined to stay with her until she was ready to be alone. He and Alexis had been in and out of the house over the past day and a half, checking in on Kelsey to see how she was holding up. Their parents had been looking in on Kelsey as well, an easy feat since she'd returned to her childhood home. She'd been through quite an ordeal, and everyone in the family wanted to make sure she had the smoothest possible transition to being on her own again.

He looked down at his sister, resting in his embrace, and smiled. His mother and his two sisters were the most important women in his life, and he assumed it would remain that way until he found the right woman to settle down with. Parts of him wondered if that would ever happen, because he was loath to give up his freedom. *Could I really give my heart to someone and be okay with having her keep tabs on my whereabouts?* He didn't know the answer to that.

What he did know was that if he ever found the right woman, he'd treat her a hell of a lot better than Scott had treated Kelsey. After all, what was the point of being in a relationship if you weren't going to do it right?

No, the woman he ended up with could expect to be treated like a queen. Because if he was going to give up his freedom, he'd settle for no less.

Chapter 21

ALEXIS CLIMBED THE STAIRS TOWARD THE SECOND floor of her parents' house, her bare feet sinking into the carpet. At her mother's request, she'd shown up with her overnight bag about an hour ago, prepared to spend the night in the suite over the garage. It might seem odd to anyone else, this impromptu sleepover on a Thursday night, but Alexis didn't mind. She'd do anything to see Kelsey's bright, bubbly personality return.

Now, wearing a pair of red silk pajamas, she found herself bopping her head. The narrow stairwell vibrated with the sounds of the hip-hop music her sister was pumping, and by the time Alexis reached the top step, she was ready to do the cabbage patch. Finding the door to the suite ajar, she poked her head in.

"Kelsey?"

"Come on in," came the shouted reply.

She eased inside, shutting the door behind her. Even though this part of the house went unused most of the time, Delphinia Devers's decorating scheme continued here. The walls in the room were painted a muted shade of pink, and the plush beige carpet beneath Alexis's feet was protected by several strategically placed Oriental rugs. On the wall hung a hand-selected assortment of old family portraits and paintings, mainly landscapes featuring ocean scenes. The space was furnished with expensive but simple pieces—overstuffed beige leather furniture, oak tables, and ceramic and crystal decorative pieces. The scent of their mother's favorite cinnamon potpourri hung in the air.

Finding Kelsey in the small kitchenette, she gestured to the stereo system on the counter. "Is that *The Hamilton Mixtape*?"

"Yeah. You know I love it." Kelsey bopped across the room, setting a tea kettle on one of the two burners on the small stove. "Want some tea?" She was dressed for bed as well, in a Ro James tee and a pair of black cotton drawstring pants.

"Yeah." Reaching over, Alexis turned down the stereo system. "Sorry, but I don't want to have to yell so you can hear me."

"It's cool." Kelsey set the temperature on the stove, then went to the small, circular table and sat down in one of the two chairs.

Alexis claimed the seat across from her. Taking in her sister's face, she could see the remaining vestiges of anxiety painting her expression. Kelsey smiled, but it didn't reach her eyes, and Alexis knew it would take time for her sister to adjust to her new reality. "Listen, if you want to talk, Kelsey…"

She shook her head. "Not yet, Lex. We may as well wait until Mom gets here."

"Fair enough." As much as Alexis wanted to comfort her sister, she didn't want to pressure her. "Is Mom spending the night up here with us?"

Kelsey nodded. "Yep."

Her brow hitched in surprise. "She didn't tell me that. Plus, I would have thought her much too attached to her memory foam mattress to sleep up here."

Running a hand through her short cropped curls, Kelsey shrugged. "You know Mom. She's not one to miss out on fresh gossip."

Alexis pursed her lips. "Come on, Kelsey. That's not fair. You know Mom's just concerned about you. We all are—me, Maxwell, and Daddy, too."

She sighed. "I know, I know. Sorry. It's just been a rough week." Her gaze shifted downward.

Alexis felt her chest tighten at Kelsey's palpable sadness. "What's going on with Naji? Is he okay?"

Kelsey's expression brightened at the mention of the little boy's name. "Yeah. I spoke to Tammy this morning. Naji's going to stay with her and her husband while Scott goes to anger management."

"He's going to counseling now?" Alexis found that somewhat hard to believe. After all the crap he'd put Kelsey through while Kelsey all but begged him to get help, and he'd waited until things had ended between them to seek it. All Alexis could do was shake her head.

"Finally. I hope he doesn't think I'm going to take him back because of it."

Alexis eyed her sister silently.

Her voice firm, Kelsey said, "I mean it, Lex. I'm done with Scott. I went down to the police station yesterday and took out a restraining order against him. And look at this." She rose from the table, grabbed her purse from the counter, and returned. Taking a small, black rectangular object from her purse, she held it up for Alexis to see.

Confused, Alexis asked, "What's that?"

"It's a stun gun. Maxwell bought it for me." Kelsey moved her finger along the side of the device, clicking a switch. An extremely bright light accompanied by a loud cracking sound emitted from one end of it.

Alexis jumped. "Geez, Kelsey. Put that thing away."

Kelsey smiled. "Don't worry, I wouldn't use it on you. But Maxwell told me that if Scott ever steps into my personal space again, I'm free to 'light his ass up.' That's a direct quote, by the way." She switched the device off and returned it to her purse.

Laughing, Alexis shook her head. "Sounds like something Max would say." Their brother wasn't one to mince words.

The whistling of the tea kettle filled the space, and Kelsey got up to attend to it. "Earl Grey okay?"

Alexis nodded just as a soft knock sounded on the door of the suite. At first, she wasn't sure if anyone had knocked because of the music still flowing from the speaker. Then she heard her mother's voice.

"Girls, it's me. Are you decent?"

Alexis laughed. Their mother had been tapping on their doors and asking that question before entering rooms ever since they were teenagers. "Yes, Mom. Come on in."

Moments later, Delphinia walked into view. Her gray hair was secured in a set of plastic hair rollers. She wore a long, white cotton nightgown. The floral pattern of blue and pink roses repeated on the robe she wore over it. Seeing Kelsey at the counter, she smiled. "Looks like I'm just in time for tea."

Once everyone had their cup of tea prepared to their liking, the three of them moved to the sofa in the living room area of the suite. Each daughter took up a cushion on one end of the sofa, with their mother sitting between them.

Wasting no time, Delphinia announced, "I feel my daughters have some things they need to tell me. Alexis, you start."

Alexis tensed as two sets of curious eyes landed on her. "What do you mean, Mom?"

Delphinia frowned. "Honestly, Alexis. Did you really think I wouldn't have any questions about this so-called engagement to Bryan? I mean, it all seems a bit sudden to me."

Alexis cringed, and she couldn't help noticing how relieved Kelsey looked not to be in the spotlight for now. "It was sudden, Mom. But I really do love him."

Delphinia's brow scrunched together, indicating her skepticism. "If you say so."

Alexis could feel herself crumbling under her mother's scrutiny. Drawing a deep breath, she told her mother and sister an abbreviated version of how her relationship with Bryan had started.

When she'd finished, Delphinia gave a slow nod. "I'm not going to lecture you about how I taught you better than to pull that kind of stunt, Alexis. But you say you're in love with him now? How has he been treating you?"

She felt the smile tilt her lips. "Like a queen." Her gaze fell on the engagement ring he'd purchased for her.

"Based on the look in your eyes, I'd say it's more than the ring that has you saying that." Kelsey looked in her direction.

Her cheeks heating, Alexis responded honestly. "It's much more than that. I know this thing started in the craziest of ways, but we are actually, factually, in love."

Delphinia smiled. "I believe you."

"Good. Because I was having a hard time believing it

myself for a while. But ever since we went to New York for that interview, everything has changed between us. It started out as a game, but it's certainly not a game anymore." She wriggled her fingers, as she'd developed a habit of doing, just so she could watch the light play over the facets of the brilliant stone on her hand.

Kelsey's eyes shifted, and she released a soft sigh.

The mood in the room changed.

Immediately, Alexis realized how what she'd said must have sounded to her sister. Guilt gripped her, because now she felt like she'd been rubbing her happiness in her sister's face. "I'm sorry, Kelsey. It can't be easy for you to listen to this right now."

Kelsey shook her head. "It's not, but I would never begrudge you happiness, Lex."

Delphinia reached over, placed her arm around Kelsey's shoulder. Giving her a squeeze, she said, "You're going to be all right, Kelsey."

Kelsey wiped at a tear as it fell down her cheek. "I don't know, Mom. After what I've been through with Scott...I'm not sure I can trust another man."

"I understand that, baby. But thankfully, there are plenty of good men out there, men who wouldn't dream of hurting you the way he did." Delphinia leaned over to kiss Kelsey's forehead, then scooted forward on the sofa. Standing, she grabbed each of her daughters by the hand. "You girls come here. I want to show you something."

Alexis rose, letting her mother lead them to the old oak buffet that occupied the wall between the living room and the kitchenette. There, Delphinia released their hands and picked up a small, silver-framed portrait. Holding it in both hands, she looked at it for a few silent moments.

Regarding the beautiful, smiling, brown-skinned woman in the portrait, Alexis spoke. "Mom, I've seen you looking at this picture before. Who is that?"

"My sister, Rose Marie." Her voice was tinged with emotion as she spoke the name.

Kelsey's eyes widened. "I didn't know you had a sister."

Alexis nodded, because she couldn't recall her mother ever mentioning this before, either.

Delphinia inhaled a long, slow breath. "Rose Marie was ten years older than me. She moved out of the house when I was seven years old. Moved in with her boyfriend, Murray."

From the way her mother's hands shook around the silver frame, Alexis could tell this story wasn't going to have a happy ending.

"I remember how your grandmother fought with Rose Marie, trying to convince her not to go. And how we both cried after she left anyway." A tear slid down Delphinia's cheek. "My sister wasn't living with that sorry excuse for a man more than a month before he beat her so bad, she ended up in the hospital. One of her wounds got infected, and next thing you know, she was gone from us."

Kelsey's hand flew to her mouth, her expression conveying shock and horror. "Oh, no."

"We buried her two months before her nineteenth birthday. Your grandmother was never the same after that." Delphinia ran her fingertips reverently over the edge of the picture frame.

Alexis dashed away her own tears, recalling the recalcitrant woman her grandmother, Lula Mae, had

COULDN'T ASK FOR MORE

been. "Now I understand why Grammy seemed so mean when we were kids. Oh, Mom. Why didn't you tell us?"

"Didn't want to dredge up that old pain." She returned the picture to its spot on the buffet, then turned to Kelsey. "Baby, I know you're hurting right now. But I'm so proud of you. So proud that you had the heart to try and protect that child and the courage to get up and leave when you had the chance. I buried my sister, but I'm so glad I didn't have to bury my baby." She touched Kelsey's tear-dampened cheek.

Seconds later, the three of them fell into a tight embrace. Alexis, with one arm around her sister and the other around her mother, let the tears fall freely. They were all a mess but with good reason. And she hoped now that everything was out in the open, they could move forward.

Bryan sat at his desk Friday afternoon, looking over the latest batch of brochures the graphic designers had sent for his approval. Royal Textiles typically created new brochures every fiscal quarter. Barring any unforeseen circumstances, he evaluated designs two quarters ahead of the time they were scheduled to be published. The designs he pored over now, if approved, would grace the print and digital marketing materials they'd release in the third quarter, next spring. This design set employed a new color scheme, and taking in the muted greens, blues, and yellows, he thought the designs very appropriate for spring.

Oscar tapped on the open door of his office. "Son, have you got a minute?"

Looking up from the mock-ups, Bryan gestured his father in. Noticing the old man's unusually cheerful expression, he asked, "What's up, Pop?"

Oscar clapped his hands together. "I've got great news. I just got a call from Esposito Couture."

Bryan's brow hitched. "Esposito Couture in Milan?"

Nodding, Oscar continued. "Yes. Bella Esposito is ready to sign with us to produce the clothes for her American line."

Now Bryan understood his father's excitement. "Really? That's easily a half-million-dollar account. So what do we need to do to seal the deal?"

"Go meet her."

His eyes grew wide. "Pop, I can't go to Milan on this kind of short notice."

Oscar smiled. "That's the best part. You don't have to. Bella is vacationing stateside, at La Jolla Beach. She's expecting you in San Diego within thirty-six hours."

Bryan frowned. "Sounds like you already told her I'd be there."

"I did."

Bryan groaned, ran his hand over his face. "Pop, you can't be serious. Are you really springing a cross-country flight on me at the last minute?"

"Sorry, Son. I didn't have a choice. Besides, you know how Bella is. She only brokers deals in person." He shrugged his shoulders. "Who knew someone her age could be so old-fashioned?"

Bryan rolled his eyes. His father loved to pull this kind of stunt on him. Bella Esposito had a very high opinion of herself and expected every man she encountered to share her opinion. While very beautiful, Bella wasn't his type. She seemed determined to be flirtatious with him, despite his overt displays of disinterest. When given a choice between spending his Saturday night with Alexis or with Bella Esposito, the choice was clear. "Pop, I had plans for tomorrow night."

Oscar waved his hand dismissively. "For a potential half-million-dollar account, you'll just have to change your plans."

"Pop." He stared at his father. "You can't be serious."

"Do you want Wesley to go in your place?" Oscar posed the question pointedly, letting his son know he had no intention of giving an inch.

Bryan rolled his eyes. "Pop, do I have to remind you that Wesley is a car salesman? He knows next to nothing about textiles and even less about how to handle a woman like Bella Esposito." Bella, by her own admission, considered herself a "connoisseur of men." Wesley, overconfident and underequipped, would undoubtedly draw her attention and subsequently be devoured.

"So you'll be taking the next available flight to San Diego, then?" Oscar winked.

With a sigh, Bryan nodded. "Fine. But I expect to go business class." If he had to deal with the hassle of airport security lines in the middle of the night, he should at least be able to fly in comfort.

"No problem, Son," Oscar called back his response as he disappeared into the corridor.

Left alone in his office, Bryan leaned his head on the backrest of his executive chair, staring at the stark white ceiling. He'd have to cancel his evening with Alexis, thus further postponing their important conversation. He wasn't looking forward to disappointing her, and he'd been looking forward to their night together as well. *How am I going to do this without upsetting her?* He hoped an answer would present itself if he stared long enough, but after a few fruitless minutes, he sat up.

Seeing no point in putting it off, he grabbed his desk phone and gave Alexis a call. After greeting her, he shifted to the reason he called. "I'm sorry, Lex. Pop is sending me to California, and I won't be back until Sunday, Monday at the latest."

"Aw." Her tone held disappointment. "This must be a pretty big deal, then."

"Yeah. It's potentially a six-figure contract, and you know my dad isn't going to let that opportunity pass."

She let a few moments go by in silence.

"I'm really sorry to have to cancel on you, baby."

"It's okay. I understand. But I will expect you to make it up to me when you get back."

He didn't miss the meaning behind her words. "Oh, don't worry. I plan on making it up to you fully, thoroughly, and in every room of my house."

She giggled. "Get back to work, Bryan. Bye."

He smiled at the sound of her laughter. "I love you."

"I love you, too." She disconnected the call.

Replacing the phone in the cradle, he turned his attention back to the brochures. Seconds later, he received a page from his secretary.

"Mr. James, Rick and Peter Goings are here to see you."

He'd been so distracted by Alexis, he'd almost forgotten the meeting he'd scheduled with his mentee and his father. He pressed the intercom button. "Send them in, please."

When Peter and Rick walked into the office, Bryan stood from his seat. This was his first time meeting Mr. Goings, and he noticed right away how much Peter resembled his father. Both were tall, over six feet, with the same brown eyes, deep complexion, and ready smile. Rick, dressed in a white button-down shirt and khaki pants, stuck his hand out. "Rick Goings, I'm Peter's father."

Bryan met them in the center of the room and extended his hand toward him. "Mr. Goings. I'm Bryan James. Very nice to meet you."

Rick shook his hand. "Nice to meet you, too, sir."

"Please, have a seat." Bryan gestured to the two armless upholstered guest chairs facing his desk.

Peter spoke then, extending his fist. "What's up, Mr. J?"

Bryan fist-bumped his young mentee. "Same old, same old. You doing okay?"

The teen nodded as he and his father took their seats.

Back in his chair on the other side of the desk, Bryan leaned forward over the desktop. "So, thanks for coming by today. I wanted to talk you about something, Peter, and I wanted your father to be here."

Rick offered a smile. "I just wanted to thank you for everything you've been doing for my son. I really appreciate it, especially you coming to the school for career day."

Bryan nodded. "You're very welcome. Peter's a good kid, very bright, and I think he'll go far in life."

"I couldn't get off work that day. The tailor shop was slammed with tuxedos for three different weddings." Rick settled back in his chair, an indication of his comfort. "Worked till almost ten o'clock that night."

Rick's mention of his work got the gears of Bryan's mind turning. "Mr. Goings, how long have you been tailoring?"

He shrugged. "Seems like forever. But it's been about seventeen years. Took the job not too long before my late wife got pregnant with Peter." He reached over, ran his hand over his son's short hair.

"Dad." Peter looked appropriately embarrassed for someone his age being given parental affection.

"I see." Bryan laced his fingers together. "So you've been sewing by hand and machine that many years?"

Rick nodded. "Hand sewing, machine sewing, trimming, even some embroidery. Not glamorous work by any stretch, but it keeps my son and me fed."

Bryan nodded. Hearing more about Rick's work helped to shed light on Peter's interest in the machines downstairs. "Nothing wrong with that. Now, back to the reason I asked you both to come here. Peter, how would you feel about taking a summer internship on the textile floor?"

Peter's eyes widened. "Really?"

Bryan nodded. "Yes, really. It would give you a chance to learn more about the business. Based on what I saw during the tour a few weeks back, you're interested in how it all works."

Peter nodded. "I am."

"Well, you're welcome to spend the summer here, working. Three days a week, nine dollars an hour. If it's okay with your father." Bryan looked to Rick.

Leaning forward in his chair, Rick furrowed his brow. "What does the job involve?"

"He'd start out observing and acting as a runner between departments. If he shows promise, he could possibly be trained on the embroidery machines." Bryan remembered the way Peter's interest had been sparked during his visit to that department.

Rick looked thoughtful. "I don't have any problem with it. I think it will be good experience for him."

Peter looked between the two men like an audience member at a tennis match but said nothing.

Finally, Bryan asked, "What do you say, Peter? Would you like the job?"

Peter spoke then. "Yeah. That's real cool of you, Mr. J. Thanks."

"You're welcome. Do either of you have any questions for me?" Bryan looked between father and son.

Rick stood. "No. Not at the moment."

"If you think of anything, give me a call. Peter knows how to reach me." Bryan stood, offered the man another handshake.

A few minutes later, Rick and Peter departed, leaving Bryan alone in his office again. Taking note of the time, Bryan shook his head and tucked away the mock-ups from the graphic designers. He'd have to look over them when he got back from California.

Right now, I need to get home and get ready for this flight.

Chapter 22

ALEXIS STROLLED ACROSS THE PARKING LOT AT THE North Carolina State Fairgrounds, with Sydney walking next to her. It was a sunny Saturday morning in late September, and they'd come to see the venue where the first fashion show for Krystal Kouture would be held in just seven days.

She looked around, taking in the sights and sounds as they drew closer to the building. Already, preparations were under way for the Carolina Fashion and Music Festival. Signage and décor for the event were already up on the facades of several of the buildings on the fairground property. Now, the area bustled with activity as people hauled props, instruments, and equipment out of trucks and took them into the Exposition Center, where the festival would be held.

Sydney opened the door of the center, held it open for Alexis to enter behind her. Once they were inside the lobby, Alexis swept her eyes over the interior. The space was an atrium, with high ceilings and dozens of windows, allowing the sunlight to shine freely into it. "We're supposed to meet someone here from the staff. What was her name again?"

"Claudine. She's the event coordinator for the center." Sydney leaned against the wall, her phone in hand. "Should be here any moment."

Alexis took out her own phone, glancing at the

electronic to-do list she kept in her notes app. *I still have so much to do to get ready for this show*. She'd waited a long time to showcase her art via a fashion show, but now that it was so close, she felt ill-prepared. "Did we ever fill the last model slot for the show?"

Without looking up from the glowing screen of her phone, Sydney shook her head. "Nah. Look on the bright side, though. If we don't find someone, you can always model the dress."

Alexis rolled her eyes. "I'm not a model. I'm a designer, and I do my best to stick to my skill set, Syd."

Sydney scoffed. "Whatever. You and I both know you could slay that dress."

Alexis shook her head. The dress in question, Smoke, was a dove-gray taffeta and silk creation with a high-low hemline. Personally, Alexis thought she was too short to pull off a dress like that. But if they didn't hire someone soon, she wouldn't have a choice. The unique cut of the dress called for a certain body type, a curvier frame than the other five models possessed.

A woman walked in then, wearing black slacks and a red sweater. She had brown hair cut in a blunt bob, brown eyes, and olive skin. A clipboard was tucked beneath her left arm. "Morning, ladies. I'm Claudine. Are you two from the design house?"

Alexis stuck out her hand. "Hi. I'm Alexis Devers, the designer. This is my business partner, Sydney Greer."

Claudine shook each of their hands in turn, offering a small smile before returning to her all-business demeanor. "Nice to meet you ladies. I'll be taking you on a tour of the facility so you can familiarize yourself with the layout prior to your event."

Sydney tucked her phone away. "Sounds good."

Claudine launched into a speech, one she'd obviously given many times before. "The Exposition Center is a fifty-thousand-square-foot facility with an open floor plan to allow event hosts maximum flexibility. Our staff will assist the festival organizers with staging, electrical hookups, and the like. We have ample bathroom facilities for your eventgoers, as well as concession operations, a loading dock, and drive-through access if needed."

Alexis looked to her left, pointed at the set of doors there. "Will the whole festival be in this building, or does it extend into the Graham Building as well?" The Jim Graham Building, another of the fairground's event venues, connected to the Exposition Center via a concrete breezeway.

Claudine shook her head. "You won't have to go next door. The event organizers worked with our staff to come up with a layout that allows the entire event to take place inside the center. With North Carolina weather being as fickle as it is, they wanted to keep things simple."

Sydney laughed. "Good plan."

Alexis silently agreed. Having lived most of her life in the Tar Heel State, she was all too familiar with the random weather pattern.

"Okay, ladies, follow me. I'm going to give you a complete tour so you can be as prepared as possible for what you'll be dealing with next weekend. There's going to be a lot of walking." Claudine started walking, beckoning them with her finger.

Looking down at her feet, Alexis was glad she'd

worn a pair of tennis shoes with her long-sleeved T-shirt and boot-cut jeans. Sydney, who'd worn a sweater, leggings, and black boots with a stiletto heel, didn't look so pleased.

Claudine guided Alexis and Sydney from the lobby into a cavernous space alive with sound and activity. The space resembled an enormous beehive, with folks wearing festival T-shirts moving about and carrying signs, partitions, and more. The cacophony of conversation, footsteps, and hammering echoed through the room.

Claudine's voice broke through the aural clutter. "Ladies, this is the main area where the event will take place. I'll show you more of that later. Let me show you our other areas first." She led them along the westernmost area of the building, pointing out the office, restrooms, concession stand, nurses' area, and the corridors running between the areas to allow access.

After that thorough tour, Claudine led them back out into the huge main space. "This is the exhibit area. It comprises over thirty-nine thousand square feet, the lion's share of the Exhibition Center's floor space. There's room here for two hundred and twenty booths, so we don't anticipate any traffic flow problems for the ten to fifteen thousand people we expect to visit during the festival."

Alexis's eyes widened as she heard that figure.

Sydney, as always, seemed to read her mind. "Wow. That's a lot of exposure for our designs, Lex."

"You're telling me." Alexis's gaze swept the room, watching the staff members busying themselves with outfitting the space for the festival.

Raising her hands and gesturing toward the activity,

Claudine spoke again. "The setup for the festival will include two runways, here and here." She gestured to the spaces, outlined on the floor in colorful tape. "Between the two runways, where you see that large rectangle marked out, is where the stage will be set up for the bands that are playing."

Alexis centered herself on the rectangle representing the stage and let her creative brain take over. She could clearly imagine the show in progress, with one of her models strutting down each of the runways as a band played musical accompaniment. She pointed to the huge, blank wall behind the area. "What's going to be up there?"

For the first time, Claudine seemed unsure. "I'm not a hundred percent sure on that, but from what I understand, there will be some kind of projected images behind the stage. The organizers did have us bring in a projector and a white screen."

Alexis nodded, the possibilities of that playing in her mind. "Syd, we need to curate some images to accompany our show."

Sydney snatched her phone from her pocket. "I'm on it." She glanced Claudine's way. "Where will our staging area be? Where our models can change?"

Claudine gestured to the left of the stage. "That entire section of the floor will be cordoned off and inaccessible to the public. Partitions will be put up to allow your models, as well as the band members and essential personnel, a place to prepare. Security guards will be stationed around the perimeter of the area to ensure the public is kept out."

"Great. I'll let the girls know." Alexis knew the models would feel better knowing the setup beforehand

and that they'd be protected from any would-be pervs hoping to get a peek at them in their underthings.

"So do you ladies have any questions or concerns for me?" Claudine looked back and forth between the two of them.

"What time should we be here with our staff and models?" Alexis wanted to be sure she had ample time to get things together for her very first fashion show.

Claudine tapped her chin with her index finger. "The show is Saturday night at seven, but the building will be open from seven that morning. You're free to come and go all day between seven a.m. and five p.m. After that, we'll want to limit traffic between the staging area and the public access areas."

"Got it." Having access to the space a full twelve hours before the start of the show would be more than enough.

Sydney piped up. "This isn't related to our show, but what musical acts are playing?"

Claudine smiled. "There are a few flyers in the lobby."

"We'll grab one on the way out." Sydney grabbed Alexis by the arm. "Thank you, Claudine. You've been a great help."

"Glad to hear it. I'll see you ladies in a week, then." She waved as Alexis and Sydney slipped through the doors into the lobby.

Walking across the parking lot again toward Sydney's car, Alexis listened to her partner read some of the names of the musical acts listed on the flyer.

"Wow. It's a pretty good lineup. J. Cole, the Tams, Joyce Cooling, Kellie Pickler. Nice mix." Sydney folded the flyer and tucked it into her purse.

"I might hang around for some of the performances."
Alexis fished around in her purse for her sunglasses and
slipped them on to shield her eyes from the glare.

When they reached the car, Alexis slid into the passenger seat and buckled in. As the car pulled away, she
looked back on the Exhibition Center and smiled.

Seven days.

———∿∿∿———

Bryan's flight touched down in San Diego around one
a.m. Pacific time. He disembarked the plane bleary-eyed
and grouchy, wondering why his father would subject
him to this on a Saturday morning. Barely awake, he
dragged himself through the airport and into his hired
sedan, which delivered him to the Marriott Marquis
San Diego Marina. Once he made it to his room, he col-
lapsed into bed fully dressed.

He awakened close to one that afternoon. Sitting up
in the king-size bed, he caught a glimpse of himself
in the mirror across the room. He ran a hand over his
shaggy face and shook his head. *I look like I've been up
half the night.* Determined that he wouldn't look the way
he felt, as his mother used to say, he crawled out of bed
and headed for the shower.

Once he'd showered, shaved, and put on a fresh suit,
he checked the time again. He was due to meet Bella
in the lounge downstairs soon, so he slipped into his
dress loafers, ran a boar bristle brush over his hair, and
grabbed his briefcase.

A short elevator ride took him to the lobby level,
and he crossed the broad, tiled corridor to the Marina
Kitchen. The restaurant was crowded today, and he

noticed a lot of people standing around with their smartphones in hand as if waiting for something or someone. He glanced around the space until he located the marble bar, flanked by tall white columns. He approached the bar, set his briefcase on the floor. Taking a seat on one of the stools, he leaned against the backrest and ordered a ginger ale.

He'd taken about two good sips of the cold, bubbly beverage when he paused. He could feel a set of eyes boring into his back. Setting the glass down, he turned toward the sensation. Sure enough, Bella Esposito, her smiling eyes locked on him, headed his way. She wore a flowing red sundress of her own design, the halter top secured around her graceful neck with a thin ribbon. Waves of thick black hair hung around her shoulders, and the large, circular frames of her sunglasses obscured much of her face. This dressed-down version of Bella bore little resemblance to her usual impeccably styled, coiffed, and flashy public presentation. Matching her smile, he awaited her arrival.

When she came abreast of him, she tugged the sunglasses down the bridge of her nose, just enough to reveal the merriment dancing in her ice-blue eyes. She shimmied them back into place a second later. "Bryan. So good to see you again." Her heavy Italian accent made each word sound a bit more dramatic.

He stood, pulled out the stool next to him. "Hello, Bella. It's been a while since I saw you last. How have you been?"

"*Molto bene, grazie.*" She placed a fleeting kiss on each of his cheeks, then eased onto the seat of the stool. "*Come stai*, Bryan?"

Putting his basic understanding of conversational Italian to use for the first time in months, he responded. "*Sto bene, signorina.* Would you care for a drink?"

"Of course, thank you. My usual, darling." Her eyes and her tone indicated her level of flirtatious banter was at its typical high.

Turning to the bartender, Bryan ordered for her. "A kamikaze for the lady, please. Put it on my bill." He couldn't help thinking how much the drink reflected Bella: petite, attractive, and powerful.

She caught the shot glass as the bartender slid it toward her, but her eyes remained locked on Bryan as she brought it to her lips. Per her usual way, she sipped from the glass, rather than downing the shot all at once, before setting it down again.

The noise level in the restaurant suddenly rose, and the crowd began moving toward the lobby concourse. Bryan looked around but couldn't see what had caused the commotion. "Bella, do you know what's going on?"

She shook her head as she took another sip of her drink. "The hotel has been crowded this way since I arrived. I've mostly kept in my room and the pool bar."

The bartender, who stood nearby polishing glasses, volunteered an answer. "You know the singer, Jill Scott?"

"Yeah." Bryan waited for the man to finish.

"She's doing a show tonight at the House of Blues, and she's staying here. This place has been jumping since folks found out she's here." He set down the glass he'd been polishing, then carried the tray of clean glasses away.

Bryan nodded his understanding. The lure of seeing a celebrity in person motivated people to do things they wouldn't normally do. As the sea of people began moving toward the bar, Bryan realized that Jilly from Philly was indeed in the building.

Bella said something.

Bryan couldn't hear her over the din of conversation, so he turned her way. "I'm sorry, what?"

She draped her arm over his shoulder, leaned in closer to him. "Thank you for the drink." Then she kissed him, right on the lips.

He backed away as quickly as he could. He didn't want to prolong the kiss, but he didn't want to offend her, either. Knowing the European tendency toward kissing in greeting and thanks, and Bella's tendency toward flirting, he couldn't tell what she'd been trying to accomplish. Either way, he knew his dad would have a fit if he returned to Raleigh without Bella's signature on a contract, especially since the company had footed the bill for Bryan's business class airfare.

The powerhouse singer approached the bar with two strapping security guards flanking her. Shouts of her name were accompanied by the flashing of cameras capturing her image. She smiled at Bryan and Bella, ordered herself a soda, and moved away. The whole incident took less than five minutes, but by the time Jill moved on, Bryan could see spots before his eyes.

He blinked rapidly, hoping to clear his field of vision. When he refocused, his eyes landed on the face of a man in the crowd. He frowned. *That guy looks so familiar.* The man in question didn't seem to notice Bryan looking at him as he fiddled with the controls on a large, rather fancy, camera.

Bella's voice broke through his thoughts. "Your father sent you to collect my signature, no?"

He smiled. "Yes. We know you prefer to do business in person, and we respect that." He reached down for his briefcase.

She stayed him by placing her hand on his shoulder. "Not yet, Bryan. I still expect to be sold." Mischief lit her eyes as she spoke.

He smiled despite the pang of annoyance he felt inside. "Certainly, Bella. Let me tell you about the updates we've made to our equipment and processes at Royal." For the next several minutes, he told her everything he could think of that might sway her in his favor, no matter how dull it seemed to him. He spoke of the recently updated machines in the sewing department, the new quality control procedures his workers now employed, and the revitalized training program for their machinists. "Did I mention we're the exclusive producer of J. Cole Jeans? Also, we've just locked down a contract for a new line that's generating a lot of buzz—"

She raised her hand, chuckling. "*Abbastanza, abbastanza*. Your point is made, so hand me the contract, Bryan."

Retrieving and opening his briefcase, he handed her the contract along with a pen. "If you're ever in North Carolina, you should stop by and visit the factory floor."

Bella spent several minutes in silence, reading over the four-page document. She posed a few questions as she read and responded favorably to his answers. Once she was satisfied, she scribbled her signature on the contract and handed it back to him. "I plan to. I'll have my assistant set something up when the time comes."

He took the pen and contract back, tucked them into

his case, and shut it. "We at Royal appreciate your business and the trust you've placed in us."

She finished the last sip of her drink before replying. "I have very high expectations. But since I've worked with you before, I know you'll meet them." She slipped from the stool, stood. "Now if you'll excuse me, I'm going to get back to vacationing."

He raised his glass in her direction. "*Arrivederci,* Bella."

With a fluttering of her fingertips, she walked away, disappearing into the crowd.

After she'd left, he turned back to his ginger ale. The encounter with Bella hadn't been as tedious as he'd feared. The last time they'd met, several months ago in Paris, she'd insisted he take her out for drinks. That night had been a long one, but he supposed the rapport he'd developed with her then had laid the foundation for their dealings.

After the Paris trip, Bella had signed on with Royal to produce a single item from her line. At the time, she'd made it clear that she'd submitted the same design to two other American textile mills to test the quality of the finished product and decide who to work with on her future designs. Oscar, confident in his employees and his company, had welcomed the challenge, and Royal had come out on top. Bella expressed her immense satisfaction with the dress they'd made for her once it came off the line and mentioned wanting to work with them again. With the contract she'd just signed, Royal would have exclusive American production rights on her latest collection.

The contract would also mean a monetary gain to

Royal, to the tune of four hundred and eighty thousand dollars. Bryan smiled as he drained the last of his drink. *Maybe I can convince Pop to give me a raise.*

And even if he couldn't get the raise, he hoped his success with securing the Esposito account would at least be enough to convince his father to send Wesley back to the car dealership where he belonged.

Chapter 23

ALEXIS STOOD IN THE DRESSMAKER'S SUITE OF HER office Monday afternoon, her clipboard in hand. The suite, which occupied the entire eastern third of Krystal Kouture Design House, was the domain of her master seamstress, Pam Avalon. The space held Pam's machine, dressmaker's dummies, fabric, and supplies, as well as three small changing rooms for the fit models to use.

All around Alexis, the room was alive with activity. She'd called her five models, of whom four were temporary hires, to make sure the designs for the show were properly fitted.

Pam, kneeling on the floor to adjust the hemline of a dress worn by one of the models, turned her eyes up toward Alexis. "What do you think, Ms. Devers? Higher?"

Alexis stooped to look at the current hem. "No, that's high enough. Remember, our tagline is 'Dare to Be Demure.' Any higher than that and we'll have to change it."

"Gotcha." Pam chuckled as she affixed several straight pins to the garment to keep the hem in place.

Looking around at the women trying on her designs, Alexis noticed Sydney wasn't in the room. She attributed that to the presence of Kim Wells, a reporter from the *News & Observer*. Kim had been sent over to document Alexis's perspective and the preparations for her runway debut, and she'd brought along a photographer.

Sydney could be trusted to make herself scarce whenever a camera appeared, assuming she was aware of it.

Shrugging, Alexis walked over to where Kim sat. She'd taken up a seat at Pam's sewing table while the photographer wandered around the room, camera in hand, to capture anything of particular interest.

"Is there anything else you need right now, Kim?"

"Let me ask you a few questions. Shouldn't take too long."

"Sure." Alexis grabbed a stool from the corner and carried it over to the sewing table. Sitting down, she said, "Go ahead."

Kim, with her tablet and stylus in front of her, looked her way. "The article I'm writing will be a feature, covering your preparations leading up to the show as well as the show itself. So I'd really like to get your thoughts on what this all means to you."

Glancing around at the myriad of things happening in her surroundings, Alexis smiled. "This means everything for me. As a teen, I spent hours flipping through the pages of fashion magazines. I loved Vera Wang, Tracy Reese, Anna Wintour. When I wasn't perusing the magazines, I had my sketchbook and pencil, drawing out designs of my own. To have made it through design school, interned for Tracy Reese, and opened my design house with my awesome friend and business partner has been so amazing for me. This show, my very first show, is going to be the cherry on top."

Kim jotted on the tablet as Alexis spoke. "Your story is very compelling, and to have accomplished so much at such a young age is really remarkable. Tell me, are there any other artists in your family?"

She nodded. "My brother is an artist of sorts, since he's an architect. But my mom and dad had very 'normal' jobs—he owns a chain of auto mechanic shops, and she taught biology at Shaw before she retired. Our parents never tried to force us to go into the same kind of work they did. They only insisted that we work hard and give our best to whatever we decided to pursue."

The reporter nodded as she took more notes. "Thank you. I think we're good for right now. We'll observe, take a few more pictures, and then be out of your hair—at least until the show Saturday."

"Cool. Thanks." Alexis continued past the desk and left the dressmaker's suite. The lobby was exceptionally quiet, and she noticed Dawn wasn't at her post behind the reception desk. Moving through the lobby into the corridor, she was about to pass by Sydney's office on the way to her own when she peeped in through the open door.

Inside the office were Sydney and Dawn. Both were silently looking up, their eyes glued to Sydney's wall-mounted flat-screen television.

Alexis's brow furrowed. "What's going on?"

Sydney looked her way, her expression grim. "You probably should take a look at this, Lex."

Alexis entered the office, wondering why Sydney and Dawn looked so stricken. When she looked up at the screen, she saw what they were watching. It was *The Tea*, the gossip show she and Bryan had recently appeared on.

Lynn, the same woman who'd interviewed them, was on screen now. "You know *The Tea* is all about giving you the straight dirt. Well, this weekend, our camera crew was in San Diego, covering singer Jill Scott and her show at the Hard Rock Cafe. When we followed her to the bar at the hotel where she was staying, our cameras spotted textiles exec Bryan James, hugged up with a woman at the bar. But, Tea Drinkers, this woman was not his fiancée, up-and-coming designer Alexis Devers. Put up those pictures, y'all."

Alexis watched with horror as images of Bryan, sharing a kiss with a gorgeous dark-haired woman she'd never seen before, filled the screen. Her brow furrowed as the show's producers paged through image after image, showing the two of them kissing in the background of several photos focused on Jill Scott. Apparently, their cameraman had gotten video and isolated it into a bunch of still frames, showing the kiss from beginning to end.

Lynn continued her commentary. "We reached out to the hotel, but they refused to identify the mystery woman. But we did do some digging of our own, and our intrepid reporters could find images of Bryan James in various settings with several different women, all from within the last six months. Let me emphasize that none of these women were Alexis Devers. Take a look at what we found."

Alexis tore her eyes away from the screen rather than be subjected to any more photographs of Bryan with other women. She'd seen enough but noted that Sydney and Dawn didn't look away.

Sydney cringed for the umpteenth time. "Oh, shit."

As Alexis's heart rate steadily increased, she thought her friend's assessment was spot-on. She had a few other curse words she'd like to add, but she held her tongue.

She could not, however, stop her fists from clenching at her sides.

Lynn's voice came over the television speakers again. "Now, if you recall, Alexis wasn't ready to announce a wedding date during my recent interview with the couple. I don't know about y'all, but I think this might be why."

Stalking over to Sydney's desk, Alexis grabbed the remote and shut the television off. With tears in her eyes, she announced, "That's enough of this gossip crap for the day. In case y'all forgot, we have our debut fashion show in five days." She tried to push away the knot of pain forming in her chest. She'd worked too hard for too long to get to this point in her design career, and she refused to let her emotions get the better of her at such a crucial time.

Sydney walked over, placed her arm around Alexis's trembling shoulder. "Are you okay, Lex?"

She shook her head, letting the tears fall unchecked. She said nothing, because there were no words to describe the level of hurt and humiliation she felt. She remembered him inviting her to his house for dinner before he'd been called away on business and had to cancel. He'd said he had things he needed to discuss with her, things that he'd rather not discuss over the phone. Had this been what he'd wanted to talk about? Did he really believe it would have gone over better in person? Would he have admitted outright to being a womanizer, or had he prepared some artful explanation as to why his past behavior had no bearing on their current relationship?

Dawn, never one for emotional shows, slipped out of the office.

Sydney continued to hold Alexis. "Whatever comes next, whatever you decide to do, I'm here for you, girl."

Taking a deep breath, Alexis dashed away her tears. "Thanks, Syd." She gathered herself enough to return her friend's embrace, drawing a modicum of comfort from her steady presence. She willed her breathing to become slower, deeper, pushing away the sadness threatening to overwhelm her. The more she reined in her breathing, the more righteous indignation rose within her.

As if sensing her changing mood, Sydney released her and backed away. "Lex, what are you thinking right now?"

"I'm thinking about going to his house."

"When?"

She was already moving toward the door. "Right now. After all, he did invite me."

Sydney's eyes widened. "I don't know if that's such a good idea right now."

"Whatever. It may not be a good idea, but I'm going over there anyway to tell him about himself." She stalked out of the office, stopping in her own office long enough to grab her purse and jacket.

Sydney followed her, matching her step for step as she shrugged the jacket on and headed for the main entrance. "Alexis, don't do this. If you go over there now, while you're angry, you'll wind up saying something you'll regret."

Pushing open the door, Alexis glanced Sydney's way. "I'll call you later." Then she strode out into the afternoon chill without a backward glance.

—∿∿—

When Bryan arrived home from work on Monday, he immediately snatched off his tie and sport coat. He'd stopped for dinner on the way home so he wouldn't have to bother with cooking. His body was still trying to recover from his cross-country round-trip travel over the weekend, and tonight, he looked forward to an entire evening of doing absolutely nothing.

It had been a long day at the office. While Oscar had made a big deal out of Bryan's securing the contract with Bella Esposito, that hadn't meant any less work for him. He'd been stuck behind his desk all day, when what he really wanted to be doing was talking to Alexis, touching her, kissing her, making love to her. He'd only spoken to her briefly on Sunday after returning from his trip. Today's epic workload had kept him from calling her, despite how much he missed her. *Maybe I'll call her later.*

He took some time to shower, then changed into a white tee and a comfortable pair of gray sweatpants. Crashed out on his couch, he pored over his copy of the *Wall Street Journal*. He'd been told more than once to upgrade to a digital subscription, but he'd kept his regular one anyway. Something about reading the stock reports on a screen made them seem less credible, so he stuck to his preference of reading them on paper.

He studied the textiles and fabric stocks, noting the general rising trend of the last few weeks. *Culp Industries is pulling a pretty nice profit lately.* Only a few American textiles companies that were publicly traded remained in the reports, due to the trend of outsourcing labor and importing textiles from outside the country. Royal wasn't publicly traded; Oscar thought running the business in the current climate complex enough without the added burden of kowtowing to shareholders. Bryan wholeheartedly agreed with his father's assessment.

Bang! Bang!

He jumped, dropping the paper, and turned his head toward the sound. Someone was knocking—no, pounding—on his front door. "What the hell?" Muttering under his breath, he got up and walked across his living room.

When he flung the door open and saw Alexis standing on his porch, a mixture of surprise and delight flooded him. She looked gorgeous as always, in a pair of black jeans, a green blouse, and a black leather jacket. Her hair was pulled up in a high ponytail, and she smelled like candy and sexiness. "Lex. It's good to see you, baby." Seeing her made the desire to touch her rise again. He reached out for her, intent on pulling her into his arms and giving her the kiss he'd been saving up for three full days.

She deftly dodged him, stepping to the right. "Don't touch me, Bryan."

Confused, he dropped his hands. "I was going to call you…" His voice trailed off as he took a good look at her face. The beautiful smile he'd come to love was nowhere to be seen. The lines of her face were taut, her lips were curved downward, and her brown eyes flashed with angry fire.

Arms folded across her chest, effectively cutting off any access to her body, Alexis took a step forward that brought her almost into his doorframe.

He stepped aside, gestured. "Do you want to come in?"

The stern shake of her head met his question. "No. I'm not staying."

He watched the negativity playing over her features for a few seconds before asking the question he had to ask but dreaded the answer to. "Lex, what's wrong?"

"Oh, I guess you didn't watch *The Tea* today."

His brow furrowed. "No. I was at work, and besides, I never watch that show." It was the truth. The show was basically a gossip rag, played out in real time.

"You didn't seem to have a problem with it when they interviewed us." She glared at him.

He leaned against his doorframe, sensing he'd need the support. "I did the interview because you asked me to. I never had any interest in the show, and that hasn't changed since they interviewed us."

She pursed her lips. "Well, we caught the show at the office today. Do you want to tell me what you were doing kissing some dark-haired woman in San Diego this weekend?"

He frowned, not making the connection. "What?"

"Their cameras were there for Jill Scott, and they just happened to catch you lip-locking with someone at the bar. I thought you were going on a business trip, Bryan. Is this how you do business?" Her tone was harsh, accusing.

What is she ranting about? It took a few moments before he made the connection. Then he remembered it: the guy with the camera who looked familiar and Bella Esposito kissing him on the lips to thank him for the drink he'd bought for her. *I knew I'd seen that guy before. He was the cameraman when* The Tea *interviewed us*. "Oh, you mean Bella. That was my client."

She scoffed. "Bryan, please. Do you make a habit of kissing your clients on the lips?"

He let his head drop back, then blew out a breath. Up until now, he hadn't known she was capable of such attitude. "Lex, I didn't kiss Bella. She kissed me. That's just how she is. I brought her the contract to sign, bought her a drink, and she was thanking me."

She shifted her weigh to the right, propped her fists on her hips. "The people at *The Tea* couldn't identify the woman. If that was the famous Bella Esposito, why didn't they know that?"

This is getting out of hand. How much more explaining did she expect him to do? "She had on these enormous sunglasses, which I'm sure you saw in the pictures, and she wasn't dressed the way she normally is. She did that on purpose, because she was on vacation and didn't want to be bothered. Why are you acting like this?"

"If it was just her, I probably wouldn't be acting this way. But when they started showing photos of you with all those other women, all from the last six months…" Her words trailed off, and she looked away.

He sighed. His work often put him in the position of socializing with designers, executives, and sometimes models in an effort to get them to sign on the dotted line. "All work. There have been plenty of times I had to take someone out for drinks, dinner, whatever, so I could close the deal for the company."

She appeared skeptical, with her gaze focused on the floor of his porch.

"It's true I'm an executive. But I work in marketing, which at times can mean I'm just a glorified salesman."

"I know what it means. Don't patronize me, Bryan."

"Lex, I'm not trying to patronize you. But please know, this is the first serious relationship I've had in

COULDN'T ASK FOR MORE   289

years. I'm not seeing anyone else, I swear." He wanted to reach for her again, but he sensed the folly in that.

She looked his way with tears standing in her eyes. "Did you sleep with any of those women, Bryan?"

He went silent. Memories of the nights he'd spent with women in Paris, Milan, and Madrid flashed through his mind, and he couldn't bring himself to admit to what he'd done. He also couldn't lie to her.

In response to his silence, tears flooded her eyes and streamed down her cheeks. "I knew it. I can't believe I let you pull me in, make me believe you really cared about me." She started backing away.

He followed. "Lex, please. We didn't get into all the details of each other's past relationships. This is why I wanted you to come over, so I could let you know—"

"That you're a womanizer?" She turned away, stepped off the end of the porch. "Save it, Bryan."

Frustration got the better of him, and he blurted, "Come on, Lex. It's not like you're a virgin." The moment he said it, he cringed.

She glanced his way with narrowed eyes, then turned and started walking.

"Don't leave like this. Give me a chance to explain…"

She stopped on the sidewalk, turned his way.

The pain in her red-rimmed eyes crushed his soul, silencing him.

She took a deep breath. "It's over, Bryan." She grasped the engagement ring he'd given her, yanked it off, and dropped it on the sidewalk as if it were no more important than a crumpled gum wrapper.

And without another word or glance in his direction, she marched to her car, got in, and started the engine.

Standing in his front yard, he watched her drive away. He cursed, kicking himself for screwing things up with her. He'd wanted to tell her that he'd been searching for something missing in his life, trying to fill the hole in his heart with empty, meaningless sex. It hadn't worked, though. He'd never felt fully himself, never felt whole, until she entered his life. He didn't know if she was in the right mental space to receive that, but it was true.

And now, because he hadn't been up-front with her, he'd probably lost her.

Forever.

He walked to where she'd thrown the ring, stooping to pick it up. It still sparkled, just as it had in the store. But somehow, it had lost its luster. Pocketing it, he turned and trudged back into his house, shutting the door against the rising darkness.

Chapter 24

On that Saturday morning, Alexis had arrived at the Exposition Center with Sydney in tow. She'd given Dawn, Pam, and the models specific instructions about what time they should arrive and everything they needed to bring. As she stood near the staging area, looking around the exhibit hall, she could feel her nerves fraying like a worn shoelace.

She'd dressed in jeans and a sweatshirt, choosing comfort for the early part of the day. Since they'd been unable to find another model, Alexis would walk the runway in the Smoke dress, and she just hoped she wouldn't fall flat on her face. Modeling wasn't something she had any interest in, but circumstances dictated that she step into that role, just for today.

She inhaled deeply, the smell of popcorn wafting from the concession stand to fill her nostrils. Looking around the space, she could see all the things Claudine had described when they'd toured the center the previous week. The tape outlines were gone, replaced with the real thing: two long, arrow-shaped runways, centered by a rectangular stage. The white screen for the projected images had been hung behind the stage, and a small control platform had been erected in front of the stage. Alexis assumed the person manning the platform would be responsible for the lighting and the projected images festivalgoers would be viewing.

Wearing the laminated passes they'd been given when they entered, Alexis and Sydney walked past the security guards. As one of the guards held the velvet rope aloft for her to pass, Alexis realized she felt a bit like a celebrity. Tall metal partitions, covered with fabric, had been erected to separate a space for them. The partitions touched the floor and were about seven feet tall. The way in which they were set up left no gaps below or between them, and Alexis felt secure in the knowledge that she and the models would be afforded sufficient privacy for their wardrobe changes.

The area had been outfitted with three free-standing full-length mirrors, two long tables, and eight folding chairs. It wasn't fancy by any stretch, but they had all the basics they'd need to pull off their first show.

Sydney, sitting on one of the folding chairs in their dressing area, crossed her legs. "I still think we came too early. What are we gonna do here all day?"

Alexis shook her head. "I had to get out of the house." She didn't elaborate, knowing she didn't need to. Sydney knew all about what had transpired between Alexis and Bryan.

Sydney chuckled. "I know, and I understand that. You've been complaining to me all week about what went down between you two. But you seem to have forgotten, I tried to stop you from going over there in the first place."

Alexis frowned. "I had to. Besides, it was bound to happen eventually. I said what I had to say, and now I'm through with it." She left out the fact that she'd cried herself to sleep the night she'd ended things with Bryan and every night since. She couldn't describe the yawning emptiness she felt without him in her life, but if he were the kind of man to sleep around, then he wasn't the kind of man she needed.

Sydney sighed. "Whatever. I'm here for you, just like I said I would be." She gestured toward the stage, a few feet away. "Looks like they're setting up for the first musical performance. Why don't we snag a seat and enjoy the music?"

"Sounds good. I need something to get my mind off my nervousness." *And off Bryan*.

They found seats near the front just in time for the first show, which was given by smooth jazz guitarist Joyce Cooling. Throughout the late morning and early afternoon, Alexis and Sydney enjoyed several different musical acts. Between sets, they wandered to the booths set up around the perimeter of the exhibition hall, where vendors were selling purses, scarves, jewelry, and other accessories. Local musicians had also set up shop in the space, selling recordings of their work. Alexis was impressed with the festival, and the more she mingled with the other artists present, the prouder she felt to be a part of the event.

Around five, the entire Krystal Kouture crew gathered in their dressing area. Standing amid her staff and models, Alexis felt her heart pounding in her chest like the bass line of an old-school rap track. "Ladies, I just want to say that I have so much gratitude for you all, for everything you've done and everything you're about to do to make this show a reality. I have the highest confidence in you all. Let's go out there and slay this runway, girls."

Smiles and applause met her words, and the flurry

of activity began in earnest. Alexis helped the models into their first outfits, monitored the two makeup artists working on their faces, and gave approval on hairstyles. Amid all that, she paced the floor.

Sydney tapped her on the shoulder, pulling her out of her thoughts. "Lex, it's six nineteen. Maybe you should stop pacing and get dressed. Unless you want to be seen on the runway in jeans and a sweatshirt."

"Crap." She darted away, opening her small trunk and taking out the black mermaid dress she'd designed for the show. With Sydney's help, she slipped into the dress, then did her own hair and makeup.

Regarding her reflection in the mirror, she smiled. She'd waited for this night since she was fifteen years old, doodling dresses in her sketchbook. The fantasy was finally coming true, and yet she felt a strange sense of emptiness. She didn't have to guess what was wrong. The state of things between her and Bryan had her feeling somewhat melancholy. Still, she'd worked too hard to let that ruin this day. So she put on her best smile, determined to make it a memorable night.

"Knock, knock."

Alexis turned toward the opening in their partition to see her mother, Delphinia, sticking her head in through the curtain. She walked over, threw her arms around her mother's neck. "Hey, Mom."

"I won't hold you long, baby, because I know you're busy." Delphinia returned her embrace, then stepped back. "You look gorgeous. Everybody's here, Maxwell, Kelsey, and your father, and we'll be cheering for you."

"Thank you."

Delphinia kissed her on the forehead. "I'm so proud

of you. I love you." There were tears standing in her eyes to accompany the wide smile on her face.

Alexis held back the tears threatening to ruin her makeup. "I love you, too, Mom."

They were one model short, since one of the girls had pulled out at the last minute. So tonight, Alexis would model another look before she debuted the Smoke dress. Once her mother left, Alexis slipped into the pair of low-heeled black pumps she'd chosen for her first look. Careful not to wrinkle her dress, she sat down, awaiting her cue.

As the lights went down and the announcer called her name, Alexis stood. She felt like a teenage girl, being escorted out on the football field as homecoming queen. She took slow, deep breaths in an attempt to keep calm as she made her way to her mark.

"You got this!" Sydney gave her shoulder a squeeze.

She stepped out onto the left runway and waved to the crowd. Applause filled her ears, making her smile. She gestured to Sydney, lurking backstage, in an attempt to get her to come out and share in the glory. In the end, Sydney's shyness won out, and Alexis stood alone as the figurehead of Krystal Kouture. She looked out on the faces in the crowd, saw her family sitting in the third row. Her gaze traveled further back, and her breath caught in her throat for a moment.

Is that Bryan? She could swear she saw him, sitting a couple of rows behind her parents and siblings. She pushed the thought away, hoping he'd have better sense than to show up here after what had happened between them.

The music began, signaling the models to come, and

Alexis left the runway as the first two of her models began their walk. The local soul band on the stage played a midtempo tune that provided a perfect backdrop for the show.

"We should go ahead and put you in the Smoke dress. That way, you'll be ready when it's time for you to walk out again."

Alexis nodded. "You put me last, right?"

"Yes. It makes sense because you'll have to go out last anyway to take your bows as the designer." Sydney went to the portable dress rack the seamstress had rolled in and unzipped the bag containing the dress.

Sweeping her gaze over the shimmering gray silk and the billows of glitter-laced taffeta, she sighed. "It's been so long since I've seen this dress. I'd forgotten how beautiful it is." She ran her fingertips gently over the smooth bodice, reveling in the feeling of seeing her creation so skillfully rendered in fabric. "Pam is a true master."

"She is. I'm telling you, Lex. You are gonna look fantastic in this dress."

Eyeing her creation, Alexis drew another deep, calming breath. "For our sake, I hope you're right."

From his seat near the center of the exhibition hall, Bryan had a fantastic view of Alexis's very first fashion show. Watching her models strut up and down the runway, he couldn't contain the sense of pride he felt. He loved her, yes, but even without that bias, her skill and vision as a designer amazed him. He'd been around fabric and clothing his entire life and had seen enough to know true talent when he encountered it.

He knew he'd taken a risk by coming here after what had transpired between them on Monday night. She'd left angry and would probably not be pleased when she found out he was here. But the past four days without her, including four fitful, sleepless nights fantasizing about the feel of her body pressed against his, had been absolute torture. He had to be here tonight, not just to see her first show, but to make things right with her. Whatever venom she might launch his way would be nothing compared to the misery of knowing he'd hurt her, of being without her.

His seat also allowed him a view of Alexis's family members, who were sitting a few rows ahead of him. He could see the back of Maxwell's head, and he wondered if Alexis had told her brother what had gone down between them. He cringed, thinking of the blows he might have to take if she had. Maxwell was a fierce protector of his sisters. That had been true years ago when Bryan met him in college, and it remained true today. Having been there to bear witness to Maxwell's knocking out the last guy who'd hurt one of his sisters, Bryan knew better than to think he'd be immune. When it came to Alexis and Kelsey, Maxwell wasn't to be trifled with.

He shook his head. *No use worrying about what might happen. I'll find out soon enough.*

Settling into his seat, he redirected his focus back to the show. Two models were on their way back down the runway, away from the crowd. The music changed then, an indication that the show was nearing its end.

The announcer's voice rang out over the loudspeakers. "The last dress you'll see in tonight's Krystal Kouture show will be worn by the designer herself.

Wearing a gown dubbed Smoke, here is our gifted designer, Miss Alexis Devers." She swept her hand toward the right runway.

Bryan's eyes traveled where the announcer indicated and immediately widened as he caught sight of Alexis. The dress, a form-hugging creation in shimmery, clingy gray fabric, was amazing. The strapless bodice showed off the graceful lines of her throat and shoulders while accentuating the swell of her cleavage. The fabric clung to the flat plane of her stomach and the curve of her hips, ending in a cloud of shimmering waves of fabric that resembled a broad cluster of silver roses. She was resplendent, a vision of feminine beauty so perfect, she stole his breath.

As she walked slowly to the end of the runway, carefully lifting the floor-grazing hem and stopping to curtsy toward the uproar of applause in the audience, he placed his hand to his chest. The ring he'd given her, the ring she'd discarded in his front yard a few days ago, rested in an interior pocket of his sport coat. In that moment, he wanted nothing more than to make her his bride and to spend the rest of his life loving her in every way a man could love a woman.

He continued to watch her, with his heart swelling in his chest, until she'd taken her final bows and exited the stage. The members of the audience began to leave their chairs, some headed for the booths set up around the space and others heading for the exit. When Bryan got up, he went straight to the staging area.

There, a tall, muscular guard stopped him when he reached a set of velvet ropes. "I'm sorry, sir. You can't go any farther than that. This area is for event staff and participants only."

With no other choice, Bryan backed off but lingered near the area. He knew Alexis would have to come out sometime, especially with the members of the press already gathering near where he stood. Glancing around, he saw plenty of them, standing around with microphones and cameras.

One woman, who appeared to be feeding live coverage of the event to one of the local news stations, stood about ten feet to his left. She held a microphone to her mouth and had a large camera and floodlight directed at her.

Inching a bit closer but staying out of her shot, Bryan listened in to her commentary.

"This is Phoebe McLean, coming to you live from the Carolina Fashion and Music Festival, where local designer Alexis Devers has just completed her debut fashion show. We're awaiting Miss Devers's comments and expect to hear from her at any moment."

Less than five minutes later, Alexis appeared. As she moved to the ropes, the guard lifted one so she could get out. Bryan faded into the crowd as best he could, waiting for the right moment to make her aware of his presence.

He watched and listened as Phoebe asked Alexis several questions about what inspired her designs and how she thought her first show went. Alexis smiled as she answered each query thrown her way, handling herself with grace and poise.

Until Phoebe asked a question that seemed to catch her off guard. "Miss Devers, we'd love to chat with your fiancé, if he's here. And if you don't mind my asking, where's that gorgeous engagement ring?"

Alexis froze then, her eyes growing round.

Bryan pushed his way through the crowd then, appearing at her side and well within the camera shot. "You rang?"

Phoebe offered him a smile. "Mr. James, lovely to see you. We were just congratulating your fiancée on a fantastic show. Do you have anything you'd like to say to the Channel Nine viewers?"

Turning his attention to Alexis, who still seemed to be in the grip of her shock, he picked up her hand. Placing the ring, which he'd had altered to include her birthstone on either side of the diamond, back on her finger, he then lifted her hand to his lips. Kissing it, he gazed into her wide eyes for a moment before addressing the reporter. "All I have to say is that I'm so very proud of Lex and that I'm the luckiest man in the world to have her in my life."

Phoebe looked ready to swoon. "Well, you heard it, folks. This is Phoebe McLean, Channel Nine News." The light shining on her face shut off, and the cameraman lowered his equipment. Elbowing Bryan, Phoebe asked, "Have you got a brother?"

He shook his head. "No, sorry."

"Darn." Snapping her fingers, the reporter wandered away, with her cameraman close behind.

Bryan turned his attention back to Alexis, whose hand was still cradled within his own. "Hi there."

Blinking back tears, she managed, "Hi."

"Sorry to ambush you like that, but it looked like you needed me." He ignored the crowd that continued to ebb and flow around them, keeping his focus on the center of his world.

She nodded, raising her free hand to brush away an

escaped tear. Then she spoke, her voice shaking with emotion. "That was quite a declaration, Bryan."

Keeping his eyes locked on hers, he squeezed her hand. "Baby, I meant every single word."

She didn't respond to that. Dropping her head, she brushed at the other tears that flowed down her cheeks.

He helped her, taking the handkerchief from his pocket to dab away her tears. "Don't cry, Lex. Please."

She sniffled. "I can't help it."

He moved closer to her, and when she didn't dodge or back away, he relaxed a bit. Draping his arm loosely around her waist, he leaned in close to her ear, wanting her to hear him clearly. "My past is filled with meaningless encounters, with women I used to pass the time. But nothing and no one in my past could ever compare to you, Alexis. You are my heart, my true love, and my future."

She released a weak, broken sob. "You're not...helping me...stop crying, Bryan."

He crooked his index finger beneath her chin. "Alexis, please forgive me, baby. Marry me. Let me spend the rest of my days making it up to you."

Another sob left her throat as she vigorously nodded her head, reaching up to lace her arms around his neck.

Pulling her body close to his, he crushed his lips to hers and kissed her as if no one else were around.

Chapter 25

ALEXIS COULDN'T FIGURE OUT HOW BRYAN MANAGED to kiss her so thoroughly while carrying her in his arms and nudging open the front door of his house. As they moved inside and he kicked the door shut behind them, she found she didn't care about the how. All that mattered was the growing warmth of desire radiating through her body and the sense of safety she felt being in his arms. So she kept her eyes closed, content to enjoy his lips pressed against hers and the weightless feeling of his strong arms supporting her weight.

She opened her eyes when she came to rest against something soft. A quick glance around revealed they were in his bedroom, and he'd placed her atop the comforter on his bed. He eased away from her, leaving her seated on the edge of the bed.

His eyes glittered with passion as he looked at her. "You look so beautiful in that dress."

She smiled, recalling how reluctant she'd been to wear it in the first place. "I'm glad you like it."

"I'm going to be very careful removing it." He grasped her hands, tugged her gently into a standing position.

"Why?"

Placing a few torrid kisses along the bare line of her shoulder, he whispered in her ear, "Because I want you to wear this dress on our wedding day."

Her insides dissolved like sugar crystals in a cup of hot coffee.

He followed his words with more hot kisses, against the side of her throat, her collarbone, and the tops of her breasts. Her head dropped back, her knees going weak. His strong arms supported her, keeping her from toppling over as he continued his wicked ministrations.

His large hands began to glide over the dress and over the bare skin of her arms. Then he moved his touch behind her, grasping the zipper pull and dragging it down ever so slowly. All the while, he continued to place his soft kisses along her upper body. True to his word, when the halves of the dress fell open, he eased it down her hips. She stepped out of the dress, and he moved away from her long enough to drape it carefully over a chair on the other side of the room.

Returning moments later, he grazed his palms over the tops of her breasts, above the line of her strapless bra. He kissed and caressed her out of the bra, tossing it aside as he flicked his tongue over the taut buds of her nipples. Soon, the rising sensations became too much, and she fell back against the edge of his big bed.

He followed her, continued to lavish her breasts with his ardent attentions. Her back arched against the searing pleasure as he sucked her nipples. When he rolled the tight dark tips between his thumbs and forefingers, his name fell from her lips on a strangled moan.

She felt him lift her hips, whisk away her panties. When he started to undress, she centered herself on the bed and propped herself with her elbows behind her. With appreciative eyes, she watched him strip away his sport coat and the shirt and undershirt he wore beneath it. He knelt briefly to remove his shoes and socks, then stood to take off his slacks. By the time he hooked his thumbs beneath the waistband of his boxers, she was near drooling.

Moments later, he took the boxers off and kicked them away. Seeing his dick standing high and thick in the shadows, she licked her lips. Logically, she knew it hadn't been that long since they'd last made love, but now, it seemed as though it had been an eternity. Her core quivered with the anticipation of his arrival.

She watched him go to his bedside table, where he retrieved a condom. After he'd covered his erection, he rejoined her on the bed.

She welcomed him as the mattress sank beneath their combined weight, wrapping her arms around his strong shoulders and pulling him down to her kiss. Their lips met, crushing together as their tongues mated with all the shared passion they had for one another. The heavy weight of his arousal pressed against her damp heat as he settled himself between her thighs.

A heartbeat later, he rocked his hips forward, entering her. The feel of his girth filling her, opening her to his passion, drew a long moan from her lips.

Once he settled in at maximum depth, he stilled. Looking down into her eyes, he whispered, "Forever, Lex."

She nodded, her vision of his handsome face swimming as the tears filled her eyes again. "Forever."

He began to move then, building a steady rhythm of slow, deep strokes that set her body and soul on fire. Each time he rocked his strong hips, he pushed her closer and closer to madness. She lifted her legs, clamping them around his waist and holding on to him with every ounce of strength she possessed.

Unable to keep quiet, she gave herself over to the sensations he created, letting the moans and soft cries fall from her lips unchecked. He made his own sounds, low, rumbling groans that indicated he shared in the immense, blinding pleasure. Fire, hot and searing, sparked from his body moving within hers and spread through her as if she were dry brush. Her toes curled, her hips rising off the bed to meet his thrusts. She clung to his body as he moved above her like bliss incarnate, driving her toward the edge of sanity.

And as orgasm rippled through her, she cried out his name, the sound muffled as she turned her face into his strong shoulder. As she tried to recover her wits, she heard him roar above her, felt his muscles tighten as he met his own completion.

Soon, only their breathing broke the silence of the semidarkened room. He rolled onto his side, and she shifted to face him. He wrapped his arms around her, and she settled in, her body still aglow with the orgasmic joy he'd gifted her.

"I love you," she whispered against his chest.

"I love you, Lex." He gave her a gentle squeeze.

She wanted to say more, but before she could open her mouth again, sleep descended on her and carried her away.

———— ∿ ————

Bryan awakened later in the night to the sound of someone pounding at his door. As his eyes popped open, he groaned. Pounding on the door late at night rarely meant anything good, but he knew he'd have to answer it before the person woke Alexis. Her soft snores indicated how deeply she slept, and he didn't want her disturbed by whoever was on his porch.

The minute he separated from her warm curves, he knew he would be rushing to get back to her. Easing away from her, he slipped out of bed and pulled on his boxers and a pair of sweatpants. Not bothering with a shirt, he left the room, shutting the door behind him. Then he trudged barefoot over the carpeted floor to his front door.

Swinging open the door, he was ready to smack whoever stood there.

Maxwell's face came into view under the yellow glow of the porch light. He was still wearing the dark suit he'd worn to the event, and he didn't look pleased. "I know my sister's here, jackass. How could you spirit her away like that, before her family even got a chance to talk to her?"

Bryan placed his finger over his lips, then stepped out onto the porch. Making sure to leave the door unlocked, he pulled it shut behind him. "Dude, chill. Yes, she's here, and she's asleep, so lower your fucking voice."

Maxwell tilted his head to the side, glared at him.

Bryan glared right back. "If you're gonna show up on my porch cursing this late at night, you should know that I'm gonna match you, foul for foul."

Folding his arms over his chest, Maxwell scoffed. "You know, I should kick your ass right here. Lex told me what happened on Monday."

"Fine. But since she's here with me now, doesn't that tell you that we've patched things up?"

Leaning his back against the porch railing, Maxwell sighed. "Listen, B. You're one of my closest friends,

COULDN'T ASK FOR MORE

and I love you like a brother. But I told you from the gate that I didn't like the idea of you with my baby sister."

Bryan tried to keep his tone level, because he understood where his friend was coming from. "You know I feel the same way about you, Max. But your sister is a grown woman. You can't police her decisions like this."

"I'm not trying to run her life, but I'm not going to back down from protecting her, either." His eyes communicated his immense love for his sister.

Bryan sat down in one of his resin porch chairs. "Look, I respect how much you love Lex. I love her, too. You have to believe me when I say I'm not out to hurt her."

Maxwell shrugged. "Technically, you already have. I mean, look how this thing between you two started, with this farce of an engagement. How can you expect me to trust what you say now, when I know this all began with a lie?"

Bryan settled back in the chair, tenting his fingers in front of him. "I don't know any other way to respond to that, so I'm just going to spit the truth. I love her, Maxwell. This is the realest thing I've ever felt in my life. Now, I've asked her to marry me, for real, and she's said yes."

Anger flashed in Maxwell's eyes. "Again with this? When are you two going to quit?"

"Never, if I have anything to say about it. We're in love, Max. This shit is legit, so you're going to have to get with the program."

Shaking his head again, Maxwell sighed. "I guess so, man. But you need to know right now that if she ever comes to me crying again because of something you did—"

Bryan raised his hand, stopping his friend in mid-sentence. "Max, if I ever do anything to hurt her again, you are welcome to kick my ass up and down Capital Boulevard until you get tired."

That seemed to satisfy Maxwell, because his expression softened, and he visibly relaxed. "Shake on it."

Bryan extended his hand, shaking hands with his friend. "Now that we've settled that, I'd like to get back to my fiancée, if you don't mind."

Maxwell chuckled. "I guess that's all right. Just remember our agreement."

Bryan stood, extended his closed fist. "Later, Max."

Maxwell matched his stance and bumped fists with him. "Yeah, whatever."

Maxwell stepped off the porch and strolled away. Bryan opened the door and slipped inside the house, eager to return to his bed, and his love.

Epilogue

"IS IT ZIPPED? ALEXIS CRANED HER NECK, ATTEMPT-ing to look over her shoulder at the back of her dress.

"Yes, it's zipped. Stop trying to look back here before you hurt yourself." Kelsey released her grip on the zipper pull, stepped back. "Now take a look in the mirror, Lex."

Turning forward again, Alexis took in her reflection in the full-length mirror. The Smoke dress did indeed look gorgeous on her, and unlike the first time she'd put it on, she didn't feel nervous or hesitant in the least. Adjusting the pearl-and-diamond necklace hanging above the sweetheart neckline, she smiled.

Kelsey, who stood behind her, lifted the matching pearl-and-diamond-encrusted headband and placed it in Alexis's hair, "There. I'd say you're ready."

Turning around to hug her sister, Alexis had to agree.

Sydney approached then, handed Alexis her bouquet of crystal brooches. "You look gorgeous, girl."

"Thanks."

"How do I look?" Sydney twirled around, giving her the three-hundred-and-sixty-degree picture of her lavender cocktail dress.

Alexis laughed. "You look just like Kelsey." She gestured to her sister's matching dress.

Sydney pursed her lips.

Laughing again, Alexis blew her a kiss. "What I mean is you both look great."

Later, Sydney and Kelsey escorted Alexis out of the VIP box at O'Kelly-Riddick Stadium. The cool February air hit Alexis's bared skin right away, but the glow of love kept her warm. Sydney held up the hem of Alexis's gown as they carefully made their way down the bleachers toward the field. At the bottom rung, Humphrey Devers awaited. The girls walked ahead, taking their positions as Humphrey came to Alexis's side.

Offering his arm to his daughter, he asked, "Are you ready to do this?"

She nodded, looping her arm with his and blinking away the happy tears gathering in her eyes. "Yes, Daddy. I am."

As the hired band played "The Nearness of You," Alexis walked with her father onto the grassy field. There, on the fifty-yard line, stood Bryan. Joined by a friend of his who was a justice of the peace and all four of his fraternity line brothers, Bryan looked incredibly dapper in his black suit, white shirt, and silver tie.

Her eyes met his, and she smiled, knowing that every step she took over the soft, winter-brown grass was another step toward her destiny.

When she reached Bryan, her father stepped back, and she looked up into his eyes.

"You're so beautiful," he whispered, his voice thick with emotion.

And when Bryan took her hand in his, she felt her heart expand with the joy of this day and of the life they would build, together.

After the ceremony, Alexis was standing alone in the

reception hall when she felt a light tap on her shoulder. She'd come to the punch table to spend a quiet moment taking it all in, and she assumed Bryan had come to find her.

Turning around, she smiled up into her brother's face. "What's up, Maxie?"

"Congrats, Mrs. James." He leaned down and gave her a hug.

"Thanks, bro." She returned his embrace. "What is it? You tapped me for a reason, I'm guessing."

"You're right. I just wanted to apologize, you know, for giving you such a hard time about getting involved with B."

Her brow cocked. "You already apologized. And I forgive you, Maxie. I know you can't help yourself when it comes to protecting your sisters." She loved her brother, and even though he got on her last nerve sometimes, it would never change her affection.

He shifted his weight. "I did a little something to make it up to you. So I want you and B to enjoy your two-week honeymoon."

Confusion made Alexis frown. "Maxie, what are you talking about? We only booked a week in the Maldives."

He smiled. "I know. But with a little help from Sydney, I paid for a second week. Consider it my wedding gift." He winked. "So, like I said, enjoy yourself." And before Alexis could recover from her shock, her brother strolled away, fading into the crowd of friends and family enjoying the reception.

Bryan sidled over, taking her into his arms. "What's that look on your face?"

Still amazed, Alexis told him about Maxwell's gift.

Bryan smiled. "Wow. That was really cool of Max. I'll be sure to thank him when we get back." Leaning down, he placed a kiss on her forehead. "I can't wait to get you alone, Mrs. James."

Smiling up at him, she laid her hand against his cheek. "Don't worry, baby. You won't have to wait much longer."

And within the hour, Mr. and Mrs. Bryan James were dashing out of the reception hall in a shower of bubbles and confetti. They were going to have a glorious life together, and Alexis couldn't wait to get started.

About the Author

Like any good Southern belle, Kianna Alexander wears many hats: loving wife, doting mama, advice-dispensing sister, and gabbing girlfriend. She's a voracious reader, an amateur seamstress, and an occasional painter in oils. Chocolate, American history, sweet tea, and Idris Elba are a few of her favorite things. A native of the Tar Heel State, Kianna still lives there with her husband, two kids, and a collection of well-loved vintage '80s Barbie dolls.

For more about Kianna and her books, visit her website at authorkiannaalexander.com or sign up for her newsletter at authorkiannaalexander.com/sign-up.

Follow Kianna on social media:
Facebook.com/KiannaWrites
Twitter.com/KiannaWrites
Pinterest.com/KiannaWrites
Instagram.com/KiannaAlexanderWrites

BACK TO YOUR LOVE

A successful businessman reignites an old flame in the first Southern Gentlemen book from Kianna Alexander

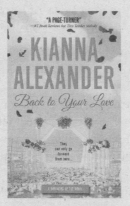

As a hardworking businessman and aspiring politician in his Southern hometown, Xavier Whitted has a lot on his plate. A weekend at the beach for his best friend's wedding is exactly what he needs—until he runs into the woman who broke his heart ten years ago.

Imani Grant is more beautiful, confident, and intelligent than ever, and their connection is still sizzling. But Imani harbors a secret that could destroy their blossoming careers. She knows she should keep her distance, but Xavier is determined to win back her heart—consequences be damned.

"Sexy and unforgettable."

**—USA Today Happy Ever After
for *This Tender Melody***

For more Kianna Alexander, visit:
sourcebooks.com

COME BACK TO ME

Welcome back to bestselling author
Sharon Sala's Blessings, Georgia series,
and the next book of her heart

After a devastating fire pitted their families against each
other, high school sweethearts Phoebe Ritter and Aidan
Payne were torn apart. Twenty years later, Aidan is called
back to Blessings, nervous about confronting his painful
past. And that's *before* he knows about the nineteen-year-
old secret Phoebe has been harboring all this time...

---

*"Sharon Sala is a consummate storyteller...
If you can stop reading then you're
a better woman than me."*

**—Debbie Macomber, #1 *New York Times*
bestselling author, for *A Piece of My Heart***

For more Sharon Sala, visit:
sourcebooks.com

RESCUE ME

In this fresh, poignant series about rescue animals, every heart has a forever home

By Debbie Burns, award-winning debut author

A New Leash on Love

Megan Anderson would do anything for the animals at her no-kill shelter—even go toe-to-toe with a handsome man who is in way over his head. Craig Williams didn't expect this fiery young woman to blaze into his life. But the more time they spend together, the more he realizes it's not just animals Megan is adept at saving—she could be the one to rescue his heart.

Sit, Stay, Love

For devoted no-kill shelter worker Kelsey Sutton, rehabbing a group of rescue dogs is a welcome challenge. Working with a sexy ex-military dog handler who needs some TLC himself? That's a whole different story…

"Sexy and fun… Wounded souls of all shapes and sizes, human and animal alike, tug at the heartstrings."

—RT Book Reviews for *A New Leash on Love*, Top Pick, 4½ Stars

For more Debbie Burns, visit:
sourcebooks.com

LOVE GAMES

Contemporary romance with heart, heat, and humor
from author Maggie Wells

Love Game

Kate Snyder is at the top of her game. So
when the university hires a washed-up
coach trying to escape scandal—paying
him a lot more than she earns—Kate is
more than annoyed. When Kate and
Danny finally see eye to eye, sparks
ignite…and they need to figure out if
this is more than just a game.

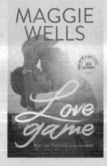

Play for Keeps

Basketball coach Tyrell Ransom is
ready to whip his team into shape
and start winning some games…until
compromising photos of his soon-to-
be-ex-wife with one of his players
go viral. When public relations guru
Millie Jenkins arrives to save the day,
things really heat up… Soon they're
going to have to work double time to
keep their own white-hot chemistry
out of the headlines.

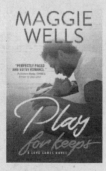

"*Perfectly paced and gutsy romance.*"

**—*Publishers Weekly* Starred Review
for *Love Game***

For more Maggie Wells, visit:
sourcebooks.com

AT THE SHORE

New York Times and USA Today bestselling author Caridad Pineiro

One Summer Night

Everyone knows about the bad blood between the Pierces and Sinclairs, but Owen has been watching Maggie from afar for years. Whenever he can get down to the shore, he strolls the sand hoping for a chance meeting— and a repeat of the forbidden kiss they shared one fateful summer night...

What Happens in Summer

Connie Reyes and Jonathan Pierce only discovered how different they were after a magical summer on the Jersey shore. Now, Jonathan is back in Sea Kiss, having made a fortune in tech. He has everything money can buy, but his bed is empty and his heart is hollow. He's never stopped thinking about Connie, and he'll do anything to show her the man he's become...

"The perfect escape! Tender, funny, and sexy."

—RaeAnne Thayne, *New York Times* bestselling author, for *One Summer Night*

For more Caridad Pineiro, visit:
sourcebooks.com